Don't You Cry For Me

A Novel of the Civil War

Based on a true story

By

Judith Redline Coopey

Don't You Cry For Me

Author's Declaration

Published by Fox Hollow Press
Cover design by John M. Coopey, Mesa, Arizona

Attention Corporations, Universities, Colleges and Professional Organizations: Quantity discounts are available on bulk purchases of this book for educational and gift purposes or as premiums for increasing magazine gift subscriptions or renewals. Special books or book excerpts can also be created to fit specific needs. Contact Fox Hollow Press.

Digitally printed in the United States of America

Also by Judith Redline Coopey

Redfield Farm
Waterproof
Looking For Jane
Juniata Iron Trilogy:
The Furnace
Brothers
Full Circle
Editor: *Dig or Die*

Acknowledgements

No book ever makes it into print without the help, encouragement and support of many, but this book in particular comes with a deep debt of gratitude. My longtime editor, Paul McNeese, passed away during the writing of *Don't You Cry For Me*, leaving me to my own devices for editing, formatting, design and innumerable other services that he always took care of with professional ease. I miss him now and will for some time in the future, but I am grateful for the experience of producing seven books with him as my guide. Rest in peace, editor and friend.

In addition, a thank you to Travis Ferrell of the U. S. Army War College Library, Pat Park, Genie Robine, Lou Coopey and Erin Coopey.

Dedication

To my mother,
Helen Samuels Redline
also known as "Nell"
who first told me this story

She Dwelt Among the Untrodden Ways

BY <u>**WILLIAM WORDSWORTH**</u>

She dwelt among the untrodden ways
Beside the springs of Dove,
A Maid whom there were none to praise
And very few to love:

A violet by a mossy stone
Half hidden from the eye!
—Fair as a star, when only one
Is shining in the sky.

She lived unknown, and few could know
When Lucy ceased to be;
But she is in her grave, and, oh,
The difference to me!

Introduction

Every spring as I was growing up, my mother would buy a quantity of potted flowers and we would make the rounds of the various cemeteries for what was then called Decoration Day – now Memorial Day. As we visited the graves, planted and watered the flowers, pulled the weeds and dusted off the tombstones, Mother would reminisce about the family members who'd gone before.

One story she told me more than once was about her grandmother, Mary Elizabeth Blackburn, (1837 – 1910) who was courted and won during the Civil War by a stranger from Georgia by the name of Joseph Berman, a circuit riding Methodist minister. They married and as the war was winding down he left to return to his southern home to settle his affairs, with the promise that he would return as soon as he could. Sadly, Joseph Berman was never heard from again, and lost to family history.

Mary Elizabeth later learned that he had been captured by Union troops while traveling south, accused of being a Confederate spy and thrown into Libby Prison in Richmond, Virginia, where he died.

According to my mother, Mary Elizabeth kept a framed copy of her marriage certificate hanging above her bed until her death. Unfortunately, that, too, has been lost to history.

Mary Elizabeth gave birth to their only child, Josephine, in November 1865, and Josephine grew up using the Berman name in most records. Two years later, in 1867, Mary Elizabeth married Jacob D. Tetwiler, a Civil War veteran, who, according to my mother's account, tried to persuade her to give up her child to an orphanage. She refused, and the marriage was dissolved. Mary Elizabeth went by the Tetwiler name for the rest of her life, while Josephine used her father's surname, Berman, until her marriage in 1888.

As an adult with an interest in genealogy, I tried to find any records to substantiate this account of the elusive Mr. Berman. I reasoned that if he was living in Blair County in 1865, he had to be living somewhere in 1860, but I found not a trace of Joseph Berman in the 1850 or 1860 census for Georgia or anywhere else. I wrote to Drew Seminary in New Jersey, the repository for the records of the Methodist Church, but they responded that they did not keep records from circuit riders, and therefore had no information on Mr. Berman. Libby Prison had no record of a Joseph Berman either.

I began to suspect that Mr. Berman might have been a figment of my great grandmother's imagination, made up to spare herself and her daughter the sting of illegitimacy. But it also occurred to me that a spy would have used an alias, so if he was captured after the war was over, he would probably have used his real name in the prison records. Since I did not know his real name, I was left at a dead end.

Still, it seemed to me that there must be some fragment of information to support this story, and I continue to examine Civil War records but so far have found little hard evidence. In one brief marriage notice in the Bedford (Pennsylvania) Inquirer, a Mrs. Mary Elizabeth Berman married Jacob D. Tetwiler on October 15, 1867, evidence, but not proof of the story.

But in genealogy one never gives up because some fragmentary record could still surface. In the meantime, I became enthralled with the story and the possibilities it opens, so I started to do research on Civil War spies and found those records to be sadly fragmentary as well. So I may never know more than I know now, but I think it makes a great story and if it is just a story, it is well worth reading and contemplating on its own merits.

Judith Redline Coopey
Mesa, Arizona
May, 2019

Chapter 1

October 1864
Milledgeville, Georgia
Carter Willoughby

I paced back and forth in front of my father's huge walnut desk, fully aware that I was spouting heresy.

"I know I shouldn't say this, Papa, but I hate war – war in general, but this war in particular. It'll ruin us yet. People talk about getting back to normal when it's over, but what is normal, anyway? I wonder if we'll ever see normal again."

My gray haired father sat back in his chair, thoughtful. He frowned, biting his lip in consternation. "Carter Willoughby, I never expected to hear talk like that from you, a son of the South. A true defender of Dixie."

I picked out a cigar from the box in his desk drawer. Papa's store of fine wines and choice cigars had so far weathered the storms of war, just like old times. Being home on leave from the CSA, drinking my father's brandy gave me an opportunity to put it all away for a day or two. Try to forget what awaited me when I got back to my unit. Here I was free to make a fool of myself, let the brandy loosen my tongue and dissolve my good sense. I continued, unable or unwilling to stem the tide of words.

"Lincoln will be re-elected. Sherman'll probably take Atlanta within the month. It's time to wake up to the truth, Papa. We're beat."

"Now, now Carter. Don't let present circumstances discourage you. England's ready to support us. You wait and see. They still need our cotton, and they'll break the damn blockade soon enough."

He sat back in his horsehair chair, his desk strewn with papers. "Wait and see. You youngsters will be our salvation. Those Yankee boys don't even know what they're fighting for."

"That may be true, but there are still too many of them. Every time we kill one, two more take his place. Wars are not won by valor alone. Resources, Papa, resources."

He peered up at me, his face a study in frustration. "We've got resources! Plenty of them! But more than that, we're fighting for our homes, our families, our way of life, Carter. You can't measure that."

I stopped pacing and sat down opposite him, reminding myself how little he knew little of what I'd experienced these last two years. And I couldn't help him know. If you haven't lived it – slept out on the ground through rain, snow and sleet, ridden all night to fight in the fog and the brambles, seen your boyhood friends scattered about the field, grotesque, misshapen piles of old rags, you just can't know.

Oh, we had our victories, and they sustained the romantics among us, but any man with a little sense could see the inevitable signs of defeat, and the worse things got, the more these fools romanticized the war. No one spoke of it, but defeat was there watching, lingering among the trees, waiting. As I took another sip of brandy, the bell rang calling us to dinner.

"Come, Papa, if we don't join mother and the girls at table right away, they'll be sending Julius round to find us."

We left the library, crossing the wide center hall toward the dining room, each carrying our glass of brandy, smiling as though we hadn't a care -- all for the benefit of my mother and sisters. I was determined to stand between them and the war. They'd already lost too much.

My brothers Randolph and Mark rode off tall and ready at the first call only to be cut down, one at some place called Pittsburg Landing and the other at a sad little town in Maryland called Sharpsburg. Unbelievable. That left me, the third son, to survive at all costs and carry on the Willoughby name, proud scion of Belfast Plantation, Milledgeville, Georgia.

Mother forced a wan smile as we stepped into the dining room, her face drawn, head bowed, the once-proud mistress of a prosperous plantation, now barely able to hold onto her dignity. My younger sisters, Emily and Ellen rushed to my side, anxious for news of their favorite beaux.

"Carter dear, what do you know of Tommie Breckinridge? I've not had a letter in weeks." My little sister Ellen looked me in the eyes, earnest, sincere, full of hope.

"No news is good news, Ellen. If he were dead, his name'd be on the lists in the papers."

"I already know Charles Foster is taken prisoner. His sister Mary Ann told me at church two months ago." Emily held her head high, always the proper Southern lady.

"Prisoner is it? Well, I hear talk of a prisoner exchange, so you may see him come riding home yet one of these days."

My sisters were sensible girls, not beautiful, but certainly attractive and refined. In another time and place they would have stepped into their roles as southern ladies and lived out their days according to tradition. Now they passed the days doing everything they could to help our cause, and while they sorely missed the way of life they'd been bred to, they and every other woman in the neighborhood supported the war effort -- rolled bandages, knitted stockings, sewed shirts, even stitched up under drawers for the Confederate Army.

It was the first time I'd been home since I'd joined, and I was soberly aware that this was to be my final visit until the war was over. Recruited as a scout for the Confederacy on detached assignment somewhere behind enemy lines -- could be anywhere, but most likely north of the Mason-Dixon Line, I was prepared to do whatever had to be done in service of the South.

A scout was a spy – a bold and deceitful actor, observer and informer whose neck, should he be found out, was destined to end this life clad in a rope. I'd find out the details when I reported for my new orders in a few days.

Now it was time to dine and drink and play frivolous games in a futile effort to reach back and touch the world we used to know. I knew it couldn't be done, but my family still believed. My mother and sisters. My father, even. So we put forth a valiant effort to bring back the gaiety and pretend the good times were still within reach and would return as soon as we whipped those damn Yankees.

I took my seat at the table, joining hands with each of my parents as they reached across to grasp my sisters' hands. I glanced at Emily as Papa said grace. She returned my look, her countenance grave. Emily was nobody's fool. She knew it was only a matter of time until the South would have to face the reality of defeat. I nodded and lowered my head.

Friends and neighbors started to arrive as soon as the word of my presence spread around the neighborhood. "Massa Carter home!" They arrived with grave faces and hopeful eyes. Did I know anything about Thomas Gregg? They said he'd lost a leg, but heard nothing more. And what about the Rutledge brothers? No one had heard from either of them in almost a year. I could offer no comfort, unwilling to lift them up with false hope. I felt shame at my clean uniform and relative good health compared to what we heard of some of our other Rebel boys.

The evening was spent in pleasant reminiscence of times past and hopeful predictions of the return of all that. I did my best to reassure, encourage and nurture hope, even though I knew the cause was lost. Gettysburg had knocked the wind out of us. Our lack of resources, our diminished ability to outfit and supply an army were not lost on me. Right then our dearest hope was to bring a blow to the Union's transportation system – slow them down and give our diplomats time and reason to shore up support in Europe and our generals time to plan a desperate final strategy.

As the evening wound down and our guests drove away into the darkness, our parents retired for the night. Exhausted, I took myself out to the veranda, where, clad in this new Confederate uniform, only the second one I'd owned, I withstood the cold for a brief communion with the land. I wondered if I'd ever see the red clay of Georgia again. An unshakeable pall of sadness seemed to hang over the land, chilling my heart. As I stood looking out over barren cotton fields, I felt a presence and turned to find Emily at my side.

"What are you thinking, Brother?" she asked, pulling a wrap around her shoulders.

"Oh, nothing. Just taking in the beauty."

"I've heard those photographers can set up a camera that swings round on its stand and takes a picture that goes from here to there." She swept her arm round the circumference of the landscape.

"Mayhap you should get someone to take such a picture, for God knows all of this may soon be gone from the face of the earth."

"Now, Em. Don't you go all gloomy on me. All isn't lost."

"Yet."

I turned and took both her hands in mine, raising them to my cheeks. "Emily Willoughby, don't take on so, if for no other reason, to spare Mama and Papa worry."

"They worry anyway. They're putting on a good face for you, but the loss of our brothers took away all pretense -- made them face reality." My sister pulled herself up to her full height. No tears. Just quiet dignity.

"Yes, well, we still need to shield them from what's coming. It may be worse than any of us can imagine."

I put my arm around her shoulders, felt her shiver whether from the cold or the fear. "What do you hear from Ivey plantation these days?"

"She's still out there, Carter. Still holding the whole plantation on her shoulders. Still waiting for Mark to come home and rescue her. She cries out his name in her sleep."

"Really? How do you know that?"

"Both Ellen and I have spent week-long visits there. And the Caldwell girls. We've all heard it. She puts on a brave face, but she's dying inside."

"Do you think I should ride out for a visit, or would that make things worse?"

"Oh, yes, I think you should. She knows Mark's dead, but she just can't bring herself to abandon hope. Seeing you might help."

"All right. Maybe the three of us should take the phaeton and go out tomorrow. Spend the day." I let go her hands and stepped back.

"With that plan in mind, I think we should retire and get a good night's rest."

Emily smiled. "I know I shouldn't say this, but I can still see you standing right behind Mark in case she might look over his shoulder and find you there. You've always had a special place in your heart for Jennifer Ivey."

I nodded. "You know me, Em. Better than anybody. But Mark's gone, and at the rate we're dying, I doubt she'll ever find another."

"None of us. Not a husband to be had, come the end of this."

I touched the back of my hand to her cheek. "I'm anxious to see her, even though I can't offer much comfort. I hope she doesn't think I'm maneuvering to take Mark's place."

"Don't worry, Carter. Jennifer knows who you are. You've always been special to her."

"And she to me, except I always knew my place – right behind Mark." I took her elbow and escorted her back into the house.

The next morning I ambled out to the stables, hands in my pockets, as though I had all day to wander. Julius, our one time butler and current overseer of what was left of slave labor stepped out from one of the stalls to greet me.

"Marse Carter, suh. You want I should saddle up the roan?"

"No, Julius. Hitch up the two blacks to the phaeton. I'm taking my sisters for an outing."

The old Negro nodded and slowly turned to tend to the task amid half empty stables. Once crowded with the finest horseflesh in Georgia, they now housed a motley-looking collection of once-was and might-have-been. I watched Julius work, slow and careful, still wearing his butler's outfit, his close-cropped hair as white as snow.

"Ya'll goin' over to the Ivey place?" he asked.

"Why, yes. Do you want to send greetings?"

"Yassuh. To my daughter, Viney. She over there now. Got me a grandson, too."

"You bet, Julius. I'll tell her you're well and send your best wishes."

Julius grinned, waved a gnarled hand and stepped aside. "My grandson name Julius, for me."

"That's nice, old man."

"He be free some day."

I mounted the driver's seat and took the reins as though I hadn't heard that. The war had made the slaves insolent. All of them. We'd see who'd be free and how long that freedom would last. Lincoln could emancipate all he wanted. He had to win the war before it would be a reality and even then the road to freedom would be long and hard. Harder for some than others, but hard, nonetheless.

I drove the phaeton around to the front and waited for Emily and Ellen to emerge, dressed in plain dresses, carrying baskets of food and sewing, very business-like. It pained me to see them so, but I was determined that this would be a happy day. I loaded up the baskets and turned toward the main road, then saw Julius standing by the stable door looking hopeful. I beckoned to him.

7

"Come on old man, drive us and you'll get to see your grandson." With a hop and a skip, he mounted the carriage and settled himself in the driver's seat beside me, the girls in the back. We were off.

Chapter 2

October 1864
East Sharpsburg, Pennsylvania
Susannah Lander

I saw the wagon coming up the road, and hurried to tell Aunt Betsy. "Looks like Thomas has done the butchering. Sent us our share."

I rushed to get a wooden tub to hold the meat that would sustain us through the winter. Uncle Thomas was honor-bound to care for his maiden sister and indigent niece, and, being an honorable man, he would meet his obligations, but not one smidgen more. We knew that. But the prospect of a good supply of beef, canned, dried or salted, to sustain us over the winter gave us leave to hope. The wagon turned in at the gate, my cousin Anthony, Thomas's middle son, driving. He pulled up to the edge of the porch and dropped to the ground, eyes downcast, avoiding my gaze. Puzzled, Aunt and I watched as he rounded back of the wagon and wrestled a burlap-wrapped bundle onto the edge of the porch. I shoved a wooden tub in place as Anthony hefted the bundle into it.

"Thank you, Anthony. And thanks to your father for us." That was Aunt Betsy, always gracious, always looking for the good in people.

I stood staring at the odd-shaped bundle oozing blood into the tub. No thanks from me. Instead of a fair share of roasts and side meat, it was clear he'd sent the leftovers, the pickings, the waste. I walked over and lifted the burlap to see a baleful eyeball staring out at me. The head. He'd sent us the unskinned head of the cow to sustain us for the winter.

I stood over the bloody bundle, feet wide, hands on hips. "Oh, yes, Anthony, thank him for us. And tell him we hope he rots in hell."

Anthony lowered his head and turned away. Always a little too meek, and therefore a perfect candidate to carry out his father's hateful schemes, Anthony could be counted on to obey his father's orders without resistance,

"Tell him God loves a cheerful giver. Tell him that. And tell him the meek, not the greedy, shall inherit the earth."

In a hurry to escape my lashing tongue, poor Anthony fairly tripped over his own feet getting back up on the wagon seat. Aunt Betsy frowned and placed her finger in front of her lips, shaking her head at me. I kicked the tub, sending it off the edge of the porch to land upside down in the dirt, then turned and stomped into the house.

To call it a house would be generous; it was little more than a shed, really. More like a closed-in corn crib. Long and narrow with a door at either end and just two windows upstairs and two down, it leaned precariously toward a ravine that ran along to the left of it. Built of logs in the early days, it had been added to and built up at various times without much skill or care. Its next life would be as a pig pen or worse, once the likes of Auntie and I were done with it.

We rented from Alonzo Riggs in return for our labor in his fields or wherever else he found a need for a couple of weak women. But Alonzo's interest in me was fed by the hope that I might someday want to marry his derelict and laggard son, Jonah. Jonah Riggs was the only man who'd ever shown an interest in me, but as far as I was concerned, he was as far from a marriage prospect as a pig, and Alonzo knew that.

Jonah was nobody's idea of a prospective husband – him being given to bragging and lying and putting on airs. Folks called him spoiled since he was the only child out of six who'd survived babyhood in the Riggs family. Five little tombstones in an iron-fenced graveyard atop a hill on their farm, each adorned with a sculpture of a lamb, bore witness to Alonzo and Martha's tragedy. No wonder they placed all their hopes and dreams on Jonah's head. It surely gave him an inflated sense of his own importance and skewed his idea of how others saw him.

After his mother died when he was seventeen, Jonah looked to replace her with a bride cast in her image. As he grew to manhood, Jonah's expectation that any woman would be lucky to be joined in matrimony to a mate such as he, swelled into just plain vanity. As a birthright Quaker schooled in the destructive aspects of pride, I wasn't that desperate – yet.

Aunt followed me into the house, gathered her basin and knives and returned to the scene of charity lived out. I stayed inside for another five minutes, pacing, talking to myself, cursing my uncle and my fate. Aunt was ever kind, charitable to a fault, ready to praise and hesitant to blame. Fat lot of good that had ever done her. I joined her in the yard, gathered kindling and set the iron kettle to boil. Unwrapped, the cow's head looked grotesque, eyes blank, tongue hanging askew. It was all I could do to heft it back into the tub and up on the porch where Aunt splashed it with a bucket of water, cut out the tongue and placed it in her basin.

"Git me the salt," she directed. "And pump some water in with that tongue."

"Think you still remember how to do this, Aunt?" I asked.

She nodded. "Course I do. My mama did it every year. Anyway, they's good meat on the head."

"Just not very much of it."

"More'n you'd think. And he left some neck meat."

She moved on to the process of skinning which she accomplished with the sharpest of knives. Once the head was skinned, Aunt took the ax we used to split stove wood and chopped off the horns with precision I had to admire. Going about her business with matter-of-fact competence, I watched, thinking how poverty makes you strong, whatever else it does to you.

The dressing, cooking and preserving of the meat took the rest of the day and the next day as well, for we pickled, salted or dried what we couldn't use right away. I spent most of the time grousing about Uncle Thomas and the unfairness of life while Aunt let me go on. She didn't chastise me or remind me that others had it worse; she just worked steadily, doing what had to be done.

That's how we got on, Aunt and me. Doing what had to be done. There was a war on, and every day we heard of death and maiming and suffering beyond anything we'd experienced. So even though I was dissatisfied with my lot in life, I was free, young and literate, so I knew things could be worse. At sixty-seven, Aunt was poor, unmarried, and without hope of anything better, but she still managed to find ways to help others less fortunate than we. Bless her.

I knew I should try to be more like her, to find the good in people, to forgive and try to live according to my inner light, but my Irish Quaker temper got in the way of good sense sometimes and my inner light had a tendency to dim and flicker. It even went out now and then, and it was in those times that I gave vent to the anger and frustration I'd felt deep down ever since I was a child.

I helped Aunt with the cow's head out of duty, fighting the urge to walk the three miles to Uncle Thomas's house and share my innermost thoughts with him. I knew I could do him some damage at Meeting. I could stand up in the business part of things when men and women met together and speak of charity and compassion for the poor, looking right at him as I spoke. But I'd done that before, and it hadn't changed anything. Uncle Thomas was still the rich relative and we were still poorer than Robbie Burns' louse.

"What do you think gets into him, Aunt?" I asked as I stood, long handled paddle in hand, stirring the kettle as the fat boiled down.

"Oh, Thomas has always been like this, child. Some of us are born with more yearning than caring. Our other brothers, John and Samuel, was good men. Thomas just had it in his head he was smarter, better, more deserving, maybe because he was the oldest. Blamed your pa for being too soft. Said he was lazy and didn't deserve better'n he got."

12

I puzzled over that. Everyone in my father's family seemed mostly good and charitable, except Uncle Thomas. He'd inherited the farm, as was his right, but then he fought my papa in court for another hundred acres papa said Grampy had meant for him -- didn't have any proof it was his and there was talk that the will had been changed so it all ended in us leaving for the west – Papa, Mama, me and my little sister Maggie, not born yet.

Papa was real mad at Uncle Thomas, and if he knew how things had turned out for Maggie and me, he'd be even madder, I guessed, but none of us had heard a word from him since he sent Maggie and me back from Iowa to be raised by his sisters.

"I wish my Mama hadn't died." I said, as though it were a new thought, not one that had been etched in my brain since I was four.

"We all do. Things'd be different for all of us. I'd a sight rather have your papa to depend on than Thomas."

"Wish he'd have come back, too, instead of just sending us. Wish I knew what's become of him."

Aunt picked up a couple of sticks of fire wood and fed the flames, her tattered dress hanging limp from her shoulders, the front hem dragging on the ground. I hated to see her looking so bedraggled, but where was she to get new? The Meeting offered charity to those in need, but Thomas was charged with caring for us, and everyone thought he did. So we went about in rags and ate only what we could produce or forage for ourselves most of the time.

"What's happened to your pa is likely what usually happens to them that goes west. They get swallowed up in a new life and forget about the old."

"Do you really think so, Aunt? Do you really think he's just gone and forgotten us?"

Most of the time I thought my pa was dead – got the fever that killed Mama or snake bit or fell off the barn roof. Something like that. But Aunt's words echoed in my brain. How could a man just forget about his children? Go on and start a new life with nary a thought? What kind of man would do that?

Aunt Betsy smiled and patted my shoulder. "I know, child. It's hard to think ill of those we love."

I stepped away from the fire and wandered to the bank of the creek that meandered through Farmer Riggs's land. I didn't want to be seen as a shirker, but I needed some time alone. I got this way sometimes when life looked bleak and my prospects bleaker. The only way out was to marry. I knew that, but my prospects there were beyond bleak. I wasn't pretty, see. Not ugly, either, just plain. I'd heard the old ladies at Meeting refer to me that way when they thought I was out of hearing range. "Too bad she's the plain one." "Not much to attract a man there." "There's some says she's shrewish, too." "Too willful. No man wants a willful wife."

Well, I was. Willful, shrewish, plain and mad about it. How was a shrewish and plain woman supposed to get on in life if she didn't have any family to support her? Anyway, being kind and gracious hadn't done Aunt any good. She was as poor as I and if I didn't care for her in her old age, who would? Her brother Thomas? Not likely.

As I wandered aimless along the creek, Jonah Riggs stepped out of the woodlot with a smile and a wave, like he was glad to see me and assumed I felt the same. Known about the neighborhood as a lazy ne'er-do-well, slow witted and somewhere on the short side of honest, Jonah liked to appear out of nowhere when I was doing chores, watch me work and make dumb comments like "Whyn't you marry me? You could have a girl to work for you and never have to muck out a barn again."

I shook my head. "No. Jonah. I've told you no before. I will never marry you." I brushed past him, still in a snit over the cow's head, meaning to continue on my way, but Jonah stepped in front of me and grabbed my hand.

"Don't be so sure of yerself, Miss High and Mighty. I know you ain't got no other prospects. Folks say 'Don't marry her. She's a shrew.' But I got ways to handle a shrew, so I do. So before you get too old and shriveled up, we should get ourselves married, is what I say."

14

Talking to Jonah was always tiresome. Younger than I by six years, he was in no way attractive. Tall and angular, stooped in his posture, he looked sideways at you with a face devoid of good sense. His mother, Martha died and left him and Alonzo to fend for themselves, and it looked like fending was beyond them. Their farm had gone steadily downhill and I shuddered to think what the house must look like after years of neglect. Jonah was oblivious to all of that, preferring to portray himself as an upcoming country squire which made him quite a catch in his own mind.

"That's nice, Jonah, but I have only one reply to your proposal. 'No.' Same as last time and the time before."

Known for his delusions and not much else, Jonah was slow to pick up on signals and not anxious to learn, so he offended any prospective bride without knowing it. Jonah Riggs was not husband material, and every young woman in the Great Cove knew it.

"Excuse me, Jonah. I have business to attend to." I moved to get around him, but Jonah side-stepped to block my path. In exasperation, I shoved him aside and kept on going, hoping walking the three miles to my uncle's place would calm me.

I stepped across the creek, made my way back to the road, out of sight of the house and continued toward Uncle Thomas's farm. I knew I shouldn't be going there – knew it would come round to spite me in the end, but anger is a powerful thing – especially when it springs from injustice. You'd think walking three miles would settle me down, but no. There was no settling me that day.

Uncle Thomas sat on his front porch – sixty-nine years old and content to watch over the workings of his farm, directing here, advising there, lifting nary a finger while his sons carried out his bidding. He saw me and took off his wide-brimmed hat, adjusted his cravat, skittering his rocking chair into the sunlight.

"Good day, niece," he greeted me. "What brings thee on such a trek on a chilly day?"

"You, Uncle. You bring me here -- to thank you for all you do for Aunt and me."

15

He could hear the sarcasm in my voice, knew he was in for a tongue lashing, but, accustomed as he was to unquestioning obedience from all other sources, he must have found my tirades novel. He nodded as though in agreement with my words. "I do what I deem appropriate."

"Yes, Uncle, as though only your view of things mattered. As though you were gifted with a divine ability to perceive what others cannot. Would that we all were so wise."

Thomas Lander rose from his hickory rocking chair and stepped to the edge of the porch, looking down into the yard where I stood, hands on hips, ready to assail him with a storm of words. "Take care, niece, not to bite off the hand that feeds thee."

"Oh, yes, Uncle, the hand that so generously cares for me in my dire need. How can you stand in meeting and condemn the indigent, berate the idle, disparage the poor and not see that your own sins are greater than theirs? What of the greedy? The pretenders to charitable works? What of them, Uncle?"

"I know not whereof thee speaks. All I hear is whining in the face of generosity, ungrateful girl. I send thee thy share – nay, more than thy share – and thee come here to berate my benevolence? 'Tis fortunate for thee that I don't turn thee out, and I would but for the sake of my dear sister."

"Dear sister! Is this how you express concern for your dear sister? Send her the head of the cow? Really, Uncle? While you sit here rich and idle, sipping apple cider?"

Attracted by the row, Aunt Hannah and her two daughters ventured out on the porch, standing close to the kitchen door in case things got ugly. The girls, younger than I by half a dozen years or more, stood behind their mother, curious and perhaps enjoying just a bit, the berating of their father. Thomas Lander was known throughout Meeting as a skinflint. A stingy, tight-fisted miser whose interest in other human beings was limited to a nod and a terse good-day, unless there was business to be conducted. Everyone knew it, but no one spoke it to his face. No one but me, his sharp-tongued indigent niece.

16

"Thee needs to find thyself a husband, Susannah. A man to tame thee and teach thee thy place. One with the will and the patience to put up with thee. Though I doubt there is such a man on the face of the earth, for art thou not six and twenty and unspoken for? Best ye leave off of berating me and take up the cause of self-improvement."

I felt a shiver of anger run down my spine. "Oh, yes, Uncle. You with the evermore solution to every woman's problems. A man to fix her. A man to guide her. A man to set her on the right path. Really? There is not a thing wrong with me that having a husband wouldn't cure? Should I exchange poverty for a lord and master and a houseful of babies coming one after the other until my body wears out?"

A picture of myself, married to Jonah Riggs, surrounded by a passel of whining, crying babies passed through my mind. I shivered again.

"'Tis the lot of the female. Thee knows that. Now get on with thee. Get back home to help Betsy dress that meat. Thee have overstepped thy bounds this time. Go!"

I turned and stalked away, agitated beyond reason. It was ever thus with my Uncle. I took his lack of charity for as long as I could, then exploded in anger; he would listen for a measured time, stand his ground and I would return to my sad and hopeless place in the world.

Judith Redline Coopey

Chapter 3

October 1864
Milledgeville, Georgia
Carter Willoughby

Jennifer Ivey, still beautiful, stood in the doorway of the sprawling plantation house, shading her eyes with one hand, a vase of flowers in the other. We drove up the gravel tree-lined drive and around the circle to the wide veranda. I could see her face, bright, awake, hopeful. She must know I wasn't my brother. Oh, surely she didn't think I was a ghost.

"Jennifer! What joy to see you," Emily called, climbing down from the rig.

"Yes, Jennifer! We've brought you a visitor!" Ellen added.

I waved and helped Ellen down, nodding to Julius to drive round to put up the horses and visit his daughter, then followed the girls up the broad stone walk. Jennifer watched me approach, her face full of hope, though she surely knew there was none.

"Carter Willoughby! I was lost for a bit. You always did look so like Mark." She turned away, lifting her apron to wipe her eyes.

I reached for her, wrapped my arms around her, felt her shoulders shake with the effort to stem the tears.

"Oh, Carter, you do look ever so much like him. Forgive me. I can't seem to get over your brother."

"Yes. I understand. I hope it's all right for me to come."

19

"Of course. You're welcome here. I'll adjust. I have to."

She led the way into the house and bade us sit, then called to Nettie, her maid, to bring tea.

Nettie appeared in the kitchen doorway, looking insolent. "Why I should git tea for these here Willoughbys? They ain't nobody. Used to think they was. Ain't no more. Git yo' own tea."

I rose as though to mete out punishment, but Jennifer stayed my hand. "No, Carter, no. She's all the help I've got left – along with Viney, who declares she's leaving as soon as she's recovered from childbirth. The rest of the slaves have gone and left us. Nettie's been a great help to me. With no men around to run the place, I'm afraid we've let it go to seed."

I stood back, abashed. I'd no idea things were so bad at Ivey Plantation. Jennifer's father had died years ago, but her brother Austin had taken over and run things efficiently before the war.

"Why did Austin feel the need to go fight?" I asked. "Didn't he know how important it was to keep Ivey Plantation in production?"

"He just felt it was his duty to fight for the cause."

Her words rankled me. "He should have known there is more than one way to support the cause. We must produce cotton for trade. Where else will we get the money to finance the war?"

Jennifer turned away to face my sisters, leaving my question hanging in the air. After a brief silence, I tried to undo the damage I'd done.

"Where's Austin now? Have you heard from him?"

"Off in Tennessee last we heard. Chattanooga, I think. Some place called Lookout Mountain."

I shuddered even more at that news. Lookout Mountain was under siege and in danger of falling to Union troops any day now. Colonel Austin Ivey could very well have perished already, or be a prisoner which wasn't much better.

My failure to reassure Jennifer cast an uncomfortable pall over the little group. It seemed I'd brought more consternation than comfort. Regretting that, I stepped out on the veranda so my sisters could help Jennifer recover from my clumsy handling of

20

things. I'd meant to make a better impression, but I saw the folly in pursuing any plans, especially any that included men now serving. By the time the war was over, who knew where any of us would be? Clinging to hope seemed a waste of energy. My feeble effort to rescue Jennifer from her grief faded in the face of deteriorating property, rebellious slaves and the fear that Austin Ivey was doomed, if not dead already.

Dejected, I stepped off the veranda and walked down to the slave quarters to tell Julius my plans had changed. Given my awkward handling of things I didn't feel comfortable staying around with the girls, so I'd decided to take my leave.

I found Julius sitting on an upturned log outside a slave cabin, talking to his daughter, Viney. "Mornin', Viney," I greeted her. "Julius tells me you've a new baby."

She gave me a sassy looking-over, head reared back, mouth twisted. "You bet I do, Marse. This one goin' be free, time he's five, I'm bettin'."

I let the taunt go by and sat down on the edge of the porch. "Anyone doing any work around here?" I asked.

"No more'n they has to. Why should they? Yankees gonna come and burn it all. Give us the land. We goin' be rich. Gonna own this whole plantation some day. Just you wait and see."

I winced at her self-assured insolence. It would be hard to pull these blacks back into line once the war ended, win or lose. They'd been let go too far. Even Julius, once a loyal servant, showed disrespect. So while my own hopes for victory were weak and getting weaker, I still entertained the notion of somehow ending the war and getting down to the business of restoration, putting the south back together.

I turned to Julius. "Think I'll let my sisters stay the whole day, but I must get back home. I've business to attend to. You stay and drive them. I'll just borrow a horse from the stable."

I rose and walked in that direction, aware of derisive stares aimed at my back. I longed to return to the Army, where we could celebrate our victories, our prowess as soldiers, our surety of winning the war in spite of every evidence to the contrary. This

place was depressing. In the stable, I looked around for a groom –
stable boy – anyone who knew anything about the stock. No one.

In the stall beside our pair was an old gray – bony and saddle
worn. I picked a saddle off the rail and flopped it over her back,
watching the dust fly, then mounted and rode up to the house to tell
my sisters my plans. I stayed astride the horse with no intention of
tarrying any longer.

"Emily! I've decided to go on by myself. I have some things to
attend to. Julius will bring you home before dark."

Emily came out on the veranda, nodded and waved as though it
were just fine that I was cutting out on our little party. No
questions. No excuses. Just, bye now. See you later. Good old
Em.

That evening after dinner with my parents, I sat on the veranda
sipping whiskey and waiting for the girls to come home. As I
waited I picked out a tune on my banjo, a relic from my pre-war
youth. When the girls arrived, dusty and tired from the journey, I
offered my chair and asked about the rest of their day.

"Oh, we had such fun," Ellen cried. "We haven't visited much
at all lately. Remember how we used to visit all the time – here
and there? Ivey Plantation was a second home to us."

She sat down beside me on a settee, leaning toward the plinking
strings. "Oh, Carter, do play for us. It's such a happy sound –
reminds me of the fun we always had before the war. Remember,
Em?"

Ellen drifted off into memory, smiling and swaying to the plink-
a-plink music. She had her own way of dealing with tragedy.
Ignore it. Pretend it isn't there. Don't let it change a thing.

Emily was different. She neither ignored nor pretended, but
met adversity head-on with strength and determination. Now she
pulled up a chair in front of the settee and looked me square in the
face.

"You certainly didn't do your cause any good at Ivey this
afternoon."

"I know. I don't know what gets into me. I want to shake people into facing reality. Make them acknowledge what's coming. Prepare. Do something about it."

"Well, I agree with your purpose, but your approach is a bit off-putting. Jennifer can't even face the fact of Mark's death, let alone the prospect that her brother will never come back either."

"I know. I'm sorry. I think I need to get back to my troops. It's too disheartening to see what's happening around here, with nothing to stem the tide."

"You mean the blacks?"

"Yes, them, but everybody else, too. Going about as though the world weren't collapsing on their heads."

She took off her bonnet and leaned back in her chair. "What do you expect them to do? They're helpless to stop it. All they can do is wait and see how it all ends. See what, if anything is left."

"Ever think we were wrong to start the whole thing?"

"Of course. We all wonder about that. If we win, we were right. If we lose, we were wrong. That's the way it is with all wars."

I leaned over the banjo, picking out a familiar melody to distract myself from stark reality and took a strong draught of whiskey .

"That's no solution," she said, nodding to the glass. "We're in for it, all of us. The blacks think they'll be the better off, but I doubt it. They just don't know what kind of mischief the Yankees can think up yet. When I look at them – so completely ignorant, I don't see how they can survive either way, slave or free."

I watched her face as she spoke. Far more intelligent than any woman was ever given credit for, she bore the burden of insight. So much easier to be an Ellen or a Jennifer with only a shallow understanding of the world.

"I wonder if we shouldn't get out of here – go west. Start over. There won't be anything left for us when it's done." Her voice sounded hollow – empty.

Peering at her, I took another drink, stretched my legs out in front of me and picked out another melody. The whiskey was starting to take hold, loosening my tongue, tearing down whatever inhibition I had about speaking out.

"Oh, yes, and I have a new assignment. Detached service behind enemy lines. If I get caught, they'll hang me. Sometimes I wonder why I'm doing it."

Struck silent by this revelation, my sister looked out over the lawn, once cared for by slaves, now let go to its natural state except for a wide swath around the house, kept trimmed by Julius. My father's authority hadn't completely eroded. Yet.

"I wish you hadn't told me that. I'll worry more now."

I reached out and took her hand. "I could tell you not to, but it wouldn't do any good. I still care about the cause – the way of life we had here – but not enough to die for it. Is that cowardly?"

"Some would say yes, but I think we've let ourselves get taken in by too many romantic notions. The truth is, there's nothing romantic about dying for a lost cause. Randolph's death was romantic. Mark's was tragic. Yours would be a cold lead tombstone, leaning crooked in a weedy plot."

I winced. "Is it lost, do you think?"

"Some will hang on until the bitter end – cause others to suffer more for their tenacity, and end up losing anyway. Yes, I think it is lost."

I sat up straighter and picked out a melody – Shenandoah. Hauntingly beautiful, the strains wended their way through the darkness, over the quiet lawn. I looked at Emily, longing to hold onto this wise, clear-eyed sister of mine. Instead I refilled my glass.

"I leave tomorrow."

"God keep you."

Chapter 4

Late October 1864
East Sharpsburg, Pennsylvania
Susannah Lander

The first time I laid eyes on him, he was astride his horse looking cold, muddy, lean and tired. He slowed to a walk when he saw me, then stopped altogether. I guess he'd never seen a woman got up like me – old pair of muddy boots, dress caught up between my knees, ragged wool jacket made up for a man and a holey slouch hat held in place by a knotted bandanna. Or maybe he'd never seen a white woman digging potatoes in a muddy field. He looked me over real good before he spoke, like he was taking in every detail so he could write it up in a letter or something. He took off his hat and slapped it on his thigh, leaned forward, hands on the saddle horn.

"Good day, my lady."

That's the kind of greeting you don't get every day around here. My lady. Sounded like he might be makin' fun, but he wasn't. He was serious, straight-faced, not a bit mocking. He talked different – soft-like, elongated and drawn out, like he was tasting every word. He wasn't from around here. That was sure. I stood by, leaning on the digging fork as he let himself down from the horse, stiff from a long ride.

"You play that thing?" I asked, nodding toward a banjo he had tied behind his saddle.

"A little. Used to be pretty good, but don't get much time to play these days. My name is Mark Randolph. I'm a circuit rider – Methodist -- looking for lodging. Know where I can find a place to stay?" He smiled and extended his hand.

I wiped my hand on my dress and grasped his, smiling too, shading my eyes with my other hand. "Susannah Lander, sir. Pleased to meet you."

"I've been riding a long time. Right tired."

Mud spattered and threadbare, he looked like a peddler after weeks on the road. "I'll be here for a while, so I'm looking for some place -- more than a haystack to rest my weary bones in."

"Looks like you could use a drink, too. Well's right over there." I pointed to the roofed-over structure between the stable and our house. "Drink up."

He led his horse across the potato field to the well. I returned to my work, fully aware of his presence but anxious to appear preoccupied with digging potatoes. Once both man and beast had drunk their fill, he led the little mare back to where I still labored. At first he just stood and watched me like digging potatoes was about the most interesting thing he'd ever seen a woman do. I wasn't put off by it. He had a gentle way about him – I could tell that – and a kind of sadness, like he'd seen something of the harder side of life.

It was seldom anyone came to East Sharpsburg looking for lodging, so I didn't want to mislead him, but I sincerely wished I could think of some way to keep him from leaving right away.

"I don't know of any lodging, sir. I'm sorry."

I straightened up and tossed him a potato, motioning back to the well.

"You could wash it and have it for your lunch. And an apple, too, if you please." I nodded toward a gnarly old apple tree laden with fruit.

He caught the potato with his left hand and, leaving his horse stand, trekked back to the well, washed the potato and returned with two bright red apples that he polished on his britches as he walked. "Thought we could share lunch if you'd like," he said.

26

I looked up at the sun riding high overhead. "Guess it's time," I agreed. "I've got a heel of bread and a bit of cheese. You?"

"Just what I've managed to forage from you. I hope you don't mind." He sat down under a tree at the edge of the field and took a bite out of the potato.

Mind? How could I mind? Lunch with a handsome stranger? That didn't happen every day out here in the Cove. I sat down a few feet away, embarrassed about my get-up. Well, it couldn't be helped. The potatoes had to be dug, so what did a fashionable young lady wear to a potato digging party? Whatever was handy. I tucked my hair up under my hat and tore the bread heel in half, handing a piece to my guest.

When I looked up, he'd taken down the banjo and sat tweaking the strings, smiling gently, his blue eyes striking against the tan of his face.

"I'm sorry I don't know of any place you could bunk around here."

"Oh, don't be sorry. I'm sure to find something. This is such pretty country."

He looked out over the Great Cove, farm after farm laid out in orderly arrangement, ripe with the promise of a record harvest.

"Where do you come from, anyway?" I asked.

"I'm from Georgia, ma'am." His voice was soft, gentle, like you had to cock your head and listen to pick up all he said.

"Georgia? A rebel state?"

He nodded. "Not what you'd expect, now, is it?"

I rose and leaned on my digging fork to give him a good looking over. "No. Not at all."

"Well, I'm not your typical Georgia Rebel. If I were, I'd be fighting your husband or brothers and cousins. I'm an anti-slavery, anti-rebellion Methodist. Not popular where I come from, but I see it my duty to roam the country bringing the gospel of truth to all."

I giggled just a little. "Why'd you come up here to do your preaching? Did you think we needed it more than the South?"

27

He grinned broadly, eyes twinkling. "Why no. But it's harder to justify not wearing gray down there than it is to justify not wearing blue up here."

"Really?"

"Really. Down there every able bodied man is fighting for the cause. Up here you can spare some to work on other things."

"Like preaching the gospel?"

"The Lord's work."

"Hmmm." As I finished my lunch and rose, brushing the crumbs off my apron, an idea occurred to me. "You want lodging, maybe I guess my Aunt and I could find room for you in our stable if you ain't too picky."

"Not at all picky. I just require a place to lay my head and house my horse."

He looked at the hovel we called home and didn't raise an eyebrow even though he had the air of a gentleman about him and the thought of bunking here must have gone against his upper crust grain.

"Looks like you could use a man around some. Your roof's in pretty bad shape. Leak yet?"

"Not yet, but a shingle or two might blow off come a storm."

He looked thoughtful, rubbed his chin like he was considering my offer. "How much?"

Now Aunt and I didn't have any reliable income. We did some sewing upon a time and sold a little produce at the market in Martinsburg. Still, letting a stranger in required some serious consideration. "Would you like to see it first?" I asked.

"Sure." He led his horse – a right fancy one for some poor circuit rider – and followed me down the path to the stable.

Once inside I nodded toward a rickety ladder leading to the loft. "Up there if you favor it. Ain't much, but it's dry. I can sweep it out for you. Give you a couple of quilts."

He climbed the ladder, cautiously peeked over the edge of the floor and looked around. The room was barren except for a bunk built against the wall and a big wooden chest at its foot. He looked back down at me and nodded. "Clean and simple. It's all I require. How much did you say it was?"

I did a desperate calculation in my head, my brain scurrying about, trying to figure out a fair price. I'd no idea what to charge, but I purely hoped he'd want to stay. "A dollar a month. Unless you want your meals. Then it's $2.50. And if you want your laundry done, it's $2.75."

The room was hardly worthy of the name, true enough. But it was warm and dry and Aunt was a good cook and clean clothes would be an added bonus.

"I could fork up same hay for your bed," I said, hoping the whole arrangement would strike him as reasonable.

He nodded and stuck out his hand in the bargain. "Fair enough."

"Thank you, sir. How long do you want it for?"

"Indefinitely. I'll probably stay around until the war is over – then who knows?" "Let's pray that comes soon, sir." But not too soon, I thought. Give us some months to build up a savings.

"Is it all right if I bring up my things and turn my horse out to pasture?"

"Sure. You can work out the board with Mr. Riggs, the owner."

I left him to his business and hurried back to the house to gather up a broom, some quilts and an old feather bed Aunt had stored away in a trunk, and plodded back outside with my arms loaded down. Aunt, sitting on the porch weaving a wreath out of bittersweet, looked up in question as I passed.

"I just rented the stable room to a man from Georgia."

"What? You're doing what?" Aunt stopped weaving and rested the wreath in her lap, her brow furrowed in dismay.

"He's a preacher-man -- from Georgia. Looking for lodging," I told her.

"From Georgia?"

"Yes, ma'am. That's what he said. Georgia."

"What's a man from Georgia want around here?"

She watched in stupefied silence as I hurried on down to the stable with my armload of quilts. I knew I was in for a time of it, convincing Aunt the sky wasn't going to fall just because we took in a boarder, but I figured to save my convincing for a more private time.

A few minutes later after I'd made up the room for him, our tenant returned from bargaining with Alonzo Riggs about horse accommodations. I led him to the porch to make introductions.

"This here is Mr. Mark Randolph from Georgia," I told Aunt. "He's a preacher."

"So you said."

But, true to her nature, Aunt put aside her wreath, rose and did an awkward curtsy in greeting. "Might happy to meet you." I noted a healthy skepticism in her welcome, but I'd deal with that later. Money was money.

"Thank you. I'm grateful for the room." As though in emphasis, he sneezed twice. Must have been the dust.

After Aunt got over thinking the preacher man was going to murder us in our beds, we settled in to a routine of mostly going our own way and him going his and meeting at the dinner table. Most evenings he brought the banjo with him and plunked out a tune or so for Aunt and me. We Quakers don't have any music in our services, so my acquaintance with music was limited, but Aunt took to that banjo music like she'd been singing all her life. She and Mr. Randolph would sit together and try to work out the words to "Ora Lee" or "Tenting Tonight" while I hummed along, conscious that the Friends would not approve.

Within a week I gave Mr. Randolph two more quilts – Aunt loved quilting and had made a lot of them. I think he was as comfortable as could be, sleeping in an unheated stable. But then one day he came riding home ahead of a wagon loaded down with a parlor stove, installed it in his stable room and kept himself quite cozy, so he said.

Meeting was another thing. People will talk, you know. As soon as the Friends heard we'd taken in a boarder the Meeting assigned a committee to talk to us about the error of our ways. Two maiden women living almost under the same roof with a man no wise related to them? Shameful. Aunt was mortified that anyone would think ill of us, but I knew well enough what they'd think. Well, let them.

I assured the lot of them that there were no shenanigans going on and that they should mind their own business. They didn't take kindly to my impertinence, but I wasn't about to worry what they thought. I had a regular income and they could just go sit on a pin.

Mr. Mark Randolph was quite the comely gentleman – tall and straight with a thatch of brown hair and those blue eyes, and a quizzical expression, like he wanted to chuckle at something you said, but was holding it in. He was ever so polite at table, always complimentary about Aunt's cooking and asking if there was anything we ladies needed done. I have to admit I wondered about him from the start; there was something too good to be true in his manner, but $2.75 a month was a princely sum and I had no intention of passing it up.

He took to fixing things around the place, mending a leather door hinge or replacing a rotten fence post. Alonzo Riggs, if he thought anything about the arrangement, didn't say a word. As long as we helped him with the farm, mucking out the barn after milking or throwing down hay for the cows, he minded his own business except for occasional references to Jonah's quest for a wife. In return for the fallen down house, he gave us a jar of fresh milk and three eggs every day.

Jonah Riggs was another story. Even though he dwelt on the far side of handsome, he was still taken with himself, and had it in his head that any woman should be honored to pair up with him. Now, I know I said I was desperate to marry, but Jonah Riggs in no way resembled my idea of a husband. His head full of pride about his place in the world, he'd set out to find him a wife. Trouble was there were no takers. None of the girls he fixed his attention on shared his interest. So he made the rounds, tried to court every unmarried woman to no avail. Most of the time I minded my own business, but I was full ready to shove him out the door if ever the need arose.

Mr. Randolph tended to rise early and get on the road before light almost daily. I guess he had some followers, for every

Sunday he was gone all day preaching to small gatherings around the Cove. He'd ride that circuit rain or shine and return with a smile and not much else. Once in a while an apple pie or a loaf of bread, but most of the time, just an amen and a God bless.

It was hard for me not to corner him and pelt him with questions, for I was curious beyond reason about this Southern gentleman turned man of God.

One evening I was sitting on the bench near the cook stove when he came in carrying his banjo, ready for dinner. Aunt and I finished setting the table and placed a big plate of stew before him. I tended to my own dinner as he ate, all the while looking for an opportunity to open a conversation.

I was uncommon interested in him – who he was, who his people were, what he really thought about slavery, the war, most anything. He ate slowly, savoring every bite and asking for a second slice of bread that I watched him butter with deliberate care. He finished and slid his chair back, patting his stomach in satisfaction.

"Fine dinner, Miss Betsy. Your cooking rivals the best I've ever had." Then he rose and stepped over to the settle by the fire. "Do you mind if I sit and pick out a song or two?"

"Why no, sir. Not at all."

I cleared the table, Aunt took up her knitting, and our guest warmed his hands, all the while making pleasant conversation. "Did you have a nice day, Miss Lander?"

"Why, yes, Mr. Randolph. Mostly spinning was all. And you?"

"Very pleasant, thank you."

Aunt usually went to bed right after supper, leaving me to read or sew or knit by candlelight, so in spite of the impropriety, this evening she climbed the ladder early and took a candle with her, on the excuse that she was feeling a bit delicate.

I took advantage of the unexpected opportunity to speak with Mr. Randolph alone, anxious to learn more about him.

"Tell me, Mr. Randolph, where do you come from in Georgia?"

He yawned and stretched. "Milledgeville. It's a small town surrounded by cotton plantations."

"Does your family own such a plantation?"

"Why, yes, they do."

"And slaves? Does your family own slaves?"

"Yes, ma'am. They do."

I cringed at the thought. All my life I'd heard Quakers rise in meeting to preach against slavery, encouraging Friends to help slaves escape and defy the Fugitive Slave Law. Our Meeting was a hotbed of abolitionism – in solid support of the Underground Railroad before the war.

"But you say you're opposed to slavery?"

"I think it unfortunate that our southern economy has been built on it."

"Really?"

"Yes, ma'am. Such an economy is doomed to failure."

I doubted his assertion, but pursued the issue further. "What about your family? Are they holding onto their slaves, or have they let them go? And what do they think of you – slacker that you are?"

Mr. Randolph sat up tall and frowned. "Tell me, Miss Lander. Do you always quiz your guests so thoroughly or am I deemed special?"

He brushed some crumbs off his trousers and rose to put another log on the fire, giving me to fear I'd been too bold. But my curiosity aroused, I brushed aside his reticence and took another tack.

How could such a practice get started? How could anyone think it was all right to take away another's freedom? Make them work for no wages and beat them if they were disobedient? These and other questions rushed around in my brain, but I liked Mr. Randolph – was more than pleased to have some income, so I continued with measured curiosity.

"How many slaves does your family own?"

"Thirty-five when the war began. Now they're down to less than a half dozen, give or take."

"Oh, did they die?"

"Ran off. They've still got that Underground Railroad running, you know. Slave gets away, he can follow the Army or find other help along the way."

"Yes, I know about that. My Uncle Thomas used to be a conductor. He still moves slaves along when need be."

Mr. Randolph looked thoughtful. "Hmm. So you come from a family of abolitionists, do you? Hated where I come from. What about your father?"

"Gone west, but he was anti-slavery, too. He's out in Iowa somewhere now. My mama died and he sent my sister and me back to be raised by our two maiden aunts."

"Doesn't look like you've fared too well," he said, giving the threadbare room a good looking over. Then, by way of apology, he added, "Pardon me if I'm getting too personal."

I let the remark pass, more interested in learning about him than in reviewing my own condition. "What does the rest of your family think about you being a slacker?" I tried, but just couldn't let that one go by.

He frowned, looked around with a bit of a scowl. "Not much. My two older brothers died in the war, and my sisters will probably never marry. Too many possible bridegrooms have perished."

"You've lost two brothers? Oh, my. How can you justify abandoning their cause?"

He rose from the bench looking down at me. "A man has to live by his principals. I turned to Methodism in my youth and it teaches that all men are equal in the sight of God. So when the war started, I knew I couldn't fight along with my brothers, nor against them. That meant I had to find some other way to live."

I listened to his explanation with equal measures of admiration and skepticism. The man was a puzzlement, to be sure. If he was all he claimed to be, I could admire his dedication. But I still wondered how he could abandon all he'd ever known to ride circuit in abject poverty and be content with that. Besides, he seemed rather calm for a Methodist. I'd heard they were given to raptures and loud, boisterous expressions of faith. I found that strange, but Mr. Randolph didn't seem bombastic or ardent enough to be a Methodist, which made me wonder the more.

"Are your parents still alive?"

"Yes. Barely. My mother is in perpetual mourning for my brothers, my father consumed by helpless rage at the loss of all he holds dear. He's spent his life building Belfast Plantation."

"If the South wins, will you go back home?"

"Yes. I'll go either way. My family will need me more than ever."

"And if the Union wins?"

He frowned. "That would be a disaster."

"A disaster to save the Union? How can you think that?"

"Our way of life would be gone. We'd have to build a whole new economy. There'd be hatred and bitterness to last a lifetime. Remember, I hate slavery, but I don't hate the South."

I struggled to understand his complicated relationship with his roots. How could he hate slavery and still love the South? The South *was* slavery. It was built on it, depended on it for its whole way of life.

As I voiced my confusion, he shook his head. "Maybe we should talk about other matters You shouldn't concern yourself with such as this. Perhaps when you get married, you'll be busy with more feminine concerns -- not what happens in the broader world."

That did it! My inner light went out and I thrashed about in the darkness of indignation, anger and Irish temper.

"Oh, really, sir? You think women should only concern themselves with 'feminine' things? Do you think our brains too weak to solve weightier problems? Think the issues of human bondage and righteousness are beyond our ken?"

"No. No, Miss Lander, that's not what I meant. I meant you seem... Oh, never mind."

I winced at the ever-present need to keep the peace, but I knew it was the only way. We needed that $2.75 per month, and here I was on the edge of a tirade that could leave us destitute again. Now Mr. Randolph turned and laid a hand on my shoulder.

"My dear lady, I'm afraid I've insulted you. You misinterpret my meaning. I have nothing but respect for all women."

I took a deep breath and rose to face him. "Yes, I'm sure you do, Mr. Randolph. But if you stay around here, you'll find that Quaker women are different from those you're used to. We're educated and consulted and expected to share responsibilities. In short, a Quaker woman is much more than a mere ornament."

"Are all Quaker women as feisty as you, Miss Lander? I didn't expect to find them so prone to argue."

"Some are and some aren't. But at any rate, you'll find little sympathy for your homeland and way of life here. This war has dragged on far too long. In my opinion, the South should admit defeat and end the suffering. To hang on to the last bitter moment is to bear the guilt of thousands of unnecessary deaths."

"So, you think we've already lost, then?"

"You lost at Gettysburg. Your General Lee should have asked for peace then, and our General Meade should have followed him and demanded surrender. Now here we are more than a year later and men are still dying. The South can't win. Why continue the agony? The outcome will be the same."

Mr. Randolph rose and stepped away from the fire. "You certainly have a passel of opinions for an unm... Pardon me. I'm sorry to be so harsh, but your rhetoric sounds odd coming from a plain country girl."

"Plain I may be – and unmarried – and without prospects – but none of that impairs my ability to think or precludes my right to an opinion.

"True enough, Miss Lander. Forgive me. I'm not accustomed to arguing with women."

"I welcome the opportunity to broaden your realm of experience, Mister Randolph."

I couldn't resist a warning. "Oh, and Mister Randolph. No preaching your Methodism here. We're Friends. Birthright Quakers. Never been anything else."

He nodded and smiled. "I'll remember that."

Chapter 5

November 1864
Susannah

I knew as soon as I let Mr. Randolph rent the stable room that there'd be trouble at Meeting. Two unmarried women letting a man sleep in proximity to them would set the tongues wagging and the imaginations agog. I'd weighed it in my mind and decided that I didn't care what they thought, said or did. Life is hard, but it's harder when you let convention run it – let others make your decisions for you. They could do what they would. My destitute condition required a different way of looking at life. Being properly conventional and above reproach had yielded little.

When I went to meeting the first Sunday after Mr. Randolph arrived, several women approached me in a group and asked the obvious questions: who was the gentleman and what was his business? Then one or two screwed up their courage and asked the questions burning in all of their minds: Was I really renting to him? How long was he going to stay? Didn't I think it improper to let a strange man into our midst? Harriet Pringle, with more nerve than good sense, even asked if I had any idea how people would look at such an arrangement.

"Yes, Harriet, I do. I know there will be those who judge with little information to guide their judgment, but I must see to my own needs and my Aunt's."

"Your needs? I thought your uncle saw to your needs."

"Far be it from me to judge my uncle, but, no. He does not see adequately to our needs, so I must take care of them myself."

Harriet fell back in surprise. "Really? Why I saw your cousin Anthony drive by with a load of meat for you earlier this fall."

"If you can call the severed head of a cow a load of meat, perhaps."

A few other women joined in. "Isn't righteousness more important than material goods?" one asked.

"Indeed it is, but my aunt and I have committed no sin. He sleeps in the stable. That is all."

"And eats at your table," another observed.

"And plays the devil's music on that banjo thing."

"I hear he's a priest. Some Methodist or other."

The old Quaker prejudice against the clergy of other religions -- based on years of persecution of their own faith – came to the fore at the least opportunity.

"He is a Methodist circuit rider, not that that has anything to do with my relationship with him. Mr. Randolph is from the south, as well, but I don't expect you to hold that against him."

Looking around the group I noticed my old friend Mary Mickle among them, hanging back and looking very uncomfortable. So old alliances crumbled in the face of such 'outrageous' behavior. Let them.

We entered the meeting house and participated in silent meditation until at length, Harriet Pringle rose to speak. "I wish to reiterate my conviction that any familiarity with the opposite sex should be confined to tradition and among Friends, and any violation of our moral code should be dealt with."

That was all she said, but it spoke volumes and set in motion the process of condemnation. It was all too familiar to me; I'd witnessed it often growing up. A woman went astray in the eyes of the Friends for whatever transgression, great or small, and was read out of Meeting until she disavowed her behavior and promised never again to stray from the path of righteousness. The friends were gentle in their reprimands and forgiving if one renounced her error, but nonetheless firm in their demand that the offense discontinue and be renounced. In most cases other family members could be expected to reason with the offender and lead them back to the fold, but in my case, there was no such relative and therefore, no such influence. Aunt was too meek to do more than raise an eyebrow and I was too hard-headed stubborn to listen.

After Meeting, Aunt and I walked home in silence. She'd always been good to me, and it pained me to bring any kind of judgment upon her, but the prospect of another desperate winter weighed more than my regret.

"I'm sorry, Aunt. I wish there were another way to support us, but Uncle Thomas leaves me no choice."

"Aye, but where will we be without the support of the Friends?"

"They'll still support you. I'm the one who'll bear their disapproval."

"We could ask Mr. Randolph to leave. Things would be all right then."

I sighed. "All right? With no meat and little else to sustain us? No one knows our plight and no one is going to rescue us as long as Uncle Thomas has them convinced that he's taking adequate care."

"Couldn't you denounce him outright at Meeting?"

It took every ounce of courage she could gather for Aunt to say a thing like that. If the meek were to inherit the earth, Elizabeth Lander would be first in line, but even she couldn't deny our need.

"I could – in fact I've done almost that more than once, but it only stirs him for a brief moment before he goes back to his stingy ways."

"Maybe I'll talk to Hannah. She might be able to bring him round."

Aunt always tried to find the good in people. I wanted to believe in it too, but my own life had been a series of disappointments – enough to make me cynical – and had taught me to rely on myself.

"Aunt Hannah is as meek as a lamb – even more so than you. That's how she gets along with him. A shrew like me would only make him worse."

Aunt smiled in agreement. "Yes, dear, I'm afraid you would."

Walking home, we were approached by a man on horseback – someone I didn't know. He reined in his horse as he drew up alongside and tipped his hat to us.

"Simon Tolliver, ladies. I live up near Curryville. I hear you're renting out your stable room to a preacher. That right?"

I looked askance at him, asking after something that was none of his business. "Why do you ask?"

"I ask because I care what happens around here, and if what I hear is true, you might be bringing trouble into our midst."

Standing in the road looking up at him, I noted that he was carefully balanced in his saddle, one leg missing above the knee. Then I recalled hearing about a man from Curryville who'd lost a leg at the Second Bull Run.

"What kind of trouble is that, sir?"

"Spyin' kind of trouble is what I suspect."

"Oh, surely not, Mr. Tolliver. Mr. Randolph is a fine gentleman, here to preach the gospel. If I thought he was any other, I would never have rented to him."

Tolliver pulled in his chin. "I'm just trying to warn you. You could be harboring a Confederate spy, and if that's the case, I hope you'll turn him out immediately."

"If that is the case, rest assured I will. Now good day Mr. Tolliver. I'm confident you're mistaken, but I'll keep a good eye on Mr. Randolph just in case."

Irritated that people thought I wasn't smart enough to have considered the possibility that Mr. Randolph wasn't what he claimed to be, I started walking on down the road, motioning to Aunt to follow.

"Good day Mr. Tolliver. I don't see the situation as you do, but I will give your warning serious consideration."

Mr. Tolliver nudged his horse and continued in the opposite direction, not at all pleased with my response. All right. The

Meeting had warned me. Aunt had shown doubt and now this Mr. Tolliver was looking out for my welfare. It seemed to me they'd all rushed to judgment and I was prepared to hold fast to that $2.75 a month until some real evidence showed up.

As we approached home, I fell silent, contemplating my relationships with men – relationships that had forged low expectations and nurtured resentment. Papa. Samuel Lander, third son, lesser son in the eyes of many. Uncle Thomas was seen as a stalwart Quaker, prosperous, righteous and upstanding, while my father was seen as the weak, sniveling yielder to temptation. He'd married out of Meeting, you see, and been drummed out, refusing to admit his fault or return to the fold. Mama, not a birthright Quaker, continued in her own Presbyterian ways and ignored the whole entanglement. Weak? Well, perhaps he was, or perhaps he ended up that way for how he was treated.

At any rate I was only three when Grandpa Lander died and the will was read and Uncle Thomas got the farm and practically everything else, followed by Uncle John who got seconds, followed by Papa who got miserly thirds – a hundred dollars. That was all. Not enough to buy a farm – start one, even. In a fury, Papa used his money to buy and outfit a wagon to take us away from Pennsylvania forever.

Mama was with child when we left, and people warned Papa to wait until she delivered, but Papa was so mad, he couldn't hear a sensible word. We traveled west, Mama looking more tired and gray, losing ground every day. I wasn't much more than a baby myself, but some memories stick by you forever, and I recall that when we crossed the Mississippi into Iowa, Mama barely knew it. Papa kept telling her to hold on, that we were almost there, and she could rest for sure, but I think she was beyond hearing him. She died abirthing in Louisa County, Iowa three days after Papa staked his claim to a quarter section and set to building us a house.

The baby, my little sister Maggie, cried all the time for lack of mother's milk and Papa was frantic trying to get her some from a neighbor's cow so she wouldn't die, too. Snuggled in a corner of the wagon, I sucked my thumb and missed my mama, waiting for

Papa to take away the hurt. He didn't. Looking back, I guess he did the best he could, but the affect was the same as if he'd left me along the side of the road.

After a couple months, he heard of a family from Pennsylvania who'd had enough of pioneering and were going back home, so he asked them to take us, Maggie and me, back to be cared for by his sisters, our maiden aunts. Those people, the Clarks, were dirt poor and hopeless, but they agreed to take us, so there we were, a pair of waifs dependent on the charity of others for the first time, but not the last.

When you're too young to understand the meaning of folks' actions, you just accept the way things are, so when we got back to Pennsylvania, our relatives, the maiden aunts, didn't want us. I guess I shouldn't say they didn't want us like they just took a look at us and said no. It was more like one of them, Aunt Rachel, was sickly, and the other one, Aunt Betsy, had her hands full taking care of her sister, but the end result was that Maggie was handed over to the Edwards family of Martinsburg, and I was given over to Amos Sparks. No relation, either of them, but since Maggie was just a baby, the Edwards's took to her right away and she never knew rejection.

Amos Sparks was a steady, hardworking, dull witted farmer who ruled his family with an iron fist to make up for how he was treated elsewhere. He wasn't mean to me – he just looked right through me. If he spoke to me at all, it was to remind me how lucky I was to have a roof over my head and food on my plate. His wife, even duller than he, had no room in her heart to love another child, given she had six of her own and didn't show them much concern either.

I quickly learned to fade into the background, ask for nothing and do their bidding without question. Along with that I learned that I was no one, not important and certainly my needs were not to be given the slightest consideration. So my papa was the first man to teach me I shouldn't expect a man to take care of me, but not the last.

I grew up to about ten in the Sparks household, with two older "brothers" who used me alternately as their punching bag and their slave and four "sisters," all younger who mostly ignored me. No one knew how it was with the boys, and if I'd told, it would have gone worse with me, so I was relieved when sick Aunt Rachel died and kind Aunt Betsy offered to take me off the Sparks's hands.

What Aunt Betsy got was damaged goods. I was hurt and mad and ready for a fight, and I conjured all kinds of reasons why I should get one. Little girls were expected to be neat and clean and prim and obedient, but I was none of those. I ran around like a wild thing, spending long hours in the woods or down by the stream. I hated all the chores Aunt laid out for me –did everything I could to avoid them. I knew I should be nicer to her – she was unfailing kind, but there was too much rankle in me.

Then when I was twelve I was out picking berries one afternoon – by my lonesome as usual, when I heard a twig snap and turned to see Robert Larkin and Will DuPont standing near, watching me. They were older – maybe fifteen or so – and immediate when I saw them, I had a bad feeling.

"What'cha doin' Miss Susannah?"

"You can see what I'm doing – picking berries."

"Gonna share 'em with us?"

"Don't see why I should. You can pick your own."

Will had started to circle around behind so I wouldn't have a clear place to run.

"What if we don't want to?" Robert asked. "What if we'd rather have yours?"

I backed away, but Will already had my escape route covered, and Robert started a slow walk toward me. I knew what was coming. Knew it like I knew my name. A girl alone in the woods and a couple of toughs come along, and what's she going to do? I put down my pail of berries and stood my ground, ready to defend myself, but Robert's punch in the stomach doubled me over, knocking the wind out of me.

I crumpled to the ground, unable to breathe giving them freedom to carry out their business. One held me down while the other ravaged me, then they turned about. I screamed and struggled to no avail, and within five minutes I lay alone among the raspberry bushes, bloody and bruised. I crawled to a nearby brook and washed myself as best I could and went back to my berry picking. No need to think there was any cause to do otherwise. From then on I carried a sharp blade in the waist of my dress, determined never to get caught alone and defenseless again.

After Aunt took me in, she had all she could do to keep bread on the table and we struggled to survive until the meeting declared that Thomas Lander, Aunt's and my father's brother, should be our guardian. Aunt was relieved at that, but it didn't take me long to figure what kind of guardian he'd be.

Grinding poverty maddens you or it makes you strong. In my case it did both. I had a little schooling growing up. Enough to know that I was quick to learn – quicker than most – but not enough to give me a way to make a living. I learned all the female skills from Aunt: Spinning, weaving, knitting, sewing – all useful in a household, but since everyone else had mastered the same skills, there was small market for them outside the home.

The first house we lived in was right on Uncle Thomas's farm, but when his oldest son, Thomas Jr. was ready to marry, Uncle took the house over and told us we had to move. I always thought he felt better when we were out of sight. He made up an arrangement with Alonzo Riggs to let out his tenant house to us, such as it was, so that's how we came to live at East Sharpsburg.

Uncle Thomas made a great show of getting us settled and seeing that our needs were met, but as soon as that was done, he was gone from our lives except for an occasional skin-flint donation to our larder. I expect he thought I'd attract a man sooner or later and his responsibility would be done, but he didn't reckon on my plainness or my devilish personality. Both combined to make the chances of any coupling highly unlikely and that was fine with me for I now possessed a finely honed hatred of men.

So there we sat, impoverished and without hope when along came Mr. Mark Randolph. Handsome specimen that he was, I was unmoved by anything but his ability to pay us a monthly rent. My expectations for men were by then deeply rooted in cynicism, watered by resentment and nurtured by a long memory. In short, I discouraged all comers, denied any interest in men and kept myself out of reach. That's how I came to be twenty-six, unmarried and hard as nails.

Indeed my two main interests in a circuit riding Methodist minister from the South were to gain his coinage and challenge his beliefs at every turn. It was a long practiced way to sharpen my argumentation skills and hold him at arm's length, avoiding any chance of a closer relationship. So if the Meeting chose to assign a committee to look into my behavior they would find me up to the task of defending myself. In a way I blamed the Friends for my lot in life and was more than ready to point out shortcomings even to them.

Judith Redline Coopey

Chapter 6

November 1864
Mark Randolph

I've only been here just over a month and I'm about to turn into a block of ice. I don't know how these people stand the winters. Snow up to their knees. Ice under that. Winds blowing down from the mountains. God, I miss Georgia. Next time a general asks for a volunteer to go behind enemy lines, I'll get me behind the door and not come out until the volunteering is over. I don't know if I'll live till spring.

The thing is, I've a job to do – a serious job – maybe more important than anything I've done so far. I'm here to reconnoiter the engineering marvel of the century. That's what they call it around here – the Horseshoe Curve. They've engineered a gigantic bend in the railroad that gentles the rise and makes it possible to haul trains up the Alleghenies and beyond, and they're right proud of it. If we could blow it up – disrupt it for a good long time, it would slow their freight – harm their ability to transport goods, troops, whole armies for a while at least. That's what I'm here for. To figure out a way to put the Horseshoe Curve out of service.

They guard it – troops of Union soldiers stand guard twenty-four hours. It isn't as if they don't know how valuable it is – strategically and as a matter of morale. If we could get to it and put it to ruin, it'd scare the B-Jesus out of them – show them we can strike anywhere, anytime. Plus we'd interrupt supply lines all

47

over the Yankee kingdom, maybe not completely, but enough to slow them down.

In the meantime riding circuit was mighty uncomfortable in those dark November days. Alone and cold, often hungry, I plodded through snow or mud looking for chimney smoke or a light in a window, always ready to offer to work for a meal, just to get a foot in the door. Most folks were welcoming, at least at first. They'd invite me in and offer me whatever they had, listen to my story, even consider my creed. The Quakers were always polite and generous, but they made sure I knew Methodism held no interest for them. The town folk usually had some kind of religious attachment so few of them were willing to listen beyond the first five minutes. But the country folk, always glad for company, seemed more open, easier to persuade and it was among them that I had most of my success.

One family in particular befriended me, the Nobles, Everett and Maude, newcomers themselves, recently moved up from Berks County when Maude's father died and left her some money. They bought a farm in the Cove and were doing well, except for the local reluctance to embrace strangers until they'd lived here for twenty or thirty years. The Nobles saw me as a kindred soul, a fellow outsider whose need for acceptance might match their own, and the Nobles had two unmarried daughters, Olive and Beatrice, either of whom they'd have been glad to see married to a man of God. Careful not to encourage one more than the other, I led both Noble girls on, always the charming gentleman, full of fun and implied promise. Ashamed to be so duplicitous, I was careful not to pay too much attention to either girl. I had to stay vigilant and focused on the real task at hand, blowing up the Horseshoe Curve. Problem was, I hadn't reckoned on Susannah Lander.

Just last week I let myself get into another argument with her. Should have known better. These Yankee women – the Quakers especially -- have been raised to forget their place – assume themselves entitled to opinions far beyond their ability to deduce.

Well, I've learned my lesson. I'm more careful not to call attention to myself, especially negative attention. No need to make an enemy where I need a friend. Unabated, Miss Lander's curiosity could wreak havoc with my primary purpose. Paying too much attention to any young woman would be just dangerous enough to bring about my undoing. I resolved to keep my head, be patient, build trust, not get into endless arguments about slavery, the war and who was at fault, let alone who was going to win.

Still, Miss Lander had a disarming way about her. She wasn't pretty – she did little to fix herself, and her nose was just a little too long, but she had long, full chestnut hair and brown eyes that seem to know all about you. In the south, she'd have been a spinster aunt, living off the charity of a brother or uncle, not unlike her lot here, but at least there, she'd have a more comfortable life. But why should I care? She was nothing but an irritant to me -- way too curious for my purposes.

Just the other day she made it her business to advise me on the friendships I've made around here. Said I should watch who I take up with. I told her I'm a man of God and I'll take up with any soul who needs saving. She just laughed at that. Pretty self-possessed for a spinster with no money and no prospects.

"Mr. Randolph," she addressed me. "Excuse me for meddling in your business, but I think it warranted to warn you that you may be treading on dangerous ground with Helen Sperry."

Now Helen Sperry, a widow with five children in one of my congregations, was in need of a man to run her farm The gossip was that Mrs. Sperry might be willing to share her bed with anyone who'd take on the tasks of farm and family, so her neighbors tended to take offense at what they judged as her lack of morality. The Warren family from out near Henrietta befriended her, but it seemed their charity was tied to her joining their church and marrying Mr. Warren's indigent brother, so I and others suspected a plan to eventually turn her and her children out. I'd been trying to help her through these hard times.

"Local gossip, Miss Lander. I can't be concerned with it. Thank you, though."

"It's just that if you're not careful, they'll be accusing you of taking the same advantage. She's vulnerable right now. She wants to keep her farm and her children, but there are so many looking to take advantage of a poor woman -- take her property, which anyone could do once they married her. She needs protecting."

"I'm aware of that, Miss Lander. What she needs is a good husband, and soon."

"Such a shame that a woman in need of a husband is seen as prey."

"A woman with five children as prey? Hardly, Miss Lander. No man in his right mind would take that on."

"That farm is hers free and clear, but any man who marries her owns it outright the day she says I do. Lots of men would be more than happy to 'take that on'."

Why did every conversation with Miss Lander have to end in a diatribe on slavery or rebellion or women's rights? Didn't she ever think about women's subjects, like sewing and cooking? What made her so contentious?

In order to avoid another prolonged confrontation, I excused myself and went on my way, more interested in mail from my sister Emily than in persuading Miss Lander of the error of her thinking. Emily and I had arranged for her to send her letters to headquarters and they forwarded them by courier. There was an old abandoned barn down south where the courier left orders for me and took my reports. I never knew when he'd be by, so I just tried to check it now and again. This day there was a letter.

According to Em, things were getting worse by the day at home. The slaves had all but abandoned us. Mother retreated farther into her own world where my brothers were still boys and her greatest concern was what she'd wear to this year's parties. Father sat staring into space. Emily tried to put a good face on it, make light of it, but despair inevitably crept in. Em worried about Ellen, who'd taken to wearing Mark's old clothes and working in the barn and stables like a man. Em tried to stop her, but she insisted someone had to keep the place going. If I were there, they wouldn't have had to do that. Papa was no help. Em was afraid they'd run out of food before spring. Sometimes I thought I should desert and go home to take care of them, but I knew what it meant if I were caught.

It would take time, but I was building up a good little group of believers around the Cove. My congregation – one of them, at least – was even talking about building a church. I had to pretend enthusiasm for such a project, for I knew I'd be long gone before it happened. Anyway, one farmer gave us a piece of ground to build on and folks were talking about having a church-raising amid endless discussion about the size and shape of the new building. So I settled the issue by drawing up a plan for a simple chapel and everyone agreed it was perfect. When I signed on for this assignment, I'd no idea how persuasive I could be. Sometimes I thought I could get them to do just about anything in God's name. Maybe even blow up the Horseshoe Curve.

Anyway, my main group here in the Cove was growing fastest. The rest were just little clusters – one or two families that met in peoples' houses, content to sing a few of Charles Wesley's hymns to the accompaniment of my banjo and listen to me preach. I couldn't get over how they took everything I said for absolute truth and were willing to turn themselves inside out on my say so. Just calling myself a preacher gave me unquestioned status and respect. Sometimes I'd get so involved with my church work I'd forget that my job here was deception and destruction. Folks were unfailing nice, for Yankees.

Still I was uncomfortable with Susannah Lander's interest in me, where I came from and why I was here. I might have to move to get shut of her, but I found living in their stable a right comfortable arrangement. Warm room, good bed, clean clothes and fine cooking. The aunt could bake a pie to make you forget your purpose. It was better than the life I left – sleeping out on the ground, foraging for food and no question of clean clothes or body. Still, I worried that Miss Susannah was paying me too much mind – watching me – perhaps getting suspicious. She could complicate things.

Just the other day she was going on at a great rate about her sister's husband getting his notice to report for the Army. These

Quakers were a strange lot. Didn't believe in war – the older ones wouldn't fight for any reason. The younger ones might entertain the notion, but they'd been persuaded against it all their lives. I wished all the Yankees thought like that. The war would be over before it started.

It seems this Joshua, her sister Maggie's husband, got his notice and went to Harrisburg to find a substitute. A substitute! Can you believe a man would pay someone to go to war in his place? I guess that's happened in the South, too, but not in my circles. These people weren't rich. They had to scrape the bounty together and hope they could find someone who'd take what they could offer. I guess there were some willing to do it, 'cause Maggie came over here yesterday all aglow because Joshua got home the night before, a free man. Found a substitute -- some poor Irish immigrant with nothing to lose and no means of support -- and now everything was fine. I guessed a sum of money, a uniform, a cot and three meals a day were enough of an enticement. Better than he'd get in Lee's Army -- the three meals, for one thing.

I didn't say what I was thinking when Susannah told me this. Bit my tongue to keep from letting her know how happy it made me to know Yankees were paying substitutes to fight for them. Gave me slim hope that we'd beat these buggers yet and I could go home and save my family and the plantation.

In the meantime I kept up my pretense, careful not to arouse suspicion. Last Sunday there was a man at one of my meetings – grizzled-looking fellow with one leg amputated just above the knee – stood in the back, face all gnarled, and didn't say anything. When the preaching was over, he lingered until everyone else was gone and hobbled up on a crude crutch to speak to me.

"You really from the South?"

"Yes sir, I am."

His eyes narrowed. "How come you ain't down there fightin'?"

"Because the Lord called me to do his work."

"The Lord or the exalted Mr. Lee?"

"Oh, the Lord, I assure you. I've never met Mr. Lee, and I don't share his blind devotion to the South."

"Looks mighty suspicious to me. Us Yankees don't take to Rebs nosin' around, preachin' and studyin'. Mighty suspicious."

I shivered involuntarily. "Think what you will. I come to do the Lord's work. No other."

Leaning heavily on his crutch, he stepped away. "You'll bear watching, Reb. Lost my leg at Second Bull Run. Ain't worth much no more, but I know a damned spy when I see one."

That unnerved me. I expected a measure of suspicion until I could build trust, but this came from deeper than I'd expected. Building trust would take some time.

I asked Susannah about the man the next time we had a moment. "Who's the man lost his leg at Second Manas… aah, Bull Run? Big guy, heavy beard. Out by Curryville."

"Simon Tolliver, I expect. He's the only one I know lost a leg."

"Seems a might angry about it."

"Yes, wouldn't you be?"

"'Spect I would. He got on me pretty harsh about being a Reb. Like I was the one shot off his leg."

"I guess he's a might resentful about somebody like you walking around on two good legs while he…"

I shook my head. "I didn't start this war, and I don't support it. Why can't people accept that?"

"Because you're whole and it was your people who did start it. You can't blame folks for wondering about you. What are they supposed to think? Hale and hearty Southern gentleman walking around on two legs while our boys from the Cove lie dead at Antietam and Gettysburg."

I turned away. No use talking to her. Still, I was pretty sure that, given time, I could gain her trust and the others as well. I'd always had a way about me. Call it charm – it had served me well. I could joke and tease and cajole my way out of any situation, and I put my skills to work around the Cove. Smiled, joshed, tickled babies, complimented ladies, sneaked a slug of whiskey with the men behind the barn. It wasn't hard, really. Just make them think you're one of them – hard workin', common folk. The rest will take care of itself.

Judith Redline Coopey

Chapter 7

December 1864
Mark Randolph

It seemed Miss Susannah Lander had her own ideas about just about everything from religion to slavery to war to educating women. In short, she found every way she could to challenge and annoy me. You might wonder why I didn't just move in with the Nobles and have an end to her, but I enjoyed her company – found her interesting for the very differences that nettled me. She worked harder than any woman I'd known, without complaint, accepting her impoverished state. She demanded little and expected less, and yet I found it needful to try to please her – to ease her burden – to gain her approval.

One afternoon around Christmas, on a blustery day with no relief from the wind, I came upon her mucking out the sheep pens, her hair bound up in an old apron, her feet clad in boots probably discarded as worn out and beyond repair by some farm boy.

"Good day, Miss Lander. How goes life with you?"

She stopped, unembarrassed by her pathetic condition, leaned on her shovel, and peered at me over folded arms. "Well enough, Mr. Randolph. What brings you home so early? I thought you were gone for several days this time."

"Seems I'm needed closer to home. Mrs. Pheasant – the elder one – has had a stroke of apoplexy and isn't expected to live. Her son Malcolm sent a rider to fetch me from down near Williamsburg. Said she asked for me."

"Oh, your preaching has taken hold then?"

"Some." I leaned against the rail fence of the sheep pen. "Can I help you with that?"

"Nay. You'd get your clothes dirty. Can't have that if you're going to sit by a bedside. The smell alone might revive Mrs. Pheasant."

I chuckled. "It pains me to see you work so hard at men's tasks. Seems you should be indoors, baking or sewing."

"Work is work, Mr. Randolph. If it needs doing, it doesn't bear a label – women's or men's. We do what we must to keep ourselves."

"Where's Miss Betsy this morning?" I ignored the edge in her voice, sensing another "discussion" in the offing and moving to thwart it.

"Taken to her bed with a colic. She's getting frail. I try to ease her load by doing more."

"Yes, I see."

Out of nowhere a fleeting vision of what this poorly clad soul might look like in a new dress, hair coiffed in a becoming style and the latest bonnet flashed before my eyes. Just fleeting, mind you, for the picture before me belied any possibility of style. Still I wondered.

"Are you taking a break for lunch?"

"Yes, I suppose so. I brought lunch with me." She dug into her apron pocket and produced a chunk of corn bread, crumbs and all. "There's a stew on the back of the stove at home. You can help yourself if you've a notion."

"I was hoping you'd join me for some conversation. Maybe look in on your aunt. Save your Johnny Cake for an afternoon snack." What was I thinking?

She tilted her head and peered at me, hesitant. "Well, I guess I could. The sheep can muck about on their own while I lunch."

So we walked back the quarter mile to the house, discussing, of all things, poetry. It seemed Miss Lander was enthralled with the Quaker poet, John Greenleaf Whittier. She even owned a copy of his work, and found him inspirational.

56

"I'm sorry, but I haven't heard of Mr. Whittier or his work. Is he well known hereabouts?"

"Yes, of course. He's an abolitionist and a naturalist. A New Englander. Quite romantic, really. Surely you've read some of his poetry. "Barefoot Boy", perhaps? Or "Memories"?"

I shook my head. "I regret that I haven't had the pleasure. Not that I'm averse to poetry. It's just that my experience is limited."

She smiled. "It's all right. If he weren't a Friend, I probably wouldn't know of him either."

As we came up to the house Miss Lander paused to remove those wretched boots. I thought of asking where she got them, but restrained my curiosity, not wanting to offend her, even though it seemed impossible to do that. She took no pride in appearances. Distained it, really. So unlike the young women I knew. I turned away as she slipped out of the shoes on the doorstep, in an effort to maintain decorum that I well knew *was* important to her.

As soon as she'd dished out a plate of stew to set before me, she climbed the steep stairway to her aunt's room to check on her. I sat eating my stew and a handsome chunk of the cornbread, hoping she'd join me at table. For a fleeting moment I thought of my own sisters probably eating less well that day and wished I could change places with them, at least for the meal.

"Mr. Randolph, would you like a tankard of cider?" She reappeared, making her way down the stairs stepping sideways on the narrow treads.

"Yes, please. How is your aunt?"

"Still poorly. I may have to call Sister Barkley to tend to her if she isn't better by tomorrow."

"Sister Barkley?"

"Yes. The doctor for this little community."

"Doctor? A woman? Really?"

She brought her plate to the table and sat down before she addressed me. "Certainly a woman doctor. Educated in Philadelphia. Don't you approve?"

"No. Not at all. I mean, it's just that I've never heard of a woman doctor before." I noticed Miss Lander's back stiffen. "It just isn't done in the South. For birthing, yes, but surely she wouldn't tend a man."

"And why not?" Her tone was challenging, warning me to tread lightly.

I stared at my plate, took a drink of cider, looked out the window, stalling. "On the plantations the mistress tends the slaves, but no one calls her a doctor. They've no training. When the need arises, we call a doctor out from town. Not for the slaves, of course."

Her back stiffened even more. "Tell me, Mr. Randolph, do you think it right to treat the slaves with an untrained hand, but to reserve the best trained practitioners for the masters only?"

"I... I don't know. That's just the way things are done. We don't question the rightness of every act. Sometimes we just do things as they've always been done and don't subject every practice to moral judgment."

"I see. So a number of wrongs continue because no one bothers to examine the rightness of them? Your southern society baffles me. Surely someone sees the transgressions. Don't they ever speak out about them?"

"Speak out? Where would they speak out? And to whom?"

"I would assume they would rise in church and speak about the wrongs being daily perpetrated on the slaves. On the wrongness of slavery itself. Doesn't anyone do that?"

"No. That wouldn't happen in one of our churches. Slavery is an institution – the very foundation of our society."

"I would think a man of God, like yourself, would rise in opposition."

"Yes, ma'am, but if I were to stand and speak against it, I'd bring wrath upon myself. That's why I came here, to preach to willing ears. Perhaps one day I'll be able to return to my roots and condemn the practice publicly, but until this war is over, I'd fear for my life if I took such a stand."

Miss Lander rose, cleared the table and reached for the latch. "I'm sorry you don't feel compelled to witness where your voice should be heard, Mr. Randolph. Now if you will excuse me, I have business with some sheep."

She tied on her bonnet, stopped outside the door to struggle her feet into those despicable shoes and was gone. I sat drinking my cider, feeling perplexed. This woman held strong opinions and was in the habit of expressing them with conviction. I was at a loss to convince her otherwise, maybe because of my upbringing and maybe because she was so sure she was right. At any rate, I sometimes gave serious consideration to moving in with the Noble family, except that would complicate my life even more. Keenly aware of my mission, I tried to put Susannah Lander out of my head, and I did – most of the time.

✳ ✳ ✳

Susannah

I slogged out to the sheep pens, my work shoes slipping up and down on my heels. By the time I arrived, I was out of breath and my feet ached from the miserable shoes. I had one other pair, but one trip through the muck would ruin them, so I made do.

Once there I was caught up short by the presence of Jonah Riggs, and stopped in my tracks, uncomfortable to find myself alone with him, even in the open field.

"Seen your cousin Anthony here back a ways. Said he brought some meat. Seems like you had to work pretty hard for nothing but brains and tongue. Your uncle doesn't do more than he has to, am I right?"

I took a couple of steps back, uncomfortable with him standing so close. I knew Jonah's reputation and I was pretty sure his pa treated Aunt and me better than he needed to in hopes of gaining a daughter-in-law at some point. Alonzo Riggs could go suck an egg. I'd die before I let myself get paired with his derelict son.

"That's true enough. Aunt knows butchering. Handles a knife like a man." I mentioned that just to remind Jonah that two women living alone couldn't be counted as helpless by the likes of him. It was true Aunt Betsy had cut a few bull calves into steers in her time. I wanted Jonah to be aware of that.

"How you getting' on with yer preacher?"

There was always something about the way he asked any question that made me suspect he had a plan in his head – a plan I wouldn't like.

"Right well."

"Folks is talkin' ya know."

"Well, let them talk. There's nothing to concern them, really."

"Bet I could make them talk all the more. Just tell it that I saw you goin' down to the shed t'other night in yer nightgown."

Anger welled up within me. "Why would you do that?"

"Jist for the fun. You actin' all high and mighty since you got yerselves a boarder. You're thinkin' you're a cut above common folk, but you still ain't got a nickel to rub against another one, so jist git over yerself."

"But you know it's not true, that you never saw me go down to the stable in my nightgown. Surely you wouldn't tell lies about me." I struggled to keep my voice steady.

"Might if I wanna. Lessen you treat me nice."

I shuddered. "How nice?"

"Nice as I please. Oh, yeah. My pa says I should marry up with you." He turned to spit, grinning a wicked grin. "No need to answer me now. I'll let you think on it. But you might's well tell that there preacher he gotta go."

I felt rage rising up. "Don't ever think you can make me marry you, Jonah. Tell whatever lies you want, but I'll never let you near me. I'd rather drown in the pig muck than let you touch the sole of my shoe."

Jonah looked down at my muck-covered shoes and laughed. "That's all right, Missy. You go on and keep pretending you're quality. I'll just start my little rumors aflyin'. We'll see who gets believed."

Seized with a desperate need to get away from him, I backed away, then turned and ran back down the track toward the house, head down, shoes clopping off my feet. Rage blinded me to anything but keeping myself from tripping over stones until I ran straight into Mark Randolph coming out the lane. He caught me as I was falling, clearly concerned at my distress.

"Miss Lander, what's wrong? Was that young man bothering you?"

I stood in the middle of the lane, catching my breath, holding back tears, my hands shaking -- no place to turn. Jonah Riggs would have his say. I could only stand by and hope people wouldn't put any stock in his lies. As we stood in the lane, Jonah walked on by us, brushed against me, his jaw set, looking out of the corner of his eye at Mr. Randolph as he passed.

Judith Redline Coopey

Chapter 8

November 1864
Mark Randolph

Concerned as I was about Miss Susannah Lander's curiosity, I couldn't let myself be distracted from the task at hand. I set myself a weekly circuit that took me around the Great Cove and back to Altoona, skirting the mountains close enough to edge the Horseshoe Curve without arousing suspicion. On occasion, I'd stop by a spring not far from the great engineering marvel, water my horse, do a keen observation and maybe strike up a conversation with one of the soldier guards who often lolled about in front of their fire, leaning on their rifles or napping in the rough lean-to they'd built as shelter against the wind. I was careful to take in any changes in personnel or numbers of troops, making note of the train schedules and, when I could, the kinds of freight being shipped.

On one such afternoon as I let my horse drink her fill, I was approached by an older soldier, a sergeant with a mean eye and a suspicious way about him. "What's yer business around here?" he demanded. "Don't you know this is restricted territory? Ain't no civilians supposed to be near the rails."

Putting on my best imitation of humility, I replied, "Oh, no, sir. I didn't know. I was just giving old Lady Legs here a good drink."

He stepped up close – obviously meaning to intimidate, but I held my ground. "Well, best you move on afore I git it in my head to move you."

63

"Oh, sir, you wouldn't molest a preacher, would you?"

"Man of the cloth? Just 'cause yer wearin' a black suit don't make you no man of no cloth."

"I guess you have to take my word for it. Black suit or no, nothing stops me from preaching God's word."

"What ere kind a preacher are you? And where's yer church? I know every church hereabouts, and every preacher, and you ain't one of 'em."

"Circuit rider. Methodist. Got a couple little congregations in the Cove and one good sized one hereabouts."

"Methodist?" The man almost shouted it, his tone derisive. "By God, that's a good one. Methodist. I heard of them. Kinda crazy. Hootin' and hollerin' and praising God like they know him personal. That's what you are?"

I nodded. "Come to one of my meetings, friend. I suspect you're not as happy with your lot in life as you might be. Come join us, worship with us and see how wonderful life can be with Jesus."

"Not happy? Well, how happy should I be, stuck out here watching trains go by and wondering how my woman's gettin' on keeping the farm. And you. Why ain't you wearing this here uniform? What are you, one of them draft dodgers?"

"Seems to me your duty here is preferable to dodging Confederate bullets. Your uniform looks clean enough and barely worn. As for me, I've got a condition." I tapped my chest and coughed just a little.

The sergeant stepped back to avoid exposure to my 'condition.' "Well, you still ain't allowed to dawdle around here. We gotta protect this here railroad from the damn Rebs, though if you ask me, they ain't got the smarts or the courage to come all the way up here and try any shenanigans. They're beat. They just don't know it yet."

"What makes you think they'd want to do harm to this engineering marvel?"

"Hell if I know. It's just one bit of rail. Hundreds of miles of it all over the north. They could blow up any of it if they had the gumption. Can't guard all of it. But some general somewhere thinks this is a target, so here we stand, day and night, all year round, watching trains go by."

"Must get pretty boring."

"Yes and no. They's always someone happening by – farmers, railroad bosses, track crews. Get up a card game now and then. And they's a girl or two wanders by on her way to pick firewood or visit a neighbor. Once in a while you can strike up a conversation – if you know what I mean." He let out a loud guffaw, wiped his rough beard and hitched up his pants.

"I been conversatin' just this morning. – afore you showed up. Over there." He jerked his thumb back toward a little grove of trees. "Them farm gals is sump'in. Know more about conversatin' than any city gal I ever met."

I watched him carefully as he went on about his romantic exploits, sizing him up for what I hoped him to be – lazy, irresponsible and easily distracted.

"What's your name, soldier?"

"Myers. Baxter Myers from Shamokin. What's yers?"

By the time I'd moseyed on a couple hours later, Baxter Myers and I had established a cordial relationship and I'd collected a peck of information about troop strength, schedules, guard posts and officers -- which were strict and which were lax.

Slowly, carefully, my plan began to take shape. I mounted my horse and rode down the slope toward Duncansville, lost in thought. The weather was fine for December and I took off my coat, all the while paying little attention to the trail. Once I thought I saw a rider approaching, but he ducked off some distance away. Still I'd seen enough of him to recognize the one-legged horseman: Simon Tolliver.

In the meantime, three small congregations were forming in the Cove – one not far from where I lived. I was watchful because Miss Susannah Lander was close enough to keep an eye on my comings and goings. While she made a point of minding her own business, I could tell by the tilt of her chin that she was interested in my enterprise and skeptical of my purposes.

Judith Redline Coopey

Chapter 9

November 1864
Mark Randolph

Those three small flocks were starting to keep me busy – the most serious by far, was the one near Williamsburg in Catherine Township. We met in a little clapboard church near Mt. Etna, an iron plantation along the Pennsylvania Canal. The countryside was dotted with iron furnaces, all producing cannon, shot and caissons for the Union army. I found the breadth of industry amazing. It made me wonder how the Confederacy was going to compete even if we did win the war. In the south one could ride for miles and see nothing but cotton fields, tobacco fields, all kinds of agriculture, but factories, railroads, any industry at all is scarce.

A second little church group I was nurturing was just on the southern edge of Hollidaysburg, the terminus of the old Pennsylvania Canal. Folks around here were almighty proud of their transportation system. That canal was a marvel of its own not long ago, and the Portage Railroad that took the canal boats up the mountain and sent them down to Johnstown was unparalleled by anything we had in the south, even though it was obsolete already. Now it was the railroad, snaking around through the valleys and winding its way up the mountains. I was thoroughly impressed with the industry and the agriculture these Yankees had developed.

The best part of my ride was traveling north from Taylor Township through the Great Cove, looking out over those beautiful, orderly farms. These people had carved out a fine life for themselves without a slave in sight. I admired them for that and wished the south had grown up the same way. Too late now.

But lest one get too complacent, riding up through Houston and Woodbury Townships on a sunny but cold afternoon, there was always the possibility of a less than pleasant encounter, like the time I met a man with a wagonload of vegetables stopped along the side of the road, a light skift of snow covered the ground and the vegetables. Red-faced and sweating profusely in spite of the cold weather, the man waved away my offer of help at first. I got down from my horse and persisted, for I could see that it was a job for more than one man – maybe five.

"What happened here?" I asked, rolling up my sleeves and stooping in the snow to assess the situation.

"Axle broke down at the hub. Hell of a fix. Won't get to market today."

"You'll have to unload and bring another wagon."

The man looked disgruntled. "Trouble is, I ain't got no other wagon, nor anybody to bring me one."

"Well, let's unload the produce and see if we can get the axle off. I can stay here and watch your load while you take the axle to be fixed."

His impatience now came to the fore. "Cain't be fixed. Needs a whole new axle. I'm done fer. This produce will get stole afore I can get the wagon fixed."

"Isn't there somebody who could come and help you?"

He sat down, back up against the wagon wheel, head in hands, mumbling. "Who are you, sir? You ain't from around here, are you?"

"No. I'm a circuit rider. Minister of the Gospel."

He seemed uncomfortable, looking around with apprehension, but he made no move to unload the wagon, which to me seemed like the first logical step.

"Come on, let's get to it," I urged.

"No! Leave that stuff alone. This ain't yer affair."

I stopped, puzzled that he'd refuse help. "No, but I'm here and you need help, so I'm offering."

"Just git on yer way and leave me be. I'll think of something."

Just then I heard a sneeze. Loud, close by, and unmistakable. I looked at my companion, frowned and stepped nearer to the wagon.

"Hold there, Mister. Don't go no closer to that wagon. Just be on yer way and fergit you met up with me."

"Why? Who's in the wagon?"

"None 'o yer damn business. Now git gone before I have to do you harm."

I stepped closer to the wagon and lifted a couple of cabbages out of the way. Beneath the produce I could see rough boards laid lengthwise and nailed in place with space in between.

"You haulin' people?" I asked.

The man stepped up real close to me. "Too late now, I guess. Slaves. Bound for Canada."

"They're free. Ain't you heard of emancipation?"

"Course I heard. That don't mean they can just come and go. Some slave catchers still hunt them down and sell them off to Jamaica or some other God-Forsaken place. We're just tryin' to get 'em along toward Canada. They's hundreds of them wandering around in the south right now. Followin' the Army, gittin' along any way they can. These ones is tryin' to get to Canada where they got family."

"Okay. I see your problem. Can't blame you for being testy, but we have to move along before things go sour."

I looked around for any place to hide the fugitives. It was just past noon, so darkness was a long way off. "Tell you what. Let's get them out and I'll lead them to that creek over there. I'll keep them in the shallows until dark and then take them back to my house. My land lady is sympathetic. She'll hide them out until you can get your wagon fixed and come for them."

The man chewed his lip. "That there's Piney Creek. But hold. How do I know you ain't gonna steal them away – sell them to some slave catchers?"

"You don't. You don't have anything but my word as a preacher and a man. But you're in dire straits, so I guess you'd better make up your mind soon."

Unloading the produce in the snow made us both sweat a gallon. I hadn't worked so hard in six months or more, but it felt good to flex my muscles again, all the while wondering how I'd gotten myself into joining hands with the hated and infamous Underground Railroad. But there it was.

I had to play the role to keep this man from questioning who I was or what I was up to, so I put my back into it and within about ten minutes we had the produce unloaded and piled on the ground. Once that was done, I gave the man my name and told him how to find the Lander place.

"Oh, yeah, I know that name. Lander. Heard the whole family been active in the railroad for years."

"Right. Well, I don't know them well. I'm new around here."

He looked at me with skepticism. "Where you from then?"

"South. I mean, south of here. Down in Bedford County."

"I knew right well you wasn't from around here."

I nodded and jumped up on the back of the wagon, picked up a crow bar and proceeded to pry up the boards. Opening up the false bottom took only a few minutes, and soon the blacks, three men and two women, climbed out of their wagon-coffin. I looked around for anyone who might happen by, saw safety and motioned for them to follow me. The six of us crossed the empty field, bending down to keep out of sight. Fear was writ large on the fugitives' faces, but I was confident we'd be all right if we could make it to the creek bottom where high banks would shield us from view. As we trekked across an open field of corn stubble, hurrying to reach the safety of the tree-lined creek bottom, my thoughts traveled to Georgia and what my family would think if they could see me now – or my soldier friends. God! What have I got myself into?

Chapter 10

November 1864
Susannah

By the time he'd been with us more than a month, I'd formed a strong opinion of Mr. Randolph. Hard-headed, closed-minded, typical man. And yet... I looked forward to his coming home for dinner every night – enjoyed hearing him play the banjo and wished we'd get some time to talk about more than casual things. Even Aunt seemed in a better humor those evenings when he stayed and talked awhile. Imagine then, how my take on him softened when he appeared on a dark night, muddy, wet and accompanied by five fugitives – three men and two women.

Awakened by banging on the door, I rose and went to see what the trouble was. There stood Mr. Randolph, shivering and so dirty I hardly recognized him, with these poor unfortunates in tow.

"Mr. Randolph! Whatever have we here?"

"Former slaves, Miss Lander. I thought you'd know what to do with them."

"Why, yes, but..."

"Hurry, Miss Lander. I fear we might have been followed. Please, can we come in?"

Since I hadn't lit a lamp, the house was dark, so I stepped aside as the bedraggled group trooped in. Good thing Aunt was a heavy sleeper. I wanted to help these people, but even lighting a lamp could be dangerous.

I felt in the dark for a loaf of bread and a knife and proceeded to cut off slabs and pass them around. The fugitives took it hungrily and ate in silence.

I turned to Mr. Randolph. "How did you get involved in this?"

"Met a man who was having wagon trouble. Turned out they were part of his cargo. I wouldn't have thought there was any danger any more, but I guess there are still slave catchers out and about. Anyway, I kept them sheltered by Piney Creek until after dark, and we made our way here. Three horsemen passed close to us – tough looking lot – and I thought I heard mumbling about one able bodied man going for as much as $1000. I just hope they didn't turn and follow us."

I breathed deeply and looked around the room. Unnerved by the prospect of trouble, I felt compelled to talk as I worked.

"In the days before the war, we took care of a regular stream of fugitives – almost everyone in our meeting did something. My Uncle Thomas, skinflint that he is with us, was well-known among the Quakers as a conductor."

I nodded toward the slaves, huddled near the fire. "We'll keep them in here as long as we can. I'll send somebody for my Uncle Thomas at dawn."

Mr. Randolph's eyebrows rose. "That uncle? The stingy one? I wouldn't expect much from him."

"If he can't do anything, he'll know someone who can."

I set about pulling quilts out of Aunt's trunk, handing them out to the fugitives. Aunt would have cringed at her quilts being used to cover such dirty, muddy bodies, but it couldn't be helped. I sat down at the table, wondering aloud how I could feed such a lot.

"Aunt and I have some food put by, dried corn and canned beets, tomatoes and beans. There's a little flour, so I can mix up some bread dough. What I have won't last more than a couple of days with eight people to feed."

Mr. Randolph rose and announced he was returning to his stable room to clean up and care for his horse. He returned about an hour later, a pistol stuck in his waistband.

"What's that for?" I asked. I couldn't hide my dismay at the prospect of violence.

"One has to be ready to defend oneself."

"But I don't want anyone to get hurt."

"Nor do I, but if I wasn't prepared to defend these people, why would I have brought them here in the first place? Why not just leave them by the roadside?"

I turned away from the argument, maybe for the first time ever. Reality broadened my vision.

"Mr. Randolph, can I ask you to ride to my uncle's after sunup and tell him of our predicament? I should stay here and bake the bread so we can feed these folks."

"Of course. I just hope your uncle is of a mind to help."

"Oh, he'll help all right. Besides I don't mind giving him a chance to see how spare our larder is and maybe encourage a little more charity on his part."

Aunt descended the steps in the early morning light to find her kitchen occupied by a sad-looking lot. Always one to take things as they came, she set right to work helping me get food on the table. She mixed up a measure of corn meal for Johnny Cakes while I carried in a load of wood for the stove. The two black women stepped up to help with the cooking, but the men were, of necessity, confined to sitting on the floor, waiting for breakfast.

Once the men learned that my name was Susannah, they began to sing, softly, "Oh Susannah, don't you cry for me..." As Mr. Randolph joined them and the song was taken up by the women, I hummed the now-familiar tune. "The sun so hot, I froze to death, Susannah, don't you cry."

Singing broke the tension and for a few minutes, we were just a group of friends singing together and clapping softly to the tune. I laughed as they sang, delighted at the novelty. The joy of singing was new to me.

When a wagon drove up and stopped a little before ten o'clock, I stepped out to greet Uncle Thomas, accompanied by his sons, Anthony and Stephen. "What's this thee's got us into?" Uncle asked, his tone full of bluster.

73

He gave the place a critical looking over while I told him what little I knew about the fugitives.

"Do you still have connections to pass them on?" I asked.

"Yes, if need be. Seems to me though, they could just go on by themselves. No need for secrecy any more. Let them pass in broad daylight and give them names of places they can spend the nights."

"But what about slave catchers? Aren't they still around?"

"Some, but just one armed scout would be all that was needed to keep them at bay."

Mr. Randolph interjected. "I thought you Quakers were opposed to violence."

Uncle shrugged. "Not opposed to anyone else using their own means of persuasion."

Mr. Randolph added to his stock of information. "I think we ran into some slave catchers last night. I'd prefer we took care of them until they got up as far as Erie, at least."

"Very well, then. I have a contact in Altoona – railroad man. He might be able to get them on a freight train for Pittsburgh, then others can get them on up to Erie."

I breathed a sigh of relief. It seemed once involved, Mr. Randolph stood ready to do whatever he could, especially if there was a quick and happy solution.

"We'll wait until dark to take them to Altoona," Uncle continued. "My man there can hold them until he gets the train arranged." Nodding to his sons, he moved to the door, but, seeing my chance to call his attention to our needs, I stepped up.

"Oh, Uncle! I'm sorry to bring up a sore subject, but as you can see, our food supply is in need of replenishment. Perhaps you could send some stores over for us?"

My approach was as feminine and compliant as I could make it. If I didn't ask, and do it in front of everybody, Uncle would conveniently forget Aunt and I existed.

He looked around with a sour face and said, "Yes, yes, I'll take care of it. I always do."

Once he was gone, Aunt and the two black women and I prepared lunch for the refugees, after which I found time to sit down and rest on a bench near the fire. Mr. Randolph stayed close, apparently feeling it his responsibility in case there might be trouble. He settled in beside me, laying his pistol on the bench between us.

"So this is how you've spent your time Miss Lander? Sheltering runaway slaves?"

"Some. Others have served more than I. I understand you don't approve of slavery, but I'm surprised to see you put yourself in harm's way for them."

"They're human, aren't they?"

"Of course, Mr. Randolph, but you being a Southerner…"

"Really, Miss Lander. I think if you knew me better, you'd not find so much to dislike."

I smiled at that. "Dislike, sir? More likely much to disagree with, but I strongly defend your right to whatever opinions you hold."

In truth, I was beginning to find him quite likeable, his background notwithstanding. In bringing these slaves to my care he'd enhanced his standing more than a little. I moved over to give him room on the bench, amused by the circumstances. Always guarded around men, here I was, stripping down the barricades to conversation. Becoming more open. Even accepting.

"Please call me Mark. I'm not used to being Mr. Randolph," he continued, his warm smile engaging. "I feel a certain satisfaction in helping the fugitives."

Such an admission had me wanting to hold back the night. Give us more time. More reason to talk. Though I struggled against it, I could feel myself falling under the spell of this puzzle of a man.

My reverie was interrupted by the sound of a wagon approaching. I thought it must be my uncle coming early, but no. The wagon, rough and weather-beaten was driven by a man none of us had ever seen before. Grizzled and dirty, he pulled up and stopped within a few feet of the front door, and sat looking at the house, studying it. I rose from the bench, opened the door and greeted him.

"Good day, sir. What can we do for you?"

Mark positioned himself behind the door, the pistol in his right hand, just in case.

"Why I been told to come here and pick up some n_____s needin' passage to Canada." The man reached into his pocket and withdrew a couple of dirty, wrinkled papers and held them up. "Got my orders right here."

Skepticism came to the fore. "May I see those papers?" As I reached for them, the man folded the papers and shoved them back in his pocket.

"No need. They's all in order. Now, about them n_____s." Mark stepped past me onto the porch, easing his way down the steps, eyes on the driver, pistol in hand.

The wagon driver reached under the seat, lifting out a shotgun, but Mark was too quick for him. He cocked the pistol as the man lifted the gun. "Lay that aside now, Mister. I don't know who you are or what kind of business you're in, but I'm not giving these people over to anyone but Thomas Lander or his sons."

Holding the shotgun at the ready, the man whined, "Mr. Lander ain't coming. He's got business elsewhere. That's why he sent me."

Mark looked over his shoulder. I shook my head. "No one but Thomas Lander or his sons."

Suddenly from around the side of the house, two men stepped out, armed with shotguns, taking aim at Mark. He ducked and rolled under the horses' legs, shooting at first one, then the other. Didn't even wait for them to start it. By the time he'd rolled out the other side, the man in the wagon had stood up, aimed the shotgun and fired in Mark's general direction. Mark rose on one knee, took aim and shot the man square in the shoulder. Just that quick. Three wounded men lying in the dooryard, writhing in pain, but in no danger of dying. They'd live to fight another day.

Mark held the pistol steady and ordered the three to take themselves away before he felt inclined to shoot again. It all

76

happened so fast I barely had time to react. I was relieved to see Mark standing upright, still holding the pistol and held my breath as the two men got up and staggered toward the wagon, clutching their wounds. Aunt came hurrying out, expecting the worst, but stopped short when she encountered me.

"Steady, Aunt. They wanted to take the black folk. Mr. Randolph stopped them."

The old woman's hand went to her throat as she breathed a long ooooh. Without another word, the two wounded men mounted their horses and rode away while the third hefted himself into a sitting position in the wagon, did a wide turn and followed. I said we should send for the sheriff, but Mark shook his head and we went back inside to wait for Uncle Thomas.

For more than two hours the fugitives, frightened beyond sensibility, sat on the floor, their backs to the wall. One of the men recognized the slave catchers as the same troop that had tracked them through Maryland a few days before.

When Uncle Thomas and his sons came driving up after dark, I told them about the gunfight, and, discomfited at the violence, they muddled about, talking and shaking their heads. Pacifist Quakers, dedicated to settling every dispute by talking quiet and civilized, they couldn't take in that Mark had resorted to shooting, and that there were three wounded men out there roaming the countryside. I assured them that the devils would survive and probably deserved worse than they got.

Later I told Mark I was mightily impressed with his prowess with a gun, but it did puzzle me how a preacher got so good at shooting and rolling around under horses' legs. I added that I admired his willingness to defend the helpless. Rebel or not, this was a man to be reckoned with.

Judith Redline Coopey

Chapter 11

November 1864
Mark Randolph

Once Thomas Lander and his sons arrived, my job was over, but I stayed on at the house in case the slave catchers got it in their heads to come back looking for me. I didn't think their wounds were serious, just inconvenient. They'd find sympathizers to help them – even a doctor, maybe. The constable came by around ten o'clock that night as the Friends loaded the slaves in a wagon to take them to Altoona. I gave him a vague description of the intruders, suspecting he wouldn't be of a mind to pursue them very far. I was surprised at the quiet efficiency with which the Friends carried out their mission. It seemed long practice had served them well.

I saw the adventure as shoring up my position in the community – diverting suspicion from me, if there was any. And there was. Simon Tolliver gave me the eagle eye every time our paths crossed, always with a sneer to assure me he still had doubts. Thankfully Miss Lander's opinion of me seemed to soften after the slave incident, while the members of my three little congregations now held me in such high esteem I wished there were some transgression from my youth I could confess to bring them back to reality.

In short, the time to act upon my assignment to put the Horseshoe Curve out of commission was drawing nigh. After several trips around the area, keeping well out of sight and hearing of the guards, I determined that the most damage could be done with several black powder charges, set at wide intervals on both tracks around the curve itself. Trouble was, that was a job for four or five men, not just one, so I'd have to arrange for a troop to be ready at a moment's notice. As soon as the first charge went off, the place would be crawling with Bluebellies and there'd be one hell of a fight, guaranteed.

Then there was the problem of obtaining the kegs of black powder and storing them until the time was right. The Yankees guarded their munitions carefully, so I'd have to find a way to get what I needed from a Rebel supply depot twenty-five or more miles to the south or maybe from one of the many stone quarries that dotted the county. Again, a job for more than one man. My orders were to gather the information and make the plan, but help was definitely needed to carry it out.

I drew up some plans, mapped out my proposal and left it where my courier could pick it up and deliver it to my commanding officer. Timing had to be just right so that the Confederates could take advantage of the destruction and raid the disabled trains before a force of any size could arrive. The disturbing abundance of everything in the north made me doubt my chances for success, but I went about the preparations as though sure of myself. I fervently wished the war would end sooner rather than later for this assignment loomed large in my mind. I'd need half a dozen or so men to help me carry it out, and that in itself was well nigh impossible, with troop strength dwindling by the day.

Once I'd set out my plan, I waited for a response from my commanding officer. I was on my own here among Yankees whose only purpose would have been to hang me from the highest tree should my true identity be revealed. In a way, I felt regret about deceiving this community, for I'd found the people to be nice – decent, civil, honest and fair -- all attributes I'd been told were beyond Yankees, not to mention abolitionists. So it was with a quiet sense of shame that I pursued the opportunity to bring terror upon them.

It seemed I'd impressed Susannah with my ability to handle a gun. Like many young ladies, she was uncomfortable around firearms, but war had given her to understand the practical value of knowing how to use one. Now she seemed to accept the idea that I'd been around a little and knew more about the world than she did. Still, she pounced on every opportunity to test my knowledge of or my dedication to doing the Lord's work. It seemed to me the only way to deal with her suspicion was to ignore it. Let her go on as she pleased. The world would keep on turning.

The grinding poverty in which Susannah and her aunt lived set my mind to thinking of ways to help her. True, my own family was even then being ground under the heel of the enemy, but I didn't give myself over to feelings of hatred or jealousy. In fact, if anything, my anger and resentment toward the Union had begun to abate. I would have saddled up and ridden away on any given afternoon if there'd been an adequate opportunity. Here I was helping fugitives get away to Canada, a point of view I'd never considered before. I shuddered to think Miss Lander was getting to me. Such feelings brought discomfort, even as I tried to ignore them and force myself to concentrate on my mission.

In grave trouble with her Meeting for sharing her abode with an unmarried man, Susannah never mentioned her distress. She just kept doing what had to be done. Then one day late in the afternoon, a buggy drew up to Susannah's dooryard occupied by three stalwart Quaker ladies in black shawls and bonnets, sent to point out Susannah's sins and entreat her to turn away from temptation. Oh, these ladies were convinced of the rightness of their mission, but I doubt that they'd anticipated the kind of reception they were to receive. Bold Susannah invited me to stay and hear the proceedings, as she greeted them at the door and graciously invited them in for a cup of tea while I stood in the background, listening.

Once inside the hovel Susannah called home, surely they could see the state of her existence. I really think she expected them to understand her predicament and relent. But they came as representatives of the established church, defending practices whose origins were lost in the mists of time, not just with Quakers, but in society as a whole.

Ill at ease with my presence, the committee women stopped and looked questioning at me. "Well, who is this?"one of them asked.

"This is the Reverend Mr. Randolph, my tenant." Susannah replied. "He is the reason for this meeting, so I thought he should be here so you could see just what you are dealing with."

Taken aback, the women hesitated, discussing among themselves the propriety of having me there. I expected them to reconsider and retreat, but one of them, apparently the chairwoman, was determined to conduct the meeting at any cost. With tension crackling in the air, the trio presented a halting and stiff accounting of Susannah's transgressions, ending with the inevitable question, "Why? Did thee never stop to think of the consequences? Why?"

"Because I am poor," Susannah replied. "Without a husband, father, brother or uncle to care for me and my aunt. In short, we need the money Mr. Randolph pays us."

"Now, now. I happen to know that your Uncle Thomas provides very well for you as he is called to do by the Meeting." The chairwoman straightened herself up with a little sniff.

"But he doesn't."

"Doesn't? How can you say that?"

Susannah rose and pulled back the curtain that covered her food supply. The three biddies took turns looking in, taking careful note of the barren interior.

"Are you saying Thomas Lander doesn't live up to his responsibilities?"

"I'm saying that and more. Uncle Thomas is directly responsible for my taking in a boarder. If he'd fulfilled his obligation, there'd be no need for boarders."

Susannah addressed the old birds, standing before them, clear-eyed and clothed in truth. She seized the opportunity to state her position on the kind of treatment allotted to the poor, especially women.

"Being poor is not a sin. It is a circumstance, hopefully temporary, but when a woman is prevented from owning property or casting a vote or being seen as anything but chattel, how can they run their lives with dignity? My Aunt and I have to almost beg to receive the most basic of stores. Why should we have to be dependent on anybody, let alone those who resent our very existence?"

It must have occurred to all these women at one time or another that women's rights were given lip service but little else, especially among the common folk. The accepted pathway for a woman was through a husband and children. Those who lacked one or both became invisible in the community.

The three women, taken aback by Susannah's position, looked around at one another, their faces grave. "Why, I've never really thought about the lot of the poor beyond what the Meeting does for widows and orphans. I thought everyone should take care of themselves. It never occurred to me that they couldn't."

"In today's world, women are tied to their husbands or the charity of their male relatives. It isn't fair to *them* either. Who wants a spinster sister or aunt to support?"

Now the committee was abuzz with thoughts about how better to help the indigent.

"We need a means of gaining a livelihood – a bit of land to grow our own food, the chance to take in a boarder without being considered fallen women." Susannah was warming to her subject now. "We could be self supporting if they'd give us our fair share when our fathers die. Any one of us could be reduced to this level of poverty. It's humiliating to be seen as a burden when one could support oneself with a bit of a boost."

Of course the committee was nonplussed by Susannah's refusal to admit she'd been wrong to hire out a room to an unmarried stranger, and when she refused to stop her transgressions and turn away from sin, their concern was what they would report to Meeting. I guess they expected her to be contrite and promise to send me away and never cross that bridge again, but she stood and looked them in the eye and refused to change any aspect of her behavior.

After their departure I watched her for any sign of regret, wondered if she could withstand the loneliness of being shut out of the Society of Friends, but no. She went about her days with purpose, gave Mr. Riggs two days of labor per week and still attended Meeting – only now she sat outside the room where she could hear everything, but was forbidden to speak.

Within the month the ladies reported back to the Meeting that Susannah Lander had refused to show contrition, and continued to rent space to a circuit riding minister – a priest -- but nothing further was done. Instead the matter was shelved to be taken up again at a later date.

Chapter 12

Late November 1864
Mark Randolph

S imon Tolliver had me worried, lurking in the back at my services and appearing with regularity along the roads I traveled. I suspected he was studying my schedule, keeping track of my route. I didn't relish his attention, but I had to stick to my routine. My courier continued to pick up my dispatches and bring me word of war developments. Our meeting place was down in southern Bedford County, close to the Maryland border. I only ventured to go there about once a month, but I'd ordered the kegs of black powder to carry out my mission, so I rented a wagon to haul them home under cover of darkness. Given Tolliver's untimely attention, I was concerned that he might follow me and complicate my mission.

I set out in a light snowfall to collect my stores, careful to mix my tracks with others and keeping watch over my shoulder. Once or twice I sensed someone following, but Tolliver was too smart to follow close, so I pulled up and stopped in a grove to settle my nerves. No Tolliver. Still, he could be hiding along the track just beyond visibility. Twice I even stopped and retraced my trail on foot, but still, nothing. All this tarrying could make me late for my rendezvous, so eventually I coaxed the horses into a trot to make up for lost time.

I met James Bennett, my courier, at a bend in a stream flowing through a wide, flat meadow just as darkness was falling. It was the second such meeting where we exchanged reports and Bennett brought me mail. The meeting was short – only about ten minutes – during which we transferred the black powder from his wagon to mine, covered it with a tarp and shared half a bottle of whiskey, compliments of James, and a little news. Bennett had no knowledge of my mission, a precaution in case he was captured on his way back to Confederate lines. After a brief liaison we parted – I with a handful of letters from home and a couple of dispatches.

I started up the Hyndman valley, the wind blowing at right angles to the track and the snow building in drifts. It was after seven, but dark as midnight. The horses picked their way carefully, heads down against the blowing snow, when a rider approached out of the shadows. I made like to pass with a nod when the man pulled up.

"That you, Reverend? Whatcha doing all the way down here? Saving souls?" It was Simon Tolliver, sidling his horse so close to my wagon, he could easily grab my reins.

"Tolliver! I'd business in Hyndman today. You?"

"What sort of bidness?"

"Kind of like, 'none of yours," I said, raising my right leg just enough so I could reach the knife I kept inside my boot.

Tolliver backed his horse up a step or two. "I been watchin' you, Reverend, and it appears to me you been spyin' for old Jeff Davis. That right? What you haulin'? I allow it ain't groceries."

I snorted. "I guess denying it wouldn't do any good. You have a vivid imagination, my friend, but nothing to support your suspicions, which must be mighty strong for you to follow me all the way down here in a snowstorm."

"You might say. Now I'm just gonna have a look at what you've got under that there tarp afore I take you back to Bedford. Then we can talk to the constable about detaining you 'til we can turn you over to the military. Let them sort it out." He grabbed my lead horse's reins and yanked, but found that she was more than reluctant to follow

It was laughable – a one legged man on horseback looking to subdue an able bodied soldier, trained and experienced in taking care of himself. I rose, standing in front of the wagon seat. It was nothing to launch a blow that sent my adversary sprawling to the ground. I almost felt sorry for him, inept as he was. But now I had a serious problem. If I let him go, my mission was over. I sat back down and rearranged my reins, trying to decide what to do when a gunshot shattered the silence. Bennett. I guess he'd sensed trouble and followed me. He didn't show himself, but I knew. Nothing to do now but rob the man – make it look like the work of deserters.

I jumped down and went through Tolliver's pockets. Nothing of value. So I grabbed him under the arms and dragged him off the trail a way, unsaddled his horse and gave it a slap on the rump. I noticed an opening in the near hillside, a small cave, a perfect place to hide a body you didn't want discovered for a while. I installed Tolliver in his new quarters, then climbed back up, turned the horse's heads north and kept the wagon rolling. I needed to get home before the weather got any worse. Snow clung to my shoulders through the long wet ride. The discomfort made me wonder again why I was doing this. Chances of a Rebel victory faded by the day. Even if my own mission was a success, it could only postpone the inevitable. Now a man lay dead, if not by my hand, at least by my fault.

Finally, nigh onto midnight I arrived at the broken-down stable I called home, bone tired and soul weary. I still had to hide the black powder, but elected to keep the horses and wagon and return them in the morning. I unhitched and fed the horses, then lit a lamp and dug a hole in a corner of the dirt floor deep enough to cover the kegs. It was back-breaking work, doubly insulting after a whole day on horseback. Once it was done I spread straw over the freshly dug earth and climbed the ladder to my quarters. Numb with fatigue, I stuffed the stove with kindling and curled up to sleep, hungry beyond measure.

But sleep wouldn't come. I worried over Tolliver – regretted getting him killed. After some tossing and turning I rose and opened my saddle bag, taking out the letters and dispatches. As I started to read I was interrupted by the groan of the stable door hinges below. I reached for my gun.

"Who's there?"

"Susannah."

I looked down to see a cloaked and scarved land lady standing in the middle of the stable floor holding a covered dish.

"Heard you come in. Brought you some supper."

I climbed down the ladder and took the dish from her hands, afraid she might notice the broken ground in the corner where I'd buried the powder kegs. But she smiled and rubbed her hands together against the cold. "Better hurry up and eat. It's probably cold already."

I reached for her hand. "Come. It's warmer upstairs." Dish in hand, I worked my way up the ladder, followed by a hesitant but steady climber.

I picked up my papers, stuffed them back in the saddle bag and placed the dish on the wooden trunk. "This is a welcome surprise. I was just feeling sorry for myself, having to go to bed hungry."

"No trouble at all. I was worried that you'd gotten caught in the storm. I'm glad you made it home."

"Pretty nasty weather you Yankees put up with."

"Does it make you miss Georgia?"

I paused, looking around to find a spoon, then sat down to a bowl of warm stew. "Yes, I guess it does, some."

"What's the war news?" she asked, nodding toward my saddle bag on the floor beside my bed.

"War news?"

"Yes, I thought you were reading something when I came in."

"Oh. No. I hear the war's on hold now until spring."

Susannah sat down on the end of my bunk, fingering the stitched design on the quilt.

"Really? How much longer do you think it'll last? Surely not another year?"

I wiped my bowl clean with a dry crust of bread. "I don't know. We... they can't hold out much longer. The south is worn out. I have word from my sister that General Sherman's men are laying waste to practically the whole state of Georgia."

"We?" She paused. "Do you still identify with the rebels, Mr. Randolph?"

"Just a slip of the tongue. Even though I'm up here out of harm's way, I still worry about my family. They're suffering now and will much longer. I just wish I could see to them."

"Yes. It must grieve you not to be able to help them. How big a family is it?"

"Not so big as it used to be. I've lost two brothers in the fighting so now it's just me and my two sisters."

"Parents gone?"

"You might say. They're both still alive, but they're not really with us anymore."

Susannah rose and picked up my bowl. "That must be hard to bear. Why don't you just go home right now? Get back to your preaching after the war is over?"

"I'd be hanged as a spy by either side before I'd ventured five miles into Maryland."

"Hanged? Oh, surely they'd give you a trial and keep you prisoner until the war is over."

"The Yankees might. The Rebs wouldn't bother. Any man caught in civilian clothes in enemy territory is assumed to be a spy and dealt with accordingly."

I pulled the bench over in front of the stove and we sat gazing into the flames, warming our hands, silent but for the crackling of the fire.

Susannah gazed at a spot above the stove pipe. "I still wonder about you. I can't say I understand why you're here when anyone with common sense would say you should be fighting – on one side or the other. An able bodied man riding circuit in Pennsylvania marks himself as suspect."

I watched her face as she spoke, kindly enough, but also unnerving. I'd had enough bad news and suspicion for one day, and I was almost falling asleep as she spoke. I rose and offered my hand.

"Maybe someday it'll all make sense to you. Come, let me walk you back to the house."

I followed her down the ladder where she pulled her cloak tight around her throat as we walked out into the night. I left her at the door of her house. "Thank you for dinner. Now I can sleep."

But I wouldn't – sleep, that is. Once back in my room, I rescued Em's letters from the depth of my saddle bags and began to read.

> *Dear Brother,*
> *It is with grave sadness I report to you that our dear mother has gone to be with Randolph and Mark. She'd been failing for sometime – living in a fantasy world where they were still boys getting into mischief at every turn. On her last day, she seemed to find clarity, asking after you and even yielding to Papa's kiss. She indulged in a glass of claret with dinner and talked about getting new wallpaper for the dining room.*
> *She sat down at the harpsichord and whiled away the evening playing the old songs, entreating us to sing with her. At nine o'clock she bade us good night and retired. We found her in the morning sitting in her chair by the window, a locket with our brothers' pictures clutched in her hand.*
> *Better that she leave us rather than witness what is to come. We hear terrible things about the Yankees getting ever closer. I don't know how we will fare if they come, but neither do I know how we will fare if they don't.*
> *God keep you.*
> *Your loving sister,*
> *Emily*

Reading such as that increased my discontent with my assignment. Could I just quit and go home? Only as a spy or deserter. I began to plot how I could lie and bribe and fight my way home. I left the other two letters unopened for fear of what they contained. Tired beyond weary I lay down on my bunk and slept.

Judith Redline Coopey

Chapter 13

November 1864
Mark Randolph

The next morning dawned frosty white, with heavy gray clouds promising more snow. I had a home visit scheduled for the afternoon, and, feeling just a little sorry for myself, I slogged through the snow to Susannah's house for breakfast.

Except for meals I hadn't spent much time there, but this morning the kitchen smelled of ginger and pumpkin, nutmeg and raisins. As soon as she let me in she bade me sit down for a bowl of oatmeal.

"Quite the bake shop you've got here this morning," I commented, spooning honey over my porridge.

She smiled, "We can thank you for that. It was your rent money bought the sugar and spices."

Her face glowed with the warmth of the room and the effort of mixing batter.

"Aunt has all the recipes in her head, but it's been such a long time since we had the means to bake, I'm going to write down everything I do today."

I watched her beat and stir and bake, obviously enjoying her preparations. "Who's going to eat all this?" I asked.

"Oh, lots of people. I'll take some to the Riggs – Alonzo and Jonah must really miss Martha. She was such a good cook. Poor thing. Dead at forty-two. And Aunt will take some to Widow

93

Hammond. She lives alone just beyond the Riggs place. I might even drop some pumpkin bread off to my Uncle – not that he needs it. Just to be nice."

The warmth of the kitchen coupled with the tantalizing baking smells set me at ease and before I could restrain my tongue I was telling Susannah about Emily's letter.

"I've no wish to equate our troubles with yours. My sisters have lived privileged lives up to now, but I wonder how they'll get on. "

Susannah stopped mixing and wiped her hands. Bending to the oven she took out two fat loaves of currant bread. "Your sisters will be all right. People tend to rise to the challenges life puts in their path. If you've never been challenged, you don't know what you can accomplish."

Now she stooped to place two more loaves in the oven. "Your sisters are undeniably more capable than you give them credit for. Women can take care of themselves when the need arises."

Once I'd started thinking about home, I expanded the conversation to family, growing up in the South -- opened the doors of my life for Susannah's inspection. Inhibition fell away as I lost myself in memories of Belfast Plantation.

"That all sounds like a fine place to be, but I can't help noting that the people who made it all possible were enslaved," Susannah reminded me.

"Their lives weren't *so* bad. They had food and shelter in exchange for their labor." Just that quickly I was again defending slavery. Why didn't I know when to keep my mouth shut?

"Yes. But."

"Yes, but what?"

"Yes, but they weren't free. Couldn't decide where to live, what to do. I've heard many stories of abuse – harsh punishments, selling people away from their families."

"That didn't happen at our place. Our slaves were well treated. Their bellies were full, their cabins comfortable. My father never beat a slave."

"I believe you, but it occurs to me that most any slave owner would put up the same argument. But there are too many stories of the other kind for at least some of it not to be true."

One minute we were enjoying our morning; the next we were engaged in a prickly discussion of all that divided us. There was no use talking about it. These people would never understand the Southern way of life. I rose and picked up my hat, too abruptly, perhaps.

"I guess I'll get back to my humble abode. I've letters to write and a sermon for Sunday."

"Oh, Mr. Rand... Mark. I hope I haven't offended you. Sometimes I let myself get too forthright and I forget how to temper my opinions."

"Not at all. I really have work to do. Perhaps you'll save some of your baking for a weary circuit rider returning from a long, cold day on horseback. Good day, Miss Lander."

Slogging back to the stable through slush three inches deep, I felt defensive, deflated. I wished I could make Susannah see the error of lumping all Southerners together in her mind.

Still reeling from Em's revelations I was suddenly overcome with homesickness, and being constantly called upon to defend the Southern way of life didn't help. In my stable room I stoked up the fire, but the wind still blew through the cracks between the boards, stiff enough to make my lamp flicker, I put on another layer of clothing, but still my fingers were too stiff for writing,

I looked at Em's second letter lying on the table, afraid to pick it up -- afraid not to. I raised it to my nose and put it down. Come on, Carter Willoughby, toughen up. My misery increased as I looked around the plain and barren little room. One window high in the peak of the roof let in what little light there was. The outside walls, unfinished studs, stood empty except for a board of hooks where I hung my clothes. Remembering my room at home, flocked wallpaper, brocade draperies, imported rugs, I shook my head at the contrast with this pathetic excuse for shelter.

Then thinking of Susannah living like this all the time – indeed it was all she'd ever known – made me ashamed. I picked up the letter, broke the seal and began to read.

Dear Carter,

The Yankees have come. I doubt you will even get this letter, for Georgia is naught but a wasteland now. They've burned all – the barns, the stables, the crops – everything but the house. They were disciplined and methodical, almost like this was their job and they'd just as leave get on with it.

They came riding up yesterday morning – a troop of eight men and an officer – very business-like. We'd heard tales of horrors, so we hid – Papa, Ellen and I, in the fruit cellar, while Viney stepped up to talk to the soldiers. We could hear them clumping around above our heads, breaking things, stealing, laughing like it was all a game. Three stayed outside, Viney told us, and set the fires. They burned this years' cotton crop, all the feed and fodder. The place looks like a twister went through. They broke every window, ransacked every room, carried off anything of value.

Papa cried when he saw what they'd done. You wouldn't recognize him, Carter. His hair is white, his clothes hang on him. He doesn't shave anymore. I can barely get him to eat. All he does is pace and cry. Ellen and I do our best to cheer him, but if it works at all, it is only for a short time.

They took all the livestock – horses, cows, pigs, sheep. The last chicken had been picked off long ago. I guess it's for the best for we hadn't enough food to keep them through the winter, but Ellen grieves the loss of her little mare, Val. She raised her from a foal, and now, who knows what will happen to her at the hands of the Yankees?

I think we may not have enough food to last the winter ourselves. All the slaves except Viney and old Julius are gone. He's too old to follow the Army, and Viney says she'll stay with him as long as he lives.

My only wish now is for you to come home and help us. I'm so afraid. There are bands of deserters and escaped prisoners roaming the countryside. We sleep with Papa's shotgun beside us – all of us – Viney, Julius, all -- in the dining room where we could have a fire if there was anything to burn.

I pray that this is as bad as it gets and that God will protect us until we see you come riding home.

Your Loving Sister,
Emily Willoughby

The third letter, still unopened, lay on the table daring me to touch it. Afraid of what it contained I returned to writing my sermon, my hands still stiff with the cold. Concentration was beyond me. My thoughts kept returning home, and would give me no peace, so I descended the ladder to take a walk to warm and distract myself. In the stable below I threw in some extra hay for my horse and found an old dusty blanket to throw over her back for a little warmth. Then once again I tamped down the earth over the place where I'd buried the black powder, scattered some more straw over it and stepped outside into the snowy landscape with second thoughts as to the wisdom of taking a walk.

It seemed I wasn't the only one with that idea, for down the track I could see someone walking toward me. Susannah. Hurrying to meet her, I called out, "Susannah! What are you doing out in this cold?"

"Aunt and I were delivering baked goods and when we got to Widow Hammond's place she didn't answer our knock, so we let ourselves in and found her abed with a wicked cough. Too weak to get up, so Aunt is staying the night with her. I've more deliveries to make and more baking."

"May I walk you home? Maybe try a piece of your pumpkin pie?"

"Of course. You're always welcome."

Recalling our earlier discussion of slavery, I added, "I promise not to say anything to antagonize you."

She just smiled.

I returned to the stable to bank the fire and proceeded to Susannah's humble kitchen where she opened the door with a piece of pumpkin pie on a plate. "Mayhap I should leave the door open to discourage gossip," she observed.

"As you wish, m'lady. We wouldn't want to start any tongues wagging." We both laughed, knowing how certain we were to be spied upon, but unwilling to sacrifice the precious heat to propriety.

"I don't care. I'd rather they gossiped than we should freeze to death. Besides, 'tis broad daylight. Everyone knows dalliances take place after dark." Susannah laughed.

I settled onto the bench, fork in hand, a generous piece of pumpkin pie before me, while Susannah poured me a mug of cider, hot from the stove.

"A little bit homesick, are we, Mr. Randolph? The South must seem far away this day. The papers say General Sherman marches on to the sea. Mayhap the worst is over for your loved ones."

"Or just begun. I pray every day for this damn war to be over soon."

Ignoring the profanity, Susannah cut herself a piece of pie and sat down opposite me. We ate in silence, I lost in speculation about the condition of my father and sisters, she preoccupied with her baking and caring for her neighbors.

I cleaned up the pie, rubbing my thighs to warm them as Susannah lifted a floury hand to push back a lock of hair from her forehead. I noticed for the first time the way it shimmered – a rich chestnut brown. In fact it dawned on me that Miss Susannah could have been a beauty in the hands of one who knew about such things. Her plain unadorned appearance hid assets many would have found pleasing. Sister Emily, given thirty minutes could have transformed Susannah into a true Southern Belle.

"I hope it isn't too forward of me, but I wonder why a woman like you remains unmarried."

First she smiled at my impertinence; then a thoughtful look crossed her face. "First, I think because most men find me too outspoken for their taste. Second because I'm penniless. With no material gain to be had, why bother with a woman so plain and shrewish? And third because I do not want – have never wanted – to be 'taken care of' by anyone."

I hadn't expected my question to bring about such a flurry of reason. Clearly Susannah had given the world and her place in it ample thought.

"So you've resigned yourself to your present condition? Accepted this as all you'll ever have?" I passed my arm around the pathetic little room as Susannah's eyes followed my gesture.

"Nay, sir. I expect to better myself, but I intend to lay out the path on my own. I seek neither charity nor guidance."

I rose to lay another log on the fire and moved in closer to take advantage of the abundant heat. One thing about a log house, it might settle and lean, but it was far less drafty than a board house.

"Independent, then, aren't you?" I asked.

"Learned from long experience with disappointment, sir."

"Could be that trait that keeps you solitary."

Why did I not restrain my mouth? The room was warm, my belly full, my thoughts roaming free. Why could I not just enjoy the company without probing and offering unsolicited advice?

"I'm sorry, Susannah. I've overstepped my bounds. Please ignore my prattle. I intended to engage you in pleasant conversation this afternoon, and now I fear I've spoiled it."

She poured more batter into two loaf pans and shoved them into the oven while taking a broom splint to check her earlier efforts for doneness. Reaching for a folded-up kitchen towel, she removed the loaves one at a time and placed them atop the stove.

"Nay, you've spoiled naught. 'Tis a flattery that you've any interest in me at all. After the women you've known, I must come up pale by comparison."

"Pale? By no means. You've more spunk in your little finger than I've come across in all my years."

She smiled, her cheeks coloring just a bit. "Would you like to help me ice these loaves when they cool?"

Rising to the occasion, I looked about for a towel to tie around my waist. Susannah provided one that I tied with a piece of string, wondering what my fellow soldiers would think of me now – helping a Yankee woman with her baking.

We worked in unison. "This must feel like a bounty to you after more than three years of war shortages," I observed.

"There are still war shortages, but folk learn that they can get on with much less than they think."

A pointed remark designed to make me think about peoples' attachment to their 'things'? It struck me that, whatever the topic, Susannah had given it serious thought, careful consideration and had come to her own conclusions about it, always looking at the world from the broad, rather than the narrow aspect.

Standing close to her, icing cakes, laughing at my own clumsiness, I felt better than I'd felt in the last four years. Suddenly I wanted this plain, simple life, unconcerned with material things, full of the joy of being.

"Do you think I'd make a good Quaker?" I asked.

"And give up your Methodism? How could you do that?"

I suppressed the urge to reveal my true feelings, divulge that I was not a Methodist at all, but a Southern spy sent here to do what I could to destroy this way of life.

100

"Oh, I'm just speculating. I'd never do it, but there are aspects of your religion that I find appealing."

"Like which aspects?"

"Pacifism for one. Thoughtful deliberation before picking up a gun. Acceptance of the truth that violence never solves anything. The idea of the inner light for another. We all know right from wrong – good from bad; we carry that sense with us. We don't need the threat of eternal damnation to keep us from doing wrong as long as we're guided by our inner light.

"Well said, Mr. Randolph. You could rise in meeting and set forth your views with the most pious of them. Remind them of who they are and what matters to them. Sometimes they forget."

"We all forget in the name of war, until war devours us."

That's when I began to feel myself giving way to the charms of the intellect. Here was this plain, unpretentious woman enticing me away from my roots, leading me afield, opening my mind to thoughts and beliefs I'd never allowed myself to consider.

I laid down the icing knife and turned to her. I'd never thought of her as anything but a poor, sad, lonely woman, but in truth she was none of these. She was a clear-eyed, independent thinker, unafraid to consider other points of view and, damn her, becoming more attractive by the minute.

Uncomfortable with such thoughts, I stepped away, took off my apron, picked up my cloak and moved toward the door.

"I'm sorry to leave you with more icing to do, but I still have a home visit this afternoon. I almost forgot."

"Where are you going?"

"To visit Mrs. Ruth Chamberlain. You know her daughter Althea, I'm sure. They're interested in learning more about Methodism."

"Oh, yes. I know Althea Chamberlain. She has a brother, Frederick fighting for the Union. I heard he was wounded at some battle off in Tennessee. I hope he's recovered. Give her good wishes for me."

Clapping my hat on, I ventured out to allow the cold to clear my head. What was wrong with me? Here I was risking my whole mission to build an impossible relationship with, of all things a Quaker woman. I went to the stable, saddled my horse and rode off toward Martinsburg, intent upon shaking Susannah Lander from my brain.

Chapter 14

November 1864
Mark

With Christmas in the offing, I spent more time with my parishioners, helping them with whatever seasonal tasks they were engaged in. I tried to divide my time evenly among the groups, but I found that some, especially the younger women, were intent upon getting to know me as a friend, or more precisely, as a lover. I knew better than to strike up a romance with any one of them and thus make enemies of the rest. So I went about, helping where I could, spreading cheer and building trust. It seemed to be working, for people had warmed up to me – accepted me as their leader – and did everything – especially the women – to please me.

It did get tiresome riding so much – all day, every day, I wended my way around the Great Cove, stopping to visit with my followers and widening my base of parishioners. I was quite surprised at myself. I had no idea I possessed such charms, but there it was, working.

Simon Tolliver's disappearance had to stir up some curiosity, but I avoided anyone I thought might know him, and kept to my circuit. I heard off hand talk about Simon's disappearance, but didn't ask any questions. That went well for a week or so after Tolliver went missing. Then Jonah Riggs showed up at the door to my stable one evening as I was putting my horse up for the night.

"Evening," he said, letting himself in.

"Evening. What brings you out on a cold night? Need help with something?"

"Not that you could fix." He sidled up to the stall, reaching in to touch my horse, rub her behind the ears. "I come to talk to you about a friend of mine."

Wary, I stood with the horse between us, brushing her sides down. "Friend? What friend?"

"Simon Tolliver."

"Simon Tolliver?" I frowned. "I don't think I've met him."

Jonah scoffed. "Sure you have. I saw you talking to him in front of Replogle's a week or so ago. One leg. Remember?"

"Oh, that guy. Sure. Lost his leg in the war. I remember him."

"Well, he disappeared about a week ago – ain't been seen since he rode out from the livery right after you rented a wagon last week."

"What's that got to do with me? I barely knew the man." I was getting impatient with Jonah's sneaky way of leading up to whatever it was he thought he knew.

"My thought is, he followed you where ever it was you went; you caught him and made sure he didn't spread the word about you."

"Nice story, Jonah, but there's not a shred of truth in it. Mr. Tolliver might have just gone to visit relatives or something and he'll come riding home one of these days. Now, if you'll excuse me, I have a sermon to write."

Jonah looked around the stable, taking in the details. "You know there's folk around here think you're naught but a scout for the Confederacy. That includes me. I been watching you – and so was Tolliver – and I ain't no wise convinced that you're just an itinerant preacher."

"Think what you will. I've nothing to hide." I glanced at the far corner of the room where I'd buried the black powder. The straw lay strewn over the raw earth, and I worried Jonah would notice and wonder why.

'I think they'll find Tolliver's body someplace out along the track, and when they do, your name will come up."

I stepped up closer to Jonah, putting my nose about an inch from his. "Even if it does, there's no proof I did anything to him. You don't have any evidence, so I'd think twice before I accused anybody of anything."

Jonah pulled back. "Some folks don't need any of your e-vi-dence. Sometimes folk just make things happen as they see the right."

"I'll take that as fair warning, but keep this in mind: No man has a right to flaunt the law. We've got a system of justice here, and whoever knows what happened to Simon Tolliver will testify in court. The system works."

"For you, maybe, Reverend. But they's times and places where the law don't apply. Just remember, I'm watching. That's all I say."

He turned and stepped out the door. I stayed rooted to the stable floor, wondering what I might have to do to carry out my orders, should they come.

That encounter changed the whole picture for me – made me wary. Watchful. I tried to be light hearted, far too busy with my own affairs to concern myself with the likes of Jonah Riggs. I rode my circuit daily, made sure my parishioners had their needs met.

Suddenly I felt an overwhelming need to talk to someone from the South. Someone sympathetic and wise. Someone who wouldn't be so ready to see through my disguise and suspect me of treachery. I wanted to get word to my commanding officer to send a courier to meet me on Friday. There was no quick way to send a message, so I arose early the next morning and rode off by myself to see if I could per chance meet up with James Merrill one more time.

Judith Redline Coopey

Chapter 15

November 1864
Susannah

I know I should resist the temptation to think over much about Mr. Randolph – Mark – but I find he is often in my mind unbidden. This morning we had a lively discussion, almost an argument, actually, over slavery again. This afternoon he gave voice to curiosity about Quaker beliefs. He's more open-minded and thoughtful than I judged him to be, but he does cling to his Southern point of view. The man is a puzzle, but surely I'm wise enough not to let myself wander too far. Yes, my feelings for him are beginning to soften, but I dismiss them as soon as they erupt. I'm not *that* foolish.

And that explains why I am so curious about his former life, his family, especially those sisters he seems so fond of. I really should not have let him come in the house when Aunt was away. But I did enjoy the chance to talk to him alone and without restraint.

Now uppermost in my mind is the prospect of Mr. Randolph taking Christmas dinner with us, Aunt and me. At present he takes his meals here – breakfast and dinner, every day but Sunday. He usually has an invitation to Sunday dinner from among his parishioners, so we've let that day be, appropriately, a day of rest. But Christmas is in the offing – just a month away -- surely he'll have more than one invitation from his congregation. Still I find myself entertaining the possibility of sharing the holiday with him.

I know it's just self-indulgent fantasy, but I can't seem to dismiss it. Aunt and I haven't money for a goose, but we could kill a chicken – a small one – and make our own celebration. Why do I keep dreaming up such fantasies? And yet, I'm just sure he'd love Aunt's mince pie.

The next morning I took down my bonnet and cloak preparing to go fetch Aunt from Widow Hammond's. The temperature had warmed some, making me wish I had more than one pair of shoes. Shame to ruin my only pair trekking through slush.

I opened the door to a sunny day, icicles dripping and yesterday's snow sinking into itself. As I passed the stable I glanced at the door, but Mr. Randolph wasn't astir. I carried a basket of foodstuffs to sustain the widow through more stormy weather. Her daughter lived over near Roaring Spring so I was sure she'd be around soon to check on her mother. In the meantime, since Aunt and I enjoyed good fortune, it was only right that we should share. I walked along shifting the basket from one arm to the other when I heard a horse sloshing up behind me. Mr. Randolph out and about looking after his flock.

"Miss Lander, good day. Here, hand that basket up to me."

The basket *was* heavy, so I gave it up without protest. He offered me a hand up as well, but my skirts prevented that, so he dismounted to walk beside me carrying the basket. The glare from the melting snow kept my head down as we tip-toed along skirting the puddles.

"Where are you bound for this sloppy morning?" he asked.

"To Widow Hammond's. To pick up my Aunt. And you?"

"Just making the rounds. See if everyone's all right after the storm."

We walked for a while in silence as I screwed up my courage to invite him for Christmas dinner.

"I'd enjoy that. I really would. But…"

"But?"

"Well, as you probably surmise, I get my share of invitations to Sunday and holiday dinners. But I've a bit of a problem this week. Both the Nathan Dailys and the Joseph Nobles have invited me for

Christmas and I don't know how to choose between them without ruffling any feathers."

"A particular dilemma, Mr. Randolph. Perhaps you'd just as like stop by our house in the evening. Aunt bakes a delicious pound cake."

"Now that I could do. It'd give me an excuse for an early exit from whichever place I land in."

As we approached the Widow's house I noticed the door to her stable standing open, and I was turning in my tracks to close it when Jonah Riggs emerged from the stable, looking more than a little distracted.

"Good Morning, Jonah. What brings you to the Widow Hammond's dooryard?"

"Heard she was ailin'. Figured to take care of the stock for her." He moved past us, ignoring Mark, and proceeded to a gate in the fence between the Riggs and Hammond properties where he stopped and looped the chain around a fence post. "My pa's gone." He said it without emotion, just as a matter of fact.

"What? Jonah! Your father? When?"

Without stopping for pleasantry or explanation he passed through the gate walking away, his back to us.

"Wait, Jonah. How did this happen? Was he ailing?"

"Just the lumbago was all. He went to bed last night and this mornin' he was dead."

I felt a wash of pity for this orphaned boy – man – no, boy. The fact that I didn't like him and felt no desire to know him better made me ashamed, for the moment, at least. "Oh, Jonah, is there anything we can do? Anything you need?"

He shook his head. "I got Angus Hill to come and git him. Take him to town to Bowser's. Church ladies'll take care of it." His manner was off hand, like one's father died every day. No need for concern. He dismissed us with a wave of his hand and continued down the lane toward his house.

"I wonder why he's so undismayed at his father's passing. Seems as though he was in an all-fired hurry to get shut of our company." Jonah was always a puzzlement, but this was strange, even for him.

"Yes, well, I think my presence might be part of it." Mark shifted the heavy basket to his other hand.

"Your presence? Why would he care for that?"

"It seems he has his eye on one of the Noble girls – the younger one – Beatrice, I think. Anyway, he fancies her and she, unfortunately, fancies me. Her parents are keen to attach either of their daughters to me, and I am keen to remain unattached. Hence young Mr. Riggs sees me as competition and focuses his resentment on me."

It seemed Jonah was casting a wide net in his search for a wife, and I was relieved to know he had interests elsewhere. I smiled at the thought that Jonah's interest in Beatrice Noble might release me from whatever fanciful attachment he'd conjured. The thought of Jonah Riggs having eyes for one of the Noble girls was amusing if not realistic. I wished him well, but doubted he'd have any better success with Beatrice Noble than he'd had with me. I was reasonably sure she didn't even know Jonah Riggs was alive, so any liaison between them seemed highly unlikely, but I did truly hope Jonah would find him a wife, and soon.

Now I turned to Mark. "My goodness Mr. Randolph, I wasn't aware that your presence here had aroused such interest. Perhaps you should accept the Daily's invitation and avoid a sticky situation at the Nobles'."

"I'd prefer an evening with your Aunt's pound cake, but I'm afraid there's no avoiding one or the other of those. I just hope Riggs can find himself a willing wife without blaming me for his failures."

"So you think he's just conjured up a girlfriend in Beatrice Noble -- like he did with me?"

"Looks that way. Anyway, he can have his pick of the Noble girls and welcome as far as I'm concerned."

That comment piqued my interest. What about Mr. Randolph? Did he perchance have a sweetheart at home in Georgia? Was he already promised? Why did I care? We walked up the path to

Mrs. Hammond's door where Mark handed me the basket and turned to mount his horse.

"I'm off to spread the gospel. Give your aunt my best wishes." He headed his horse out the lane to the main road and was gone.

Widow Hammond's door was unlocked, so I let myself in, setting my basket on the table. I picked the last couple logs out of the wood box and fed the dying fire while from the bedroom, the only other room in the house, I heard Aunt coaxing the old woman to eat.

"Come now, Mary, take some broth. It'll perk you right up."

The scene when I entered was dim, hopeless – as though Mary Hammond had made up her mind that this was all she wanted of life. I gave Aunt a questioning look. "Shall I go for her daughter?"

"Nay, 'tis too far to walk on such a day. If you should happen to meet someone on their way to town, you can ask them to leave a message at Replogle's."

I opened the shutter of the only window and peaked out to see if I could hail Mr. Randolph, but he was already far down the track.

Out of habit I began folding the clothes lying about and told my aunt the news of Alonzo Riggs's passing "What of you, Aunt? Will you stay here another night? I doubt you can leave her until her daughter gets word."

"I'll be all right here for the present, but ye'd better get to mucking out Riggs' barn. We've neglected it of late."

I knew she was right. The barn had gone three days without any attention from us. "I'll tend to it."

Back out the lane and up the track to our house, I kept thinking about Mark's dilemma, smiling all the while. I donned my work clothes and hiked across the corn stubble to the barn.

Grabbing a shovel I commenced the dirty work, intent on finishing before noon so I could get back to the house where my knitting waited. I was knitting a pair of stockings for Mr. Randolph for Christmas, without telling Aunt, of course. The prospect of a quiet afternoon to get them started pleased me.

My thoughts were interrupted by Jonah entering the barn from the other end. ""Bout time ye got around to muckin'. Been spendin' too much time w'yer preacher friend. Shirkin' is what. Better show some spunk in yer work or I might be of a mind to turn you out."

I turned to him with a frown, but considered my situation and forced a smile. "Actually I've been busy with baking and helping Aunt look after the Widow. I'll have this cleaned up right quick, and before I forget, I've got bread and cookies for you." I kept working as I spoke, aware that Jonah was giving me a stern eye.

"What were you doing in Widow's stable when we met you there this morning?" I asked.

"Naught but feeding her stock. Somebody has to look after them with her fixin' to pass into glory."

"That's nice of you, Jonah. I'm sure the widow appreciates it."

"How are you and that preacher man getting' on? You sorry yet for lettin' the stable to him?"

"Why, no. We're quite happy to have him." I replied, as if I didn't know the source of Jonah's distaste for Mark. "And he tells me you're sweet on Beatrice Noble. How long has this been going on?"

"Ain't actually goin' on. Me and Beatrice had a fallin' out. I just said that to dig at your preacher man."

I wondered what Beatrice's version of these events might sound like for I couldn't imagine her finding anything attractive about Jonah.

"Anyway, your preacher man's a damn Reb. Comin' up here, nosin' about. I'm bettin' he's not a preacher at all. Prob'ly scoutin' fer the Rebs."

He leaned his elbows against the top rail of the stall. "You was pretty easy taken in. Some of us ain't so sure about no Reb preacher. Better tell him to finish his business and move on afore some of us shows him his welcome is wore out. Can't tell *me* he ain't a Rebel scout."

I shivered at his words. A scout for the South? Mark? Of course such a thought had probably passed through everyone's mind, but didn't you need some kind of evidence before you went about accusing? There were those who trusted and believed every word that came out of his mouth, and those who viewed his every move with suspicion. So how did one know what was right?

"Jonah, I'm sorry about your father, and I realize that this is no time to argue with you, but, I've no reason to believe Mr. Randolph isn't everything he says he is."

"Oh yeah? Well I don't need to see no more than I've already seen. Any able bodied man up here from the South has to prove to me he ain't workin' fer the Rebs." Jonah wiped his mouth with the back of his hand, and planted himself in my way. "Besides there's others – a lot of 'em – wants explanations about what happened to Simon Tolliver."

"Simon Tolliver? What happened to him?"

"Disappeared five days ago. Ain't nobody heard a word from him. Then yesterday there was talk about how they found a body just off the track down to Hyndman. Some say it's Tolliver. Easy enough to identify a one-legged man. Shot dead."

"What does this have to do with Mr. Randolph?"

"Well, some saw him riding south last Tuesday morning. Some saw him coming home after dark. And you, Miss Prim and Proper, I saw *you* going out to the stable in your nightgown late that night. How'd you like me to spread that around?"

"You're trying to make something out of nothing – on both counts. Just because Mr. Randolph rode south one day doesn't make him a murderer."

"Well, Simon Tolliver suspected him. Then he disappeared. Sure makes *me* wonder. You just tell him to get on out of here before some of us meet him on a lonely road of a night."

He spat in the muck in front of him. "Best you look out fer yerself, too. You ain't the most popular around here, you know. Once he's gone, nobody else is gonna want some Reb's leavin's."

Of course I'd wondered about Mr. Randolph, but getting to know him had pretty well dispersed those fears. Now the fears came flooding back. Maybe I'd been too hasty in my judgment, blinded by the prospect of a steady income and a gentleman tenant. I finished my chores and plodded back across the corn stubble to the stable thinking on how easy it seemed for Jonah to stir up my fears. I knew I shouldn't let Jonah's accusations open a nagging doubt --threaten to replace my blithe trust, but now, somehow, I began to entertain the notion that maybe Mark *was* too good to be true.

As I passed by the stable door on my way home, I stopped, wrestling with my better nature. Here was an opportunity to settle my doubts once and for all, even though I knew better. Surely there had to be clues to Mr. Randolph's true identity. All I had to do was look. It wasn't exactly honorable, but if the man proved false, the world should know.

The stable was empty and cold and the ladder rungs squeaked as I climbed. Everything I'd ever learned about truth and honesty urged me to back down, and yet something strong and nameless pulled me up that ladder. I stood looking around in the dim light. His bed was neatly made up with one of Aunt's quilts tucked all around. The pot bellied stove stood open, kindling lying ready for a match, ashes swept up, wood stacked beside. His clothes hung neat from pegs on the wall, the only other furniture the plain wooden trunk at the foot of the bed. Of course I had to look.

If I were looking for the gun used to turn away slave catchers and maybe used to kill Simon Tolliver, where else but in the trunk? Apparently Mr. Randolph was a trusting soul who didn't expect his land lady to be a snoop, for the box was unlocked. I lifted the lid and found underclothes and a clean shirt neatly folded in place and a covered tray, also unlocked. That compartment contained two bundles of letters: one official-looking and impersonal, the other tied with a ribbon and addressed in a woman's hand. Beneath the letters lay a canvas bag that held what I was looking for – a Colt Navy revolver and bullets. My hands shook as I wrapped the gun in the canvas bag and put it back in the covered tray.

As I closed the lid, I looked once more at the letters. Unsure of how much time I had for my snooping, fear of discovery kept me from reading anything but the addresses. Still, the woman's handwriting on the address brought a frown. Did he have someone at home? Was he even possibly married, or at least promised? Feeling altogether traitorous I slipped the top letter out of the official-looking bundle, addressed to Maj. Carter Willoughby, CSA. I dropped it as though burned, then hurriedly picked it up, slipped it back in place and closed the lid. Shaken, I took a last look around the spare little room and, gathering my skirts, made my careful way down the ladder. Back in the house, I sat down on the settle to gather my nerves. What was he? A spy? A murderer? God help me.

Judith Redline Coopey

Chapter 16

December 1864
Mark

The winter days rolled by while I worked simultaneously on gathering information, planning my mission and keeping up my little congregations. These people were so sincere in their beliefs, so ardent in their loyalty to me, I felt more than once the pangs of guilt. As I'd been there for nearly three months, our neighbors had gotten used to me, viewed me with less skepticism, even seemed to like me. So, while I never wavered from my real purpose, I felt the pangs of duplicity with regret.

Susannah Lander proved reliable cover, for she was respected despite her pitiable lack of material comforts. It was almost as though people gave me a pass because Susannah did and brushed aside any doubts because of her openness and trust.

In fact, I was feeling so secure that on one of my rides through Martinsburg, I stopped at Replogle's store to do some Christmas shopping. Since our discussion about the Quaker poet, John Greenleaf Whittier, I thought Susannah might enjoy a volume of poetry with which I *was* familiar – that of William Wordsworth. I marked in particular "She Dwelt Among the Untrodden Ways" for it reminded me of Susanna herself. Pleased with my purchase, I stowed my gift in my saddle bag and rode on home looking forward to the upcoming holiday.

The warmth of the Christmas spirit brought on a host of memories, taking my thoughts back to Christmases past when the

Willoughby family gathered round the harpsichord to sing carols to our mother's accompaniment. Father's strong bass voice boomed out with such gusto mother feared the windows would break.

Christmas Eve at Belfast Plantation was a day-long party, a gathering of everyone on the plantation with distribution of Christmas treats to the slave children along with new shoes and clothing. Each male slave received a measure of rum and each child an orange, and Parson Davies paid a call to baptize every slave child born in that year. It was a great celebration, followed in the evening by church services and a midnight supper.

When we exchanged our family gifts on Christmas morn, there was often a horse involved – sometimes more than one – brought up to the front veranda to the delight of the recipient, followed by a horse race, a carriage ride or a parade of equine beauty.

I approached the day feeling less like the shepherd guarding his flock and more like Odysseus longing for home. Keeping up my pretense felt like a burden too great, and I set out on my rounds trying not to think of all that might be lost in the next few months. I swung around north toward Hollidaysburg feeling decidedly sorry for myself and stopped at the Newry Inn – remote enough to feel safe from prying eyes. I sat at a solitary table by the window carefully making a rather mediocre dose of Yankee whiskey last a long time. Men came and went, full of Christmas cheer, some nodding, some wishing me a Merry Christmas, a few offering to buy me a drink. Careful, conscious of the risks of over-indulging, I measured my intake, drinking just enough to take the edge off my recollections.

That third letter lay in my trunk, still unopened. I shuddered to think what news it held. Images of Belfast Plantation, gone but for the house, and that stripped bare, haunted my brain. Was I getting soft or was this war really not worth it? My decimated family needed me. Why was I whiling away precious time up here in this frozen God-forsaken Yankee hell? Why didn't I turn my horse south and ride on home? Who would blame me?

The weather turned colder as the afternoon waned, the slush molding into frozen ruts in the roadway. When snow began to fall upon the ice, I rose and settled my bill, motioned for my horse and departed. The track was treacherous – the little mare stumbled, making me chastise myself for bringing her out on such a day. Here I was on Christmas Eve, groggy, cold, muddy and damn near stupefied. I slowed her pace and gave her leave to pick her own way and she did – carrying my melancholy soul back to my sad little stable. I thanked her with an extra measure of oats.

Standing at the foot of the ladder I thought once again about the letter waiting up there, but decided instead to pay Susannah a call. The whiskey had worn off some, but not enough to put much restraint on my tongue, for as soon as she let me in I began prattling about how much I missed those old Southern Christmases.

Susannah greeted me with quiet restraint, almost as though she had reservations about letting me in, but even though I was sober enough to notice, I was still too drunk to care.

"I know you're grieving the loss of your mother, but you still have your memories, Mr. Randolph."

"Yes, but I can't get my family's present condition out of my head, and the thought that things could still get worse."

I sat down on the settle while Susannah bustled about setting the table. Very business-like she was. Short with her words.

"Where is your aunt this evening? Not home for Christmas eve?"

"Still staying with the widow. This is the waning of the light for her, I fear. Aunt probably doesn't have long to linger over her. I'll go down tomorrow and give her some relief."

My foggy brain searched for another topic – something to cheer us – but all I could think about was my mother, lying prone in the cold ground, her sons at her sides. We ate in relative silence – only the clink of forks on pewter. There in the soft glow of the fireplace I took note of how the light complimented Susannah's skin. Strange. I'd never noticed before.

When the meal was finished I returned to my place on the settle, soaking up the warmth, vaguely aware that Susannah's demeanor was still quite cool. I wondered, but didn't give voice to my concerns, too wrapped up in my grief. Lonely and far from home, I sought to lighten her mood. I hummed a few bars of "Oh, Susannah" and watched her face soften just a little.

"Susannah? Come over here and sit with me," I invited, patting the place beside me. Her reserve bothered me, but I hoped my gift would lighten the mood.

"I'm sorry. Mr. Randolph, but I don't think it seemly for us to be here alone – beyond dinner, of course."

"I've brought you something – a gift," I said, taking the parcel out of my pocket. "I hope I'm not being too forward. I saw this and thought of you. I hope you might enjoy it, even though it isn't your Mister Whittier."

She came, but something was clearly wrong. Her demeanor restrained, she granted my request but sat prim on the other end of the settle, her usual bright mind preoccupied with something.

I handed her the package but she laid it in her lap. "I've something for you as well. I made it – knowing how you hate the cold." She reached into a basket beneath the settle and handed me a packet wrapped in brown paper and tied with string.

"This? For me? Really?" I asked.

"I echo your sentiment. I never expected…"

"Go on, open it. I'll follow," I said, excited to see her reaction.

So she took the package from her lap and carefully, gently, ever so slowly unwrapped it. Her face alight, she opened the slim volume and began to read. "How beautiful. Thank you so much."

Taking it in turns I lifted my gift from the bench between us and tore it open to find a pair of soft woolen stockings – gray – that I held up for admiration.

"Susannah! Did you make these?"

She nodded.

"No finer gift is possible than one from your own hands, Thank you. These will hold off the cold." I ventured to pat her shoulder when I noted a tear in the corner of her eye.

"Now, now. No tears on Christmas Eve. What is it? A sad memory of a past Christmas?"

She wiped away the tear. "This is already the finest Christmas I've ever had."

"Then what is it?"

"Nothing. Just irrational fear. It happens sometimes. The war, I guess. Tearing us out of our natural place, making us spend Christmas with strangers."

"Surely you don't think of me as a stranger. I think of you as a friend -- a special friend in whom I can confide. Getting to know you has given me a wider vision. Why, Susannah, I would venture to call you my best friend."

The whiskey, still strong enough to loosen my tongue and addle my brain, freed me to say things I'd never have done sober. My brain didn't feel addled at all. It felt open and free and full. I reached out as though to take her hand in mine. She resisted, but, emboldened by the after affects of my afternoon drinks, I reached out to pull her toward me. She held back, then yielded, hesitant, keeping a respectable space between us.

"What is it, Susannah? You seem so distant. Can't we put aside our differences and enjoy the holiday? "

As though my words brought relief, she moved closer, almost letting herself lean against me "I'm sorry, Mark. I've so much on my mind. Please don't take offense."

Feeling her nestled there lifted my spirits, warmed my heart, made me put the war and all its ugliness out of my mind for a few moments.

She smoothed her skirts, looking into the fire. "I do think of you as a friend. I'm sorry to be so dispirited, but I had a rather disturbing talk with Jonah Riggs the other day. I know I shouldn't let him bother me, but..."

I found myself watching her lips form the words. How soft and warm they looked. How I would like to press my lips against them. Would she let me? Should I try? Her words slipped by me, lost in the fantasy. I looked at her as though for the first time. Natural, unadorned, unassuming beauty. I took a deep breath to clear my head.

Turning to face her, I leaned over close. "Who? Jonah Riggs? Who's he?" With each soft word, I leaned closer until my lips brushed her nose, felt her breath, sought her mouth.

"Oh no, Mark. No." She moved away, her face flushed by the warmth of the fire and my boldness.

"No? Why not? I can't deny the truth. I've come to care for you."

"And I for you, but..."

"But what?"

"We shouldn't be alone here together. Aunt is away. We..."

"We're not children, Susannah. Life has brought us together. We should be glad of that."

"Oh, I am. I am glad. I just..."

"Just, what?"

"Have worries."

"Worries? About what?"

"About you."

That brought me up short. "Worries about me? What worries about me?"

"Whether you are who you say you are. Jonah thinks you're a rebel spy. He says others do, too. They think you killed Simon Tolliver. That's ridiculous, isn't it? I don't think that, but I don't know what to believe. My mind is so confused, I'm all in a muddle. I don't want to believe Jonah. I don't even like him." She spoke more rapidly with every word, almost as though she couldn't get it all said if she didn't rush.

I wanted to erase the word spy from her head – wanted to make it and all the thoughts that went with it disappear. I caught her arms in my hands, pulled her to me and kissed her firmly. "Spy? I'm no spy. I'm a preacher – a poor, dispirited, lonely man. I need you, Susannah. I love you."

"Love?"

"Yes, love, Susannah Lander. Love."

That's where the conversation faded away. All that mattered, all that made any difference to either of us – love.

Chapter 17

December 1864
Susannah

I shuttled him out the door, ignored his protestations of undying love and watched his progress until I was sure he'd reached the shelter of his stable. Standing with my back against the closed door, I let my head spin where it would. Don't let this nonsense lead you astray, I told myself. Keep a clear head. He'll awake to himself tomorrow and rush to protest – explain. But I. How will I feel tomorrow? As I do now. Smitten. Completely smitten.

The feeling had been there from the start – a charming, fascinating, mysterious man in my life. I fell. Who would not? I was captivated, enchanted. He'd arrived in October. Here was late December and I'd long since lost my mind. This couldn't be real, and yet my fevered brain longed for it to be so.

That kiss changed everything. I didn't know who I was anymore. I just knew I was in love. Mark had stolen into the center of my life. I told myself the kiss was just a passing impulse. He was lonely – far from home. It was Christmas. I believed mayhap he'd even been drinking. So how was this real? Lasting?

I took myself to bed, but did not – could not sleep. What was I doing, kissing a virtual stranger? And wanting more? The man was a preacher – not a Quaker – a priest! How could I put that aside? What was he doing now? Sleeping? How could he sleep after such momentous events? Oh, yes. He'd had some whiskey. Yes. He could sleep while I lay awake in turmoil.

And what of Jonah Riggs' suspicions? And those letters addressed to someone named Carter Willoughby? Who was this Carter Willoughby? How could I put such as that aside? Surely all would be explained in due time, else how could I have fallen so in love? With a Rebel? How could I?

Morning dawned to a world encased in glittering ice. Yesterday's thaw had given way to a deep drop in temperature – freezing everything. Branches glittered and clicked together. A solid icy crust covered the earlier snow. One could walk on it, stomp on it, pound it with a chunk of firewood and it would not yield. The groaning and cracking of trees under their icy burden pierced the cold morning air.

We'd planned that I would make my way to Widow Hammond's to share Christmas dinner with Aunt and her, but there would be no travel this day. A loud crack followed by a crash and the tinkle of scattering ice crystals emphasized that. I looked out the door at the solitary little stable and noted a wisp of smoke rising from the stove pipe. Apparently Mr. Randolph was up and about. My woodpile, sheathed in ice, would have to be broken free and there was a chicken to be killed and plucked, so I pushed aside my doubts and got busy.

The realization that Mr. Randolph and I were destined to share a Christmas dinner frightened and delighted me. I wrapped myself in whatever was warm, took the ax and crept over the ice to the hen house, expecting to find frozen birds fallen from their perches. Instead they were quite lively and noisy, letting me know it would take an extra measure of corn to warm them on such a day.

With a careful eye to the egg-layers, I chose one big breasted, hapless creature to sacrifice on the altar of Christ's birth, raised the ax and did the deed. I kept my foot on it until the blood froze in a puddle, picked it up by the feet and carried it into the house where I'd set a pot to boil. The whole time I was doing this, my mind dithered on Mr. Randolph. Would he regret last night? Stay home in his stable rather than face me? I plucked the chicken with shaking hands, so unnerved and unsure of the man's intentions. Perhaps he wouldn't come at all. Maybe he'd stay home and meditate on his sins. Oh, why had I let myself entertain such foolish notions?

But I'd barely finished plucking and stuffing the chicken when there came a knock on my door.

"Mr. Randolph, how nice to see you so early on Christmas morn."

He leaned over and pecked me on the cheek. "Good morning, Susannah. I trust you had a good night's rest. It looks as though you and I are destined to dine alone. This is certainly not traveling weather."

I took a deep breath. "Mr. Randolph – about last night. I'm afraid we've been a bit indiscreet…"

"What? Susannah! No, don't apologize – last night was an absolute joy. You'll never know how free I feel – how much it meant to hold you in my arms. Please, let's spend this day in the hollow of God's hand."

"Yes. Yes, let's." I opened the oven and put the chicken in, returning to the table to grind cranberries for sauce.

"Don't trouble yourself, now, my dear. A simple dinner will suffice. Come, sit by the fire."

"Nay, I want this Christmas to be as fine as we can make it. I looked into his face for a sign of regret, a second thought, but he showed none. He stepped up behind me, wrapping his arms around me, pulling me close. My heart went wild with the joy of it.

We spent the rest of the morning talking about everything except what was uppermost in my mind: who was he and what was his business here? As we pulled the settle up close to the fire to roast chestnuts, I did my best to put my doubts away, nagging though they were and make the most of this, our first Christmas together. I hoped it would be just that – the first of many.

When dinner was ready, we sat down, made our individual thanks and ate, Mark complimenting my cooking, praising every dish. I knew he was thinking of his family, remembering Christmases gone by, so I encouraged him to speak of them, recalling memories of riding with his brothers and scheming with his sisters to pair him off with the right girl at a party. My own experiences with family, siblings, holidays were so limited as to be non-existent, so I took joy in listening to his. The more I learned of his former life, the more this liaison felt like love to me. I chased all doubt from my mind, determined to make it a memory, no matter what the future held.

After dinner we sat by the fire and continued our reminiscences. His memories were far warmer and more tender than mine, and though doubt kept watch around the periphery I took joy in hearing him speak of his childhood. Unable to sit idle for long, I picked up my knitting as we talked.

He watched me cast on stitches for a sweater destined to be his. "You seem accomplished in so many ways."

Nodding, I held up the beginning of the sweater –blue – from my own dye made of cornflowers and alum.

"For me?" he asked, humbled by the idea of my doing even more for him. "You shouldn't do so much for me, but I appreciate your kindness. This Yankee winter is just plain awful for a Southern boy like me."

"Hush your yammering, good sir. Thy lot could be far worse, methinks."

"You're right. I could be sleeping in a tent in some camp with hungry comrades, foraging for food."

"You speak with the voice of authority. Have you done such?"

His face paled, drawn into a frown. "Yes. Yes, I have." He gave that comment a few moments to take hold. "This spy talk – it's not idle chatter. People like Simon Tolliver or Jonah Riggs are not far wrong. I've much to confess, I'm afraid."

I put down my knitting, not sure I was ready to hear what came next.

"The suspicions are not without substance. I'm here on assignment from the Confederate Army – to do harm to the Horseshoe Curve. Blow it up if I can." On the one hand, it must have felt good for him to let it all go -- stop with the pretense -- rather like a caged bird whose door has just been flung open.

126

He continued, holding both of my hands, gazing into my eyes. "Your doubts are justified, Susannah. Oh, and my name is not Mark Randolph. I am Carter Willoughby of Milledgeville, Georgia, a major in the Confederate Army, not a circuit riding Methodist."

No! No. I sat silent, letting him hold my hands, looking into his eyes, taking it all in. It was my duty to turn this Rebel spy over to the local authorities, but I could no more do that than turn a fugitive slave away from my door. Still I abhorred slavery as much as war and blamed the evil practice for all the present troubles. People were dying, and every day the war dragged on, more people would die. What if Mr. Randolph -- Mark -- Carter – whatever his name was – succeeded in blowing up the curve? What difference would it make? Just extend the suffering a while longer, but to no other purpose. The South would still lose.

I drew away from him, weighing the gravity of his confession. "I really wish you hadn't told me this. What am I supposed to do now? If you were to succeed in your mission and get caught, I could be hanged along side of you. Worse, I now have knowledge of you that opposes everything I hold dear."

He reached for me, drew me against him, caressing my cheek with the back of his hand. "I know. I'm sorry, Susannah. I didn't set out to fall in love with a Yankee woman, much less a Quaker woman so sure of her view of the world. Please be patient. I've much to think about."

"Will you desert then? Is that what you plan?"

"The war is near its end. But for Lee's stubborn refusal to face reality, it wouldn't have lasted much beyond Gettysburg. So the fighting of the last year and a half has been futile. I'm hoping it will end before my orders come so I don't have to be a party to any more suffering. I'm doing everything I can to drag my feet – put this off until the South surrenders, but you've changed everything for me. Now I have a purpose beyond the empty romantic cause that used to mean so much."

He took my hand, raised it to his lips and kissed it, then drew me close again, kissing my face, my eyes, my neck, sending lightening through my soul.

"I love you, Susannah."

My brain was so addled I shuddered and drew away. "We must remember who and where we are. Indeed, I love you, too, but we aren't free to follow our hearts. The war still rages and you are still in rebellion against your country."

He straightened up, still holding my hands. "I know. It isn't that I hate the Union, but living here has taught me much. Now I just want the war to be over. It's so futile, so lacking in reason and purpose. So I'll keep stalling – to use up the time. I'm torn between my love for my home and my love for you. Think about it, Susannah."

"I *am* thinking about it." I retreated into silence, even as he enclosed me in his arms. Indeed I loved him. Had since I first laid eyes on him, but how could I do this? Keep silence and betray my faith and my country?

This new person, Carter Willoughby, rose and paced the small room, hands clasped behind his back, heaviness weighing on his shoulders. Watching him set my pulse to flying, my knees to buckling. I'd waited so long for love to find me. How could I give this up? How could I ever go back to who I was just two morns ago? And yet. And yet, was he not in rebellion against the country I loved? Did he not intend destruction, violence, bloody murder?

Chapter 18

December 1864
Carter Willoughby

I spent Christmas day in Susannah's arms, wishing, oh wishing I could die there. If you were to meet her in a casual setting you wouldn't find her remarkable, but she was. At first impression she was a plain and simple country girl, but little by little, as though one had to earn them, she divulged her charms, entangling me, drawing me in. Deep, soft, whispering brown eyes, hair that, let down, fell in chestnut cascades, soft color in her cheeks. So gentle was her touch it sent chills down my spine -- and more. Much more. A fine mind, open and caring, but steady and alert to hypocrisy. Never have I met one so clear in her thinking, so sure of her place in the universe.

I know I sound besotted, and I was, but I was also fearful that this love might not survive the complexity I brought to it. Love, even love as pure as this, is not perfect. It is the ebb and flow of two divergent souls, the drawing near and the pulling away, the need and the denial of need. Now Susannah, for all her clear-headedness, must reckon between love of country and love for me. Must reckon between loyalty to one and desire for the other.

And what of me? How did I let myself get drawn into this at a time when my mission demanded complete dedication? After all, she was simply a woman, one of many and easy enough for most men to pass by. Why not I? Now we stood at an impasse neither of us could escape without losing something vital to our souls.

She, her sense of self – her devotion to her religion, her love of country. I, my hard earned respect as a soldier, defender of ideals, son of the South.

So passed a sweet Christmas day, full of concerns, but overshadowed by hopes, plans, decisions. She treated me to a fine Christmas dinner followed by hours of delight in sharing our memories of past lives. I opened my history to her in ways that I'd never done to anyone – every achievement, embarrassment, dream, and regret – and she to me. We passed the hours in sweet communion, the world held at bay, wrapped as it was in a crystal shell of ice.

Even though we were alone and safe from prying eyes, we did not fulfill our love that day as some would have. We spoke of marriage – at that time a sincere, but unimaginable dream to be put off until the war was over. I didn't promise not to obey my orders when they came, for the idea of insubordination was abhorrent to me. I was a soldier, wasn't I? But I ardently hoped somehow those orders would never come. I offered to find another place to live to protect Susannah from being accused of collaboration, but she was firm in her desire to stay close to me, though it could be her undoing.

Finally, late in the evening I bade her good night and made my way over the treacherous, icy crust to tend my little mare and feed the stove. Once the room had warmed, I sat down to write my sister Emily, conscious that she may never see the letter, to tell her of my new-found love. Then I remembered the third letter, tucked away in my trunk. I'd forgotten it – avoided it out of fear for what tragic news it might contain. Now I lifted it and broke the seal, dated 30 November 1864.

> *Dear Brother,*
> *It seems you and I are destined to be the last of the Willoughbys. Ellen has gone – brought about her own demise just days after the soldiers were here. She watched in silence as they burned everything and took all the stores*

and livestock. No crying. No pleading like the old Ellen would have done. She watched with dull eyes, her posture sagging, hands at her sides.

We slept that night alone on the floor of our old bedroom, arms around each other, only to be jarred from our rest by the blast of a shotgun downstairs. Papa. We knew it was papa. He just couldn't live with it anymore, so he left us. It fell to both of us to dig his grave and lay him to rest with Mama and the boys.

Old Julius died days after the soldiers came, and Viney says she will follow them soon. I tried to boost Ellen – hold her up until she could stand to face all that had happened, but yesterday afternoon, a cold and blustery day, I watched her wander out to the cemetery and stand contemplating the graves – all four. Even though I felt deep in my soul that soon there would be five, I made no move to prevent her. She took a bottle from her pocket and drank deep. Laudanum. She lay down between them – Papa and Mama – and went to sleep.

So now we are two. I think I can glean enough to survive the winter, but there'll be nothing to plant come spring. No seed, no horses, no mules, no one but me to plant the seed I don't have. Mayhap when this brutal war is over and you've returned we can salvage something.

I remain your devoted sister,
Emily Willoughby

So it was as I'd expected. Gone. All of it. There was no restoring the old life. Our stubborn and romantic nature had undone us. Strangely, I was not sad to see it go. The exploitation of one people over another always ends badly. But grief for my family roiled up inside of me, overwhelming my aching heart. I rose from the table, pulled on my boots, wrapped my cloak around me and climbed down the ladder. I stood in the doorway looking up at Susannah's little hovel nestled in the darkness, arguing with myself over disturbing her sleep.

Out into the ice-covered wilderness I plodded, Emily's letter in my pocket. The way was harsh, treacherous, but comfort beckoned. When Susannah opened the door, I fell into her arms, sobbing. "Gone. Oh, God, they're all gone."

As though she'd spent her life preparing for this, Susannah guided me to the fire, stripped off my cloak, sat me down and pulled off my boots. I handed her the letter and watched her read it, watched her face cloud, her hand flutter to her throat. She tucked it away under her night dress and came to enfold me in her arms.

"Men would do this. Push for war, push war beyond endurance, push people to the very limits of their souls. My God, Carter. My God."

I felt sobs wrack her body as I pressed my face into her bosom. Here was peace. Sensibility. Here I would stay. I reached for her, pulled her down beside me, kissed her through her tears and my own. I don't know how long we stayed so. I just know I felt her pull away, rise and draw me to my feet. The way across the room was short – maybe ten steps to her bed, but surely the longest path either of us would ever take. From this day on, we would be one.

Part Two

Judith Redline Coopey

Chapter 19

Early 1865
Susannah

With the holidays past, we tried to return to the normal business of living – Mr. Willoughby in his stable room, following our customary breakfast and dinner routine, I fulfilling my obligations to Jonah Riggs and Aunt Betsy. But it would be silly to pretend that all was as usual. I could hardly stand to be away from him for even a moment, though we both understood that it was more than ever necessary to stick to our old ways. He continued to ride circuit, nurturing his little congregations, while I did what I'd always done – kept house and worked for Jonah.

Aunt returned a few days after Christmas with the news that Mary Hammond's earthly journey was over. She'd passed into eternity on Christmas night. I think Aunt perceived our situation. Carter's and mine, though she didn't speak of it. She made a habit of retiring early to give us some time alone, and of not asking too many questions about why I was so good humored all the time. When cold weather made travel unreasonable, Carter would spend the days chopping wood for his own little stove and our fireplace. I could tell he was restless, wanting the winter to be over as well as the war. He spoke often of Georgia and Belfast Plantation, always with a tone of regret.

When we spoke of marriage, which we often did, it was with the understanding that we would wait until the war was over, for Carter talked continually of going back to Georgia to settle his affairs, and of perhaps bringing his sister Emily north to live with us. There was no talk of my moving to Georgia, for I think he knew even then that Belfast Plantation was beyond all hope of resurrection.

But as January waned, our need for each other coupled with the need for secrecy began to take its toll and Carter brought forward the idea that there really was nothing to stop us from marrying right away. He could still take care of his affairs after the war ended -- no need to wait, an idea with which I was firmly in accord, even though as the wife of a suspected spy my life could be in jeopardy. So on a Saturday afternoon in early February, sunny and bright, though cold as a wind from Canada, Carter tucked me up onto his little mare's back and, walking beside, took us into Martinsburg.

Having no preference as to which church would suit our purpose, we stopped at the first church we came to -- the Presbyterian. Carter helped me down from the horse, led the way across the broad front porch of the rectory and knocked on the door. The woman who answered was a round-faced, cheerful-looking soul, wrapped in a wool shawl and wearing fingerless mitts to keep her hands warm and free enough to do kitchen chores.

"Good day, Ma'am. My name is Mark Randolph and this is Miss Susannah Lander. We wonder if the Reverend would have time to perform a wedding for us today."

Removing her mitts, the woman nodded, smiled broadly and said, "I'll ask him. He's working on his sermon for tomorrow, but he's usually willing to take a break for good reason."

She disappeared into an adjoining room and was back in a short time, still smiling. "He says yes, if you can wait five minutes. He's just at the big wind-up of his sermon."

Carter smiled at that. "I understand, being a man of the cloth myself."

"Oh, and where do you serve?" she asked.

"Everywhere. I'm a circuit rider."

"You're not a Methodist, are you?" Her brow furrowed at the word.

"Yes, ma'am, I am."

"Oh. Well, you just sit and make yourselves at home while I tend to my baking." She indicated two velvet chairs sitting side by side near the fire, and bent down to lay another log. With a smile and a nod she disappeared through a swinging door into the kitchen.

Wondrous smells already filled the house as we sat holding hands, waiting. Still in a state of wonder at my new situation -- somebody loved me! I had a future and life promised wondrous things if only we could get beyond this everlasting war. I'd long since cleared my mind of dreams of love and marriage, so it was an adjustment to reevaluate my place in the world. I'd forgotten how deeply I'd longed for love – how hard it was to believe it was really happening to me.

The minister, a tall, angular man with large hands, feet and an Adam's apple to match came out of his study in short order and gave us a thorough looking over. "Where did you say you were from?" he asked, studying us over his spectacle rims.

"Miss Lander here is a local girl – from East Sharpsburg. I'm from Georgia."

"Georgia? The state?"

Carter nodded.

The man cocked his head and frowned. "What are you doing here with a war on?"

Carter gave him an abbreviated explanation which led to a lengthy exchange about Methodism and why this particular minister found it difficult to understand why anyone would elect to follow it. Carter responded with patience, mindful of our purpose and careful not to ruffle the feathers of one who would join us in matrimony. The reverend was more staid and serious-minded than his wife, who joined us in the front parlor for the ceremony. Opposites attract.

"Lander. Isn't that a Quaker name down in Bedford County?"

Carter nodded. "Miss Lander is a Quaker, sir."

"They'll have plenty to say about her marrying with a Methodist. Are you sure, Miss?"

I looked from him to Carter, my face aglow with my impending status as a wife. "Oh, yes, sir. I'm sure."

The reverend peered again at me over his spectacles. "There's much to be said for marrying within our own people, you know. Not so much to adjust to." He cleared his throat, wiped his nose and set his Bible down on a shelf. "We'll need witnesses, Clara. Did you find witnesses?"

"Yes, Reverend Snyder. Chester and Amanda Grove will be here in short order."

The reverend pulled on his frock coat, retrieved his Bible and paged through, generally ignoring us, but we were so enthralled with our future prospects that his apparent disapproval of our religious leanings bothered us nary a bit. The front door opened, ushering in a blast of cold air and an elderly couple who stopped to remove their gloves and scarves, expressing delight in witnessing a wedding. Their good humor seemed to light up the room, and Carter and I exchanged smiles as they stopped to hang their wraps on a hall tree and joined us in the now-crowded parlor.

The minister cleared his throat again and began right away, as though in a hurry to get this task over with. "Dearly beloved, we are gathered together in the sight of God..." He gave Carter a raised eyebrow. "to unite this man and this woman in holy matrimony." He tilted his head toward me with a questioning look that indicated I could still change my mind if I were so inclined. When I nodded to reassure him that I wasn't about to backslide, he continued.

The service was short and oh so sweet for Carter and me if not for the minister. As my heart beat out a tattoo that could have been heard across the town, Carter smiled down at me and patted my hand. Our witnesses signed the pastor's record book and the lady of the house disappeared into the kitchen to reappear a few moments later with a plateful of sugar cookies and a pot of tea that she placed on a table by the window. Carter and I and Chester and Amanda sat enjoying her generosity while the reverend filled out a marriage certificate. I took it, holding it out so it wouldn't get wrinkled, folded or rolled. Even though it named Mark Randolph as the groom, I knew it would forever be my most prized possession.

When in short order we rose to leave, Carter handed the minister his compensation as we made our way out the front door to admonitions about the dangers of Methodism and an invitation to attend services in the right church at any time. I smiled at that and Carter waited until I was well situated on the little mare's back to laugh out loud.

"If I were back in Georgia, it'd be the Baptists claiming to be the only right religion. Guess we'd better not move around too much for fear of offending those whose religion *is* the right one."

"I'll follow my own inner light and thee can follow thine," I told him.

We returned home and announced our union to Aunt, and, true to her kind disposition, she hugged us both and wished us a long and happy life together.

"I knew you were leaning that way," she smiled. "It's pretty hard to keep those feelings under cover. Now if the war was just over, you could get a good start on life."

I wondered if she didn't feel just a little nostalgia for what might have been in her own life. But she showed no restraint in rejoicing for me. She was quick to suggest that we change the house around, giving Carter and me the upper bedroom and moving her meager belongings downstairs. She did little things, like insisting that we take the only oil lamp upstairs with us every night, and preparing a breakfast for us each morning

Aware that I had to decide what to call this man I was now joined to for life, I asked his preference -- Mark or Mr. Randolph -- but he chafed at that. When he reminded me it was a combination of his brothers' names, I understood why he wanted to go back to his own Christian name. But everyone knew him as Mark Randolph, itinerant preacher, so I tried to get used to calling him Mark in public, while in private, I referred to him intimately as Carter.

As soon as word reached the Dunnings Creek Meeting down to Bedford, they wasted no time in reading me out of meeting for marriage by a 'priest.' Aunt continued as a birthright Quaker and I did my best to see that she got to Meeting once a month, but my own ties were cut and that was that. I never said I was a Methodist, so I guess I wasn't anything but the same child of God I'd always been.

Carter bought a small rig to carry us to his little church gatherings, and I was accepted as 'the preacher's wife,' though one or two young ladies couldn't resist talking behind their hands when I was around. The Nobles actually fell away, maybe because without any prospects, their daughters lost faith. Carter kept up his circuit riding – staying as close to home as possible while awaiting orders from the army which we both desperately hoped would never come.

As the winter wore on, we snuggled together in an impatient world of promise and dreams. We heard no more from his sister, Emily, even though Carter kept writing letters as though they had a chance of getting through. Many of our conversations centered on the war – what would happen once the weather broke. What he would do if and when... He paid careful attention to the news for he knew the South was teetering and hopefully on the verge of surrender any day. He rode down to Hyndman once in late February, but there was no sign of Bennett, no dispatches, and he returned relieved.

I tried not to worry him about his mission, but pondered my own situation endlessly. Why, when love finally came, did it bring such distress, such complexity?

We continued through a cold and harsh February into more of the same in March with a break now and then to renew the promise of spring. Frantic for fear Carter's role would be discovered and both of us condemned, I went about the business of living, afraid when spring came and folks started getting around more, there would be more talk and probably more suspicion. How I wished for the war to be over.

When the weather broke around late March, Carter's talk about home and his need to go back became non-stop. He clung to a fragile hope that there would be something to salvage out of

Belfast Plantation – a small sum perhaps to get us started in a place of our own, and the chance to bring his sister home.

Even as he spoke of leaving, I felt life stirring in my womb. Should I tell him? No. Then he wouldn't go, maybe would never go and miss the chance to break his ties to the South for good. I kept my peace and counted the months. November. It seemed such a long way off, but still I hoped once the war ended we could turn our attention to building our life together in earnest.

April came -- typical as Aprils do. Rainy, windy, warm one day, freezing the next. I knew he was anxious to go, waiting for news of the war's end, watching the weather for a long enough break to justify travel. Then on the morning of April 10 he packed up his saddle bags.

I stood forlorn in the center of the room, blinking back tears. He watched me, hands at his sides, shaking his head. "Are you sure you can get along by yourself for a while?"

I nodded. "I've done so all my life. I can do it for a few more months."

He held me close and kissed me good-bye. I clung to him, breathed in his aura, ran my fingers over his face as though to memorize every feature. "Oh, Carter, do be careful. I worry for you."

"Now, my dear, I know how to get along. Wait and see – I'll be back by early June at the latest. I love you."

He wiped my tears, kissed me once more and was gone, humming "Oh, Susannah" as he prodded his little mare into a trot. I watched him ride down the track, back straight, eyes south, his banjo tied behind him and whispered a prayer. Our parting was fraught with fear – a fear I couldn't name – for him, for me, for our child, for the murky and overcast future.

Without Carter's rent money, Aunt and I returned to our former state of poverty. He'd left me a purse containing two folded greenback ten dollar bills with the request that I try not to spend them until his return, so I put the money away under the tread of the bottom step and tried to forget it was there.

I'd put aside seed for corn, potatoes, tomatoes, beans and cabbage in the fall, anxious for warm weather so I could put in a garden. The problem was to scrape together enough food to last until the garden came round. We could at least count on our daily ration of milk and eggs, a generous supply of apples in the fruit cellar and enough potatoes to last, even though they were withering and sprouting already. Uncle Thomas was in no way obligated, nor of a mind to volunteer any aid since I was now a married woman and read out of Meeting.

Lee had surrendered at Appomattox Courthouse on April 9, the day before Carter left, even though we didn't hear of it until the next week, and when word finally reached us I rejoiced in the belief that this turn of events would make everything come out right.

At that stage of my pregnancy, I barely knew I was pregnant. I kept up my daily routine of mucking out the barn, pruning fruit trees, planting onions or whatever else was asked of me. Jonah Riggs scrutinized everything I did, unable or unwilling to accept my new status. Aunt fell ill to her annual 'spring complaint' and took to her bed, leaving me with her share of the labor, but happily convinced that keeping busy would speed the return of my love.

Then, five days after the war ended, Mr. Lincoln was shot. The news hit me hard, like some kind of omen – a warning of things to come. Why did I feel such trepidation? Where was Carter this very minute? Maybe near halfway through Virginia. Probably rejoicing that the war was over. Making plans to gather up his sister and bring her back to the Cove. Oh, yes. Surely. Who knew? Maybe he'd get home even sooner than he'd planned.

So as April ebbed into May, I planted my garden, tended to Aunt, swept and aired out the house, sewed clothes for the baby and waited. No letter came, but that was to be expected. The south would be out of touch for some time -- men returning from the war, people wandering about, trying to put in a crop, waiting for their wounds to heal. I didn't expect to hear from him until I saw him riding up the track, so to fill the emptiness, I would wander down to the stable of an evening, climb the ladder and lie in his feather bed, remembering his touch, his scent, his loving eyes. I would try not to cry – not to tarnish the memories.

Then one May afternoon I was planting beans when I looked up and saw a young woman come out of Alonzo Riggs' house. She waved and smiled and I waved back, puzzled, so I rose and walked over to the fence as she did the same.

"Hello. I'm Susannah Willoughby. My aunt and I live over there." I indicated our house with a thumb over my shoulder. Saying my name was Willoughby gave me a thrill.

The woman, not much more than a girl, was unfamiliar, but she seemed anxious to make friends. "I'm Lizzie Riggs. Me and Jonah just got married last Friday. I live here now."

Lizzie Riggs was a pretty girl, though life had not been kind to her. She stood quite tall and very thin – with little color and no shape to her. I thought she was timid – not used to social situations, for her hands shook when she handed me a daisy she'd picked.

"Where are you from, Lizzie?"

"Over to Ore Hill. My pa works in the orchard over there."

"Oh, well it's nice to have a new neighbor. I didn't know Jonah was courting."

"Oh, we didn't court. Jonah rode by and saw me putting in the garden and he stopped and asked my pa if he could marry me. Pa said yes, if ye've got five greenback dollars. Jonah said yes he did, fished them out and handed them over, so Pa said okay."

I stepped back, not exactly surprised that Jonah would buy him a wife, but puzzled that he'd apparently given up on all those other girls, most of whom had already sent him on his way. At least I could breathe easier, since I was no longer a candidate for his matrimonial quest.

"Do you have everything you need for housekeeping?" I asked, knowing full well that Martha Riggs had left a well-stocked kitchen in her wake.

"Yes'm. But I don't know much how to cook. My ma did all that so's I could do the chores and garden and such. I might need some help learnin' to cook."

"Oh, my aunt is a famous cook around here. She'd be glad to teach you everything you need to know."

The girl's face lit up. Obviously anxious to please her new husband, she promised to come over the next day for her first lesson. As I watched her walk back to her house, I hoped Jonah would prove to be a good husband, but if I had to put up a bet, I wouldn't risk it.

Lizzie Riggs came over the next day and the day after and the day after that, eager and quick to learn. Aunt loved the chance to teach her skills, so the two of them formed a fast friendship. Lizzie wore the same dress every day until Aunt asked her if she didn't have another one.

"No'me. This is all I got. I guess I might need to learn to sew, too. Maybe Jonah'll buy me some piece goods and I can make some new dresses. Can you sew?"

Aunt was even more delighted to teach her another skill and before long, she brought a dress length of green and white gingham that Aunt helped her sew up into a summer frock. We Quakers only wore brown or gray, so getting to sew a little green gingham was fun, though Aunt kept any such thoughts to herself. Now that I wasn't a Quaker anymore, I thought I might like a pretty dress, but my expanding middle put that off, at least for a while.

"Where's yer man?" Lizzie asked me one day as we sat on the porch capping strawberries.

"Gone back to his home in the south. To settle his affairs and fetch his sister," I replied.

"South? Like Bedford, you mean?"

"No, farther south. Georgia."

"Georgia? Ain't that a Reb state?"

"Yes, it was a rebel state, but the war's over now."

"So he really is a Reb? Jonah says he's a Reb spy and he ain't never gonna come back here, cause he was only here to stir up trouble. Says you're gonna end up with a Reb baby and nothing else."

I put down my strawberries. "Well, you tell Jonah, he's wrong. My husband was not a spy and he'll be back here soon enough. Then we'll see what Jonah has to say."

Lizzie cast her glance down at my words as though afraid to contradict her new husband. "I'm sorry Miss Susannah. I was only sayin' what Jonah says. I won't tell him though. He gets real mad if I tell him what you say. I don't want him to stop me from comin' over here. He says I spend too much time with you and you're a bad inf...inf..."

"Influence?"

"Yes, ma'am. Influence. That's what he says. Says I can learn to cook and sew, but he don't want me comin' home with no smart-ass woman talk."

I smiled at that and put my arm around her. "Don't you worry, Lizzie. I won't do any smart-ass woman talk in front of you. I like having you around."

So began a friendship that I cherish to this day. Lizzie Riggs was way too smart for Jonah, but it took him a while to catch onto that. The two of them were at odds almost from the start, and try though he might to make her his obedient servant, he was in for a struggle. If I was a smart-ass woman, Lizzie was a smarter-ass woman by far. It took a while to reveal itself, but Lizzie was nobody's fool. All she needed was a little self-confidence and that came with learning to cook and sew and keep a clean house.

Judith Redline Coopey

Chapter 20

April 1865
Carter Willoughby

Leaving Susannah was the hardest thing I'd ever done. I rode away heavy hearted, resolved to quickly attend to my business and return. The war would soon be over but there was no telling what further disaster was in the offing, so I was determined to get back to Belfast Plantation and Emily -- rescue her from further mishap. I doubted there would be anything to claim except what was left of my sister, but I had another reason to return, something only I knew about – since our father was dead. Just as the war broke out, Papa had hidden away a cache of gold coins down the well. I held out hope that it might still be there, and if I could persuade Emily to leave, we could recover the money, turn around and be back to the Cove by sometime in mid-June. The army would be so busy winding things up, my absence would pass unnoticed and barring any other trouble, travel should be fairly easy this time of year.

I rode as long as I could the first day, drew up at a farmhouse and asked to lodge my horse and sleep in their barn. The farmer's wife looked askance at me – wandering about without a uniform – but I returned to the circuit riding preacher ploy and she allowed as how I might spend one night in their barn. I rose early the next morning and was on the high road before light. Riding straight south from the Cove, I crossed into Maryland and spent my second night in Cumberland, bartering a couple of hours' work in exchange for boarding me and my horse. I figured it to be about seven hundred miles from the Cove to Milledgeville – probably take about a month, barring complications.

The countryside was alive with strange company -- deserters and discharged veterans from both sides trying frantically to get back home, gangs of angry Rebels refusing to accept defeat, and just plain criminals out to take advantage of the chaos. Lincoln's death ignited a fury of Yankees bent on revenge, conjuring conspirators behind every tree. I kept to myself, took pains to blend in with the forest, traveling the back roads as much as I could. Still there were encounters.

On the afternoon of April 30, almost three weeks out from home, I was riding through a blustery shower somewhere south of Greensboro, North Carolina, keeping my head down when I sensed a rider approaching. I moved aside to give him room, nodded and kept on my way. He passed me, then stopped, turned and yelled, "You blue or gray?"

Tempted to keep riding, I barely replied, "Neither."

"Neither? How can you be neither? You just get here from the moon?"

Irritated at this interruption of my steady progress, I kept riding. The man turned, spurred his horse and caught up with me. "Where's yore manners, man? I'm talkin' to you. You blue or gray?"

"Told you I was neither."

"Cain't be neither. Everyone has a side."

"The war's over. Time to get on."

The man drew a pistol from his belt and brandished it in my face. "Speak up, man. Name yer colors."

Turning the gun aside I leaned toward him. "You want to be careful there, sir. I'm not looking for trouble, but if you persist, I might oblige." Close up, I could see he was hardly more than a boy, wearing faded, ragged, once-blue pants, liquor on his breath.

"Everyone's got to decide. This here country has made up its mind. Besides, every man has a side if he's any kind of a man, so pick yer side and defend it."

I sighed and nudged my horse forward. "I'm not from around here, so I guess I'll keep my side to myself." I dug my heels into my horse's belly and took off down the track, hoping my adversary wouldn't or couldn't keep up. He raised his gun and shot in my general direction, but I kept going, aware that he'd probably try again, but still hoping to avoid the inevitable.

He rode after me, yelling and waving his pistol, so, out of frustration I stopped again and waited for him -- might as well settle this before somebody got hurt -- realizing for the second time that he wasn't very old -- maybe eighteen or nineteen, if he was that. He rode up still waving the pistol and grabbed for my reins. I knew I could take him, no problem, but I really didn't want to hurt a young drunk trying to make sense of the outcome of the war.

"There. That's better," he said, wrapping my reins around his hand. Seeing my advantage, I nudged my horse to back up and pulled the poor lout out of his saddle right quick. As he fell with a thump, his gun clattering to the ground, his horse reared and ran off a few yards. Him on the ground and me astride set the situation to my liking, so I dragged him a little way to teach him a lesson.

"You ready to behave in a civil manner, or do I need to drag you all the way to Georgia?"

He let my reins untwist themselves and, rising a little unsteadily, brushed himself off, embarrassed. "Hell, I guess you got me now."

I waited, holding him at gun point while he retrieved his horse and relieved himself. "Where you been, soldier?" I asked.

"No place. Been wandering around for a month or so. Stole a jug of home brew from a fella up the road. Piss poor whiskey, but I been drinkin' it anyway since last night."

"Which way ya goin'?"

"Don't know. Just wanna git away from the goddamn war is all."

"War's over. Ain't you heard?"

"Yeah. I know, but I still got some scores to settle."

"You still attached to some unit?" There was no telling if those bedraggled pants were U.S. Government Issue or just something he'd stripped off a dead man.

"Thirty-third Massachusetts Infantry, but I'm done with the war. Lit out a month or so ago. I was ridin' with a gang of Rebs 'til I reckoned they was nothin' but loonies -- into robbin' and pillagin' and whatever devilment they could think up. I got enough trouble with the Army. I don't need no trouble with the law."

So, a deserter. Well, I wouldn't fare any better than he if a patrol picked us up. Rebs wouldn't believe I was a scout and Yankees would kill me first and ask questions later. I felt a sad kinship with this young drunk. Not that I was looking for a traveling companion, but I figured it wouldn't hurt anything to stop and eat, then go our separate ways.

"That where you're from, then? Massachusetts?"

"Yes, sir. Thirty-third Massachusetts Infantry. A proud regiment, sir."

"Where all have you been?"

"Every goddamn where, sir. Fredericksburg, Chancellorsville, Gettysburg, Chattanooga, Missionary Ridge, Atlanta, March to the Sea, Savannah, you name it."

"Your side won. Why quit now? Not that it matters anymore." I was suddenly interested in everything he had to say. March to the sea? Could he have been one of them burned Belfast Plantation?

"Got my belly full. I could march home with my unit a hero, but I can't just now. I just can't anymore. Anyway, my fellow soldiers marked me a coward. I ain't no coward. I just couldn't see the sense in keepin' on with the fight. But they wasn't listenin', so here I am. If they catch me, it'll be a firing squad."

I understood his predicament -- the hopeless empty sense that nothing mattered. The war was over, no matter if that made you happy or not. The South was beat and so was this young Yank. No one would ever understand all he'd seen and done, but some of those memories would never let him go.

"So you were heading north. Why turn around and follow me?"

"Oh, that was just the liquor, sir. I'm still drunk, but when I sober up, I'll turn around. Or not. Or maybe I'll head west. Don't know what I'll do yet."

"Wanna stop for some grub? I got coffee and we might snare a rabbit or a squirrel. You could put that pistol to better use getting us some supper." I didn't know what made me bother to pursue friendship with a Yankee deserter just past boyhood. I guess I'd been alone on the road too long, and there was something about this open-faced young innocent that intrigued me.

"Sure." He picked up his gun and got back on his horse. We rode along with little conversation – only a question now and then, followed by a terse answer, then silence. After a couple of miles, we turned off and found us a flat spot by a stream and built a fire.

"So what's your name, Billy Yank?" I asked.

"Jack. Jack Everett. You?"

I hesitated and settled on my preacher name. "Randolph. Mark Randolph. Preacher. I ride the Methodist circuit."

The youth's eyes lit up and he slapped his leg in a guffaw. "Preacher man? Really? Methodist?"

I nodded, curious as to what he found so funny.

He kept laughing for a full minute, then turned to me, still trying to contain his glee. "My old man was a preacher man, too. Congregational. Plain little white board church in the middle of Hawleyville, Massachusetts. Nothin' he hated more than a Methodist. He'd go into apoplexy if he knew I was cavortin' with a Methodist."

I was tempted to tell him I wasn't really a Methodist, but he seemed to be enjoying the joke so much, I let it go.

"Anyway, I ain't never goin' back there to Hawleyville. Reason I joined up with the Army was so I could get away from my old man. Preachin' all the time. Haulin' me off to church or the woodshed, one, every time I spit. Ain't no life, bein' a preacher's kid." He paused. "You got any kids?"

"No."

"Where *you* from, then? You ain't said." He seemed to be sobering up some, so I thought I'd be honest and let him know that much at least.

"Georgia."

"Georgia? Why you're a Goddamn Reb, ain't you? I shoulda knowed. Shoulda shot you when I had the chance."

I had a feeling he was all talk, so I didn't look for my gun. "Thought you were done with the war."

"I am, but I still hate Rebs. Screamin', ignorant, hard-headed bastards. Don't know when to quit."

He wandered away for a while, shot a rabbit, brought it back by the ears and threw it at me. "Here. You skin it. I'll get the fire going. I'm a great cook."

That was my introduction to Jack Everett of Hawleyville, Massachusetts, a lost and lonely soldier boy wandering around looking for a purpose to hang his life on and a way to forget about the war. His rough manner belied a tender heart, the root of his trouble. The war had repelled him, repulsed him, chewed him up and spit him out, and now he couldn't get shut of it. Turned out we would travel on south together for a couple hundred miles and most nights he'd wake up screaming at the slightest noise, or bawling his eyes out over someone called Jed. Jedediah Hawkins, a kid he grew up with and watched get his head blown off with a cannon ball. Jack was a tender soul and tender souls aren't cut out for war.

We kept going south through the Carolinas headed for Georgia. I had to admit it was comforting to have someone to talk to on the way. I told him about Belfast Plantation, and he expressed regret at burning more than one, and maybe that one, on the way through Georgia. And he told me about hiding out in a swamp getting eaten alive by mosquitoes and watching water moccasins slither up a branch and drop into the water within inches of his nose. Said it was scarier than facing a whole troop of screaming Rebs bent on sending him to the blessed hereafter. I guessed it was.

We often met fellow travelers, but made it a point to avoid them if we could. Chances of them being normal, friendly and up to

152

anything respectable were slim. One evening after our fire'd been stoked up and the two squirrels Jack had shot were roasting nicely, a troop of five grizzly-looking characters rode up and stopped for a visit. I kept my gun within easy reach, and I knew Jack could defend himself, but these looked a bit mulish -- bent on turning things to their advantage.

"You men need some help?" I asked.

"Might." said the front-most one, likely the leader. "Lookin' for Yankee deserters. Hear tell there's some of that hereabouts. Got a bounty on 'em. Met any?"

"No. Not likely here. Why would a Yankee deserter want to stay around here?"

"Take advantage of our women, mebbe. Or take over some place that's abandoned. Easy to get a fresh start. Stealin' land."

"Well, we haven't seen any such. Can we offer you some coffee? We got a couple squirrels – probably not enough to fill us all up, but you're welcome to whatever we got."

The whole troop looked pretty hungry, so I figured they had it in mind to take our supper and send us packing. Watching Jack squatted down tending the squirrels, I hoped he wouldn't do anything stupid. False hope.

Jack rose, turned and without a word fired off a shot that glanced the hand of one of the troop, making him howl with pain.

"Jack! What'd you do that for?" I yelled, reaching for my gun. I was quick enough to down two of them before they could get the drop on me, and Jack took care of the other two, leaving us with five nasty hornets, scarcely wounded but mad as hell. Jack picked up their guns, relieved their horses of supplies and saddles, and sent them each off with a slap on the rump. Then he turned to the troop.

"You best move on now, y'all. I might get testy and aim before I shoot next. Now git!"

The five of them slouched off through the woods, cussing and yelling threats over their shoulders. Jack picked up their saddles and threw them on the fire. "There. Even if they catch them horses, they won't be any use."

I stood watching him in absolute wonder. "What'd you do that for?"

"What?'

"Start up with them? They didn't do anything to us. Why'd you go and pick a fight?"

He spat on the ground. "Hell, I know trouble when I see it comin'. Them was Reb deserters. They'd was getting' set to rob and kill us. Couldn't you see that?"

"You might be right, but I'd like a little more evidence before I'd start shooting people who just rode up."

"Wait around and you'll be dead. That's all I say."

"All right, but let's be a little more prudent next time, okay? I want to get to Georgia and back to Pennsylvania with my head on straight.

"All right. We'll try it your way, but I'm just sayin' there ain't nobody roaming around here these days with any but bad intentions, and if you're going to spend time evaluatin' them, you can be sure your head won't make it back to Pennsylvania attached where it is."

I took the saddle off my horse's back and clunked it on the ground, shaking my head. Seemed I'd taken up with a man whose judgment was either immature or downright corrupt. I unrolled my blanket and lay down, thinking how to separate myself from this batch of trouble.

Chapter 21

June 1865
Susannah

Lizzie Riggs and I worked together through May, planting and sewing and cooking. I said she was an apt pupil, and she was, but it unnerved me how she could find a quicker, easier way to do any chore. If she was sewing a dress, she'd be done before I'd barely started and her stitches would be finer than mine. I can't say I was jealous, but I had to recognize her talent and hope that Jonah had sense enough to do the same.

Of course it wasn't long before Lizzie was with child, so that gave us even more to be friends about. My baby was due in November, hers in January. Without a modicum of experience between us, and no help from Aunt, we looked forward to becoming mothers with the simple-mindedness only the inexperienced can enjoy. I taught her to knit, and she knitted a shawl big enough to wrap an elephant. We engaged in endless discussions about babies with no one to correct our misconceptions. Neither of us had ever witnessed a birthing, nor held a colicky baby nor nursed one through the croup.

Still confident that Carter would be home soon with his sister Emily to help, I operated under the assumption that one or the other of them would know all the things we did not.

Jonah Riggs continued to be an obstacle to our friendship, though. Always insecure, he kept a careful watch on his new wife, monitoring her every move and asserting his authority at every turn. He didn't go so far as to forbid her to associate with me, but he did counter my every opinion with an opposing one of his own, borne more of male arrogance than good sense.

But Lizzie kept coming over – in the open at first, but as Jonah's opposition grew, she turned to sneaking and subterfuge. She'd wait until he'd gone to town or was working in one of the far fields down in the bottomland. Her visits were short, depriving us of much intimacy, but sweet because we both enjoyed them so much. We shared work and skills and dreams, taking turnabout so that by summer, we knew each other like sisters.

The waiting was hard for me. I was used to taking charge – making things happen. Patience was not strong in me and waiting for my love to return set me wild some days. Then it was a relief to talk to Lizzie – tell her how I felt like I couldn't stand another minute. She'd just smile and tell me he was right down to Woodbury, headed north and that I better comb my hair and put on a clean dress just in case he got home for dinner. We'd both laugh and the relief gave me strength to last another day.

Sometimes we sat under the old gnarled apple tree that served as a line tree between our place and theirs sewing baby clothes and having endless discussions about names. My choices were few and quickly made: Carter for a boy and Emily, after Carter's beloved sister, for a girl. Lizzie had such a fertile mind that the choice was hard for her. She read a lot and had encountered many a romantic heroine with names like Guenivere and Isolde, so every day her choices changed. She favored Gawain for a boy until Jonah told her no son of his would have any but a Biblical name, so Lizzie would bring her Bible out to the apple tree to scan its pages for the possibilities. She listed the names that appealed to her on her fingers – five choices, any one of which she hoped Jonah would favor. Micah, Ephraim, Isaac, Seth and Thaddeus. We didn't know it then, but she would have occasion to use every one of the five and two more, plus three girls' names as well. Lizzie would be the mother of ten.

One afternoon Jonah caught her climbing over the fence between our farms, and ranted at her for some time about staying home and attending to her own business. "You know I don't like you lollygagging around with that Susannah Lander."

"Willoughby."

"What?'

"Willoughby.   She's married.   Her name is Susannah Willoughby."

"I don't give a turd what she says her name is. You stay away from her. I don't want you thinkin' and actin' like her. No man in his right mind would marry up with that shrew. So you stay away, now, hear?"

"Yes, Jonah. But it ain't fair. She's nice as you please to me – helps me learn a lot of stuff, and she don't say a bad word agin' you. I don't see why you don't like her."

"Never you mind. I'm the man of this house and I tell you she ain't no wise the kind of company you should keep. You got enough work to do around here, 'stead of gaddin' about learnin' new tricks from the likes of her. Now you stay away from her and that's the end of it."

It didn't work. Lizzie had a mind of her own, and telling her what she could and could not do would buy Jonah a peck of trouble. He didn't know it yet, but Lizzie had a backbone of ramrod iron. It took him a while to figure that – a while and some wild arguments, a few nights without supper and some nights sleeping in the corn crib, but he got it through his hard head eventually. Jonah would have preferred a nice quiet, obedient girl who said yes sir and no sir and bowed to his every wish, but instead he got Lizzie. He never did know how lucky he was.

As Jonah tightened up the rules, Lizzie just took to sneaking even more – almost like she was daring Jonah to stop her. She didn't even try to keep her activities from him. He got more controlling as she got more brazen, telling him, "I don't wish you no harm, Jonah, but I ain't your property and I'll listen to you if you're of a mind to treat me civil. But if you think you can force me to do your bidding when it runs against my grain to do it, you're buying trouble."

Jonah walked away sulking and muttering about what a common scold he'd married, but it was apparent to everyone that Jonah must have found him a good bed partner and he was bound to hold on tight, even if she *was* a shrew. So Lizzie kept coming over and Jonah kept grousing about it, but nothing changed.

Through all of this I kept up my vigil for Carter, waiting, wondering, counting the days he'd been gone. June passed into July with no word. If I hadn't had Lizzie to distract me, I think I'd have gone mad. In the meantime Aunt was slipping away into the dim, misty world of the hereafter. More feeble by the day, she spoke little and when she did, it was something about the past. Aunt had a keen memory for what happened forty years ago, but she couldn't follow the simplest instruction or complete the simplest household task. I knew she probably wouldn't make it through another winter.

Then sometime in mid-July I was busy making raspberry jam when Jonah appeared at my door alone, looking sour.

"Hello, Jonah. Where's Lizzie?"

"I thought you'd know. She ain't to home."

"No, I haven't seen her. Maybe she's gone to pick berries. The raspberries are fine this year."

"You ain't hidin' her are you? 'Cause if you're hidin' her, I'll thrash you both, and that's a fact."

I stepped back from the door, a puzzled frown on my face. This was too crude, even for Jonah. I didn't know where Lizzie was, and I'd no intention of submitting to any kind of punishment for hiding her.

"Jonah, you'd better leave right now. Your wife apparently has business of her own, but it has nothing to do with me. So go. Get out of here. Be on your way."

He looked around the yard, then made a move to come in the house. I grabbed the door and held tight. "She's not here, Jonah!"

He pushed past me and stomped into the house, but it was clear the room was empty except for the two of us and Aunt, asleep on her bed behind the stairs. I tried to keep him from going up to my bed chamber, but he brushed me aside and mounted the ladder, stepping sideways.

"Jonah, Aunt Betsy is ill. You can't just walk in here and do as you please. See, now you've wakened her."

"She'll go back to sleep, won't you, old woman?" He went on up the stairs as though he had a right. "This is what you get for hiding my wife from me."

I stood in the middle of the room hands on hips waiting while he stomped around my bed chamber, then came clomping down the ladder backwards. Aunt sat up in bed, clutching her quilt as though ready to run if need be.

"Jonah, have you been drinking?" I asked as he returned to the first floor.

"A bit. Gotta do something to keep from being a laughing stock."

"Who's laughing at you? About what?"

"About what? About my crazy wife, is what. She don't listen to a thing I say. Just does as she pleases. Sasses me. Folks are talking about her, sayin' she's the man of the house. All because of you."

"Oh, Jonah, that's silly. Lizzie loves you. She just needs a little freedom, that's all."

"Well, when I git hold of her, she's gonna wish she'd stayed to home. I promise you that."

Later that day Lizzie came wandering back from a walk in the woods, a pail full of raspberries over her arm to meet Jonah, his anger primed to a fever pitch. I could hear them shouting all the way in my house.

"Where you been, woman?"

"To the woods."

"What you doin' in the woods? Huh? Answer me!"

I couldn't hear Lizzie's response, but I thought I could hear a slap – crisp and harsh -- like you'd slap a cow's rump to get her to move into milking position.

"Prob'ly met someone out there. I know what you're up to. If I find out you got someone to meet out there, it'll go bad for both of you. Now git in the house and make supper."

Lizzie laughed. "I ain't got nobody to meet, and even if I did, you couldn't stop me. Anyway, Jonah, I ain't your property, so don't think you can just order me around and slap me around and make me behave. My mama got beat just about every day I was growin' up, and I promise you I ain't gonna be like her."

Another slap. I cringed at the sound. Then the yelling. They had words back and forth until Jonah raised his hand to her, and Lizzie ducked another blow and headed for the door. They passed out into the dooryard, Lizzie running away from the blows and Jonah chasing her, meting them out. I tried to stop myself from interfering, listening with anguish as he chased her along the line fence, grabbed her and dragged her down. The chase ended in the orchard where he cornered her against the fence and beat her with his fists until his energy gave out. It was clear Jonah couldn't make himself quit. I screamed his name, but the sound of my voice just bounced off his guttural grunts. The man was possessed.

Then, suddenly everything got quiet. All I could hear was Jonah's panting. He stood over her, looking down, his eyes glazed, his hands in trembling fists. Lizzie, seated on the ground, bleeding and bruised, breathed deep and looked him in the eye.

"All right, Jonah, you done this to me once. That's all. If you ever raise a hand to me again, I'll kill you. Somehow, somewhere, when you fall asleep not expectin' nothin', I'll creep up and slit your throat. Think on it." She said it softly, laced with promise.

There was something forbidding in the way she looked at Jonah, like to remind him she was good for her word, and for once Jonah had the good sense to heed the warning.

I didn't see Lizzie for a week while her bruises healed, but when she did come over, she seemed subdued. "I done warned him," she told me. "I just hope he don't fergit."

I was pretty sure Jonah wouldn't forget.

Still in that anxious summer of 1865, Jonah hadn't *fully* absorbed the way of things yet, for a week later he appeared at my door again.

"Hello Jonah. Lizzie's not here." I said it kind of dull, like I didn't want to start anything up again.

"I come to tell you to move on," he said.

"Move on? What do you mean?"

"I mean take your aunt and your things and move on. I've had enough of you. Things between me and Lizzie would never have come to such a pass 'cept for you fillin' her head with nonsense."

"But Jonah, I never... I can't... We've no place to go."

"Well, you gotta git gone from here. You're nothing but trouble for me. So you and your aunt can just git out. Find some other place to spread your venom."

Dumbfounded, I turned away from the door, unable to speak. Where would we go? How could I survive, pregnant, alone and without a home or a meager means of support? And Aunt? She'd die within a week.

"But Jonah, surely not. Surely you're just upset with Lizzie. You can't turn us out to forage on our own."

"I can and I will. You've been nothing but trouble for me ever since I married up with Lizzie. Now gather up your things and get out of here."

I turned away, unable to take in this turn of events. Without Carter to protect and sustain me, I had no place to go, nothing to rely on. Since I'd been read out of Meeting, the only person who might be willing to have anything to do with us was Uncle Thomas, and it was certain he'd only be willing to help because of his sister. I was just added an inconvenience.

Still, it was clear Jonah was firm in his convictions, so I told Aunt I'd be back in a short while and trekked off to Uncle Thomas's farm. I didn't expect a warm welcome. Our history was dotted with confrontation, stubbornness and greed. I found him sitting on the porch as usual, looking out over his bountiful fields.

"Good day, niece. What brings thee here? I hope not my sister's health."

"In a way, yes, Uncle. Jonah Riggs has turned us out."

"Turned thee out? Why?"

"He says I'm a bad influence on his wife."

"Wife? I didn't know he had a wife." Uncle took off his broad-brimmed straw hat and fanned his ruddy face. "Doesn't surprise me that he'd think thee a bad influence. Thee've always been full of vinegar. So it's got thee in trouble, has it? Now what do thee want of me?"

"You're the only one I can turn to. Aunt and I have no place to go." It galled me to stand there and beg, for Uncle Thomas was drawing this out for his own perverse pleasure.

"What? What happened to that Methodist preacher thee took up with? Don't tell me he's run off already."

I bit my lip to keep this from turning into a verbal brawl. "He's gone back to Georgia to settle his affairs. He should be home any day now. Until then, Aunt and I are destitute."

"Destitute, is it?" He sat looking down at me from the shady comfort of his front porch, while I raised my hand to shade my eyes from the sun, sweat pouring down between my breasts. Uncle Thomas reached for a tall, cold glass of something I wished I had, took a sip, set down the glass, and looked me over.

"Well, girl, I suppose it's my Christian duty to provide a roof for the two of you, but I've no idea where it will be. Go back and tell young Riggs that I'll send a wagon for the two of you tomorrow. And just in case thee thinks thee'll leech off of me indefinitely, the minute that preacher man of yours comes back, thee will be out again. I've no intention of keeping you beyond marriage."

"Yes, Uncle. Thank you. I'm sure my husband will take good care of us once he gets here." I struggled against the urge to let my anger fly, knowing Uncle Thomas was my last hope of a roof over my head.

"Humph. I doubt it. My guess is he'll never show his face around here again now that the war is over. Rebel spy he was. Everyone knew it. Such a fool he's made of thee. He'll never come back, and I'll be saddled with thee and whatever that is you're carrying under your skirt forever."

Trembling with rage, it was all I could do to keep from screaming at him. I wanted to attack him – slap him – beat him with my fists. I stood in front of his porch, looking up at his damnable complacency, wishing a bolt of lightning upon him.

"Your assessment is wrong, Uncle. Carter Willoughby is a kind and caring man. A gentleman. And I'm certain he'll return and we will have no further need of your charity." Holding in the urge to tear into him with open and bitter hostility, I set my shoulders and stared him down.

"Get on with thee. I look forward to the day that is true."

I turned and walked the three miles back to the shack that now looked to me like a lovely home. Who knew what kind of housing my uncle would provide? I pondered how to tell Aunt – how to rouse her from her bed and subject her to the hazards of moving. I sighed, thinking of Carter, wishing him home, tamping down the fear my uncle's prediction might be right. Then I felt a strange sensation in my belly. Something moving. Something alive. The baby. Oh, God, bless this baby and keep it from harm.

Judith Redline Coopey

Chapter 22

Belfast Plantation, Georgia
Carter

Jack and I crossed into Georgia in early May. We still had some distance to go, but it already felt good to be home. It didn't take long for that feeling to pass as we rode through miles of barren land, burned out buildings and battered and broken everything. Almost every plantation was a smoking ruin; animals wandered about bony and sick, digging among ashes for food. Not a single field we passed was fit for plowing, and emaciated Negro children sat on fence rails, begging for a handout as we passed. It was already getting warm – green shoots broke the ground everywhere, signaling nature's readiness for this year's crops, but an eerie silence greeted us despite the green.

Several days into Georgia, Baldwin County loomed before us, stark and ashen. I struggled to find landmarks to tell where we were. The countryside, devastated by fire and fury, showed little resemblance to memory. It appeared unpopulated, but if we stopped, a few Negroes would wander out from the woodlots or from the ruins of a barn or house to see who we were and what we wanted. I didn't see anyone I knew, but in talking to them I'd get some kind of orientation to head me in the right direction.

I kept asking for the river – the Oconee that skirted our plantation to the east of Milledgeville. Once I found the river, we turned north and followed it to Belfast Plantation. As we moved closer to home I regained my sense of place, even though there

165

was little to affirm it. The land, barren and still, lay empty before me, flat, red earth sprouting only the heartiest of weeds. Even the trees stood ragged and bent in the face of the devastation that spread far and wide in all directions. We rode slowly as I took it all in, Jack hanging back to give me space to react as I would. When I finally saw what was left of my childhood home, I fought back tears.

The skeleton of the house stood stark against the sky, unburned, but empty of all its trappings, windows broken, grounds trampled, doors standing open. All the other buildings had been burned except three slave cabins at the end of the lane that had escaped the flames. Piles of ashes marked the places where the stables, barns and out buildings had stood. Trees that had escaped the fire stood stark along the drive, sad sentinels clinging to their former duty.

I rode up to the front veranda and dismounted, calling Emily's name. All was silent -- not a soul about. I entered the house, but stopped, unable to face the broken doors, torn wall paper, banisters ripped out and burned for fire wood. The fireplace in the parlor, marble surround, alabaster mantel, had been smashed with a sledge hammer, and the ashes of fine furniture lay in disarray over the floor. Carpets had been ripped up, draperies pulled down and shredded, vases and dinnerware smashed. Everything that didn't lay broken before me had been carried off.

I stood at the foot of the broad oak staircase, its banisters long ripped out for firewood, afraid to ascend – afraid to see more than was visible from the doorway. A broken doll lay on one of the stairs, its face smashed, its dress ripped, stuffing spilling out. A memory of Ellen, a child of eight or nine, holding it close as she climbed the stairs to bed, flashed before my eyes. I turned to step out on the veranda where Jack stood quiet, giving me leave to absorb the destruction.

All I could think of was Emily, witness to this devastation. Where was she? Was she even alive? I stepped out into what had once been a lush green lawn and called her name – once, twice, three times.

"That her?" Jack pointed to a woman stepping out of the farthest slave cabin, one hand shading her eyes. Emily.

I broke into a run down the rocky lane past the ruins of a dozen or more cabins to the last one where she stood, making no effort to run to me.

"Em! Oh, Em! My God what they've done!"

She fell into my arms, almost in a faint, saying nothing. I held her up, carried her to a rude bench in front of one of the cabins and sat her down. Only then was I aware of Viney, Old Julius's daughter standing near.

"Viney! God, I'm glad to see you're here. Did Jennifer Ivey send you to take care of Em?"

Viney nodded. "Ivey all gone. Yankees come to burn and Miss Jennifer try to stop them. They tie her up and make her watch it burn. She's not right in the head no more."

I winced at the thought of one so gentle as Jennifer Ivey losing everything. "Any word about her brother Austin?"

Viney shook her head. "He come home right after the war, but his leg all swole and full of bugs. Take off his boot and the maggots all over. I throw buckets of water to get them all off, but he die a couple weeks later."

"So you're over here taking care of my sister?"

"Good as I can. I run off back a few months, but outside a bein' a whore for the soldiers, there weren't no way to survive, so I come back. We ain't got no food left. You didn't come today, we be dead by tomorrow."

I motioned to Jack to bring food from our saddle bags. We had little, but anything would suffice to revive these two emaciated women; if we didn't find food, and soon, neither of them would survive. I sat down beside my sister as she gnawed at a hard biscuit and drank from my canteen. "Carter," she said weakly. "Carter." She laid a skinny hand on my arm, slowly rubbing it as though afraid it wasn't real.

Jack rooted in his saddle bag for some bacon we'd bought the day before from a Negro who refused to divulge where he'd gotten it. Kneeling in the red dirt, Jack pulled a fire together, and brought

167

out the frying pan I'd toted all the way from Pennsylvania. Slowly the pan heated up and the sweet smell of frying bacon filled the air. Viney tended the bacon with a stick while I tried to bring my sister back to life.

After about an hour and a hasty breakfast, both women revived enough to speak. "I thought you'd never come home again," Emily told me. "We've been starving all winter. Everyone has. Some of the soldiers have come home – Austin Ivey got here right after the war ended, hobbling on a crutch, his leg all infected. He died last week. Jennifer has gone mad. All she speaks of is dying so she can be with Mark and now Austin. Oh, Carter, take me away. There's nothing here but grief."

I turned to Viney. "I thought you'd go once your father died. What about your baby?"

"He dead. Got the colic in the winter and my milk was bad. He got skinnier and skinnier and died come Easter." She brushed away a tear.

"Viney and I had naught but each other. We had to stay together. Neither one of us had any place to go," Emily sat looking at the dirt at her feet, her face slack and expressionless.

"Soldiers come by – had their way with us – beat us, took everything. We just hide in the woods when they come now, blue *or* gray." Viney's eyes shone with hate. "I got me a Yankee baby in my belly; don't know about her." She pointed a finger at Emily. "Probably got one, too." She pulled a filthy ragged shawl around her shoulders. "Ain't all Yankee soldiers. They's Rebs aplenty, too. Everybody sick, mad and hungry."

I looked at Jack. He shook his head. "Can't hang around here long or we'll have more trouble than we can handle."

I nodded. "Okay, but I've got some business down the well. Let's take care of that and get out of here."

I walked over to the well and looked down. The casing had been broken so that the opening was only half as wide as it used to be and narrower down below. It was a sure thing I was too big to fit down there. I looked at Jack, slighter than I was, but still the passage would be too tight.

"Viney!" I called. "Come over here."

She came, eyes on the ground, reluctant and slow. "What you want?"

"There's a box down the well. My father put it there. I need you to go down and get it."

"No, sir. Not me. I ain't goin' down no well for you or nobody. I'se afraid of water. "

"Please, Viney. It means a lot to us. It's money. I'll give you a share   if   you   help   us."
She held her ground, staring down the caved-in hole, shaking her head.

"Come on, Viney!'

"Let Miss Emily do it. She little as I is."

Jack stepped up to her and took her shoulders in his hands, shaking her. "You do it! Right now. Get down that well."

Viney wrenched herself free and glared at him. "No. You think you can make me? Hell with you. I been pushed around and beat all my life. I got nothin' and nowhere to go. You can kill me, but you can't make me go down that well."

I took over. "Viney, there's money down there. A lot of money. Now you know about it, I've got to get it out so you don't just wait around 'til I leave and get it yourself. You either bring it up, or we'll have to kill you. That's sure." I was in no way of a mind to kill anybody, but Viney didn't know that.

She looked up at me, eyes filled with hate. "This how you treat the one that's took care of your sister all these days? You more interested in money than her? I coulda let her die."

"I know all that, Viney, but it doesn't change the fact that we need that money. All of us. If we don't get it, we'll never make it past Sunday. You can help us or get yourself killed. Which is it going to be?" I shuddered at the idea of violence – knew I wouldn't resort to it except in self-defense.

Viney walked away and sat herself down on another crude log bench by the next cabin. Jack and I stayed with Emily, talking quietly.

"What money are you talking about, Carter? Emily asked.

169

"Papa put it down the well right when the war started. Told all three of us boys about it. Said to leave it until we were desperate or safe."

"Do you think it's still there?"

"I hope so. It's all we have to count on."

As we spoke, Jack emptied his saddle bags and mine, looking for any small bit of food. He found the heel of a loaf of bread, a handful of beans and two more hard biscuits. He rose and picked up his gun.

"I'm goin' out in them woods and see if I can scare out a squirrel." He stalked away, giving Em and me time to talk, fill each other in on the gaps in our lives. It seemed longer than six months since we'd seen each other, and the world had changed so completely and abruptly it was hard to take it all in. Through unending tears Em retold the story of death and destruction that had visited Belfast Plantation since November. I told her about Susannah, the Great Cove, the kindness of the Yankee people, my hopes for the future. She didn't want to hear it.

"Are these the same people who marched through here, leaving scorched earth behind them?"

"The same, I'm afraid, but not really. It's war, Em. War makes people do terrible things. We would have done just as bad to them if things were reversed. We did when we could."

"Then I can't go up there and live among them and act like I'm not filled with hate. They're a vile evil people and I won't stop hating them until I die."

I resisted the urge to argue with her, to try to make her see the error of living in bitterness.

"Where will you go, then? What will you do? How will you live?"

A shot rang out in the woods giving notice that in spite of everything, we'd have supper tonight. Good old Jack. He was back in a few minutes, a dead squirrel hanging from his belt. He threw it to Viney who went into the cabin, returned with a knife and knelt to skin it. Emily and I watched them prepare the squirrel and cook up a thin stew of squirrel meat and the beans Jack had retrieved from his saddle bag. We ate as the sun went down, full for tonight, but facing an uncertain tomorrow.

Through the evening, we sat around the fire talking, but well before bedtime, I found myself nodding off, losing track of the conversation. Viney sat aside, silent and sulking, nursing her own grievances. Jack and Emily's conversation excluded both of us and it was soon apparent that something was brewing between them. Too tired to care, I rolled up in my blanket and surrendered to sleep.

The next morning Jack went hunting again, leaving me with the two women, one weak and still distraught, the other silent and watchful. I took the opportunity to try again to convince Viney to go down the well and get the money. Emily was still very weak and terrified of the well collapsing, so the only alternative was to dig out the side of the well, taking more time and energy than we could spare. Afraid of what might happen if we stayed around too long, I approached Viney with care.

"Viney, I'll help you get down there. I'll tie a rope around you and around me, so if you slip or get stuck, I'll pull you out. I won't let you drown. I promise."

She tilted her head back, looking at me in defiance. "How much money down there?'

"Lots. Gold coins, too. Not Confederate dollars."

"How much you give me?"

'I don't know the exact amount, but I'll give you ten per cent."

"What that mean? Ten cent?"

"It means if I had ten bales of cotton, I'd give you one. Just for getting it out of the well."

"You give me two bales, maybe I go. You promise you won't let me drown?" Even in the bargaining, she had an innate sense of fairness. Nobody was going to take advantage of Viney.

"I promise."

"I's afraid of de water, you know."

"Yes, Viney. I know. But I promise I'll take care of you."

There were many aspects of life Viney didn't understand, but money wasn't one of them. She knew the value of gold coins and I knew I had to persuade her to help us or lose this chance to salvage something of our former life. The guilt of slavery hung heavy on my mind as I tried to talk the woman into helping us. I'd known her all her life – from a pig-tailed little mite playing in the dust to a competent, trained lady's maid. Before the war she'd been a loyal, willing helper. Sad what this struggle had done to all of us.

I studied Viney, anxious, impatient, waiting for her to give in. "Come on, Viney. This is the best chance any of us has for some kind of life."

She looked away. "I ain't got nothin', no way. If I go down that well, I might drown, or you might take the money and turn me out. So where's my reason?"

"Loyalty, maybe. We raised you and fed you and clothed you all your life. Doesn't that count for something?"

She laughed loud at that. "No, sir, Mr. Carter Willoughby. It don't. I give as good as I got – worked and did as I'se told, and now you want me to go down that well and do for you again. Ain't you got enough of me?"

I dropped my hands to my sides. She was right. We'd argued enough. She would help or she wouldn't, but I was done. "All right, Viney, yes. I've had enough of you. The decision is yours. Do it or don't."

Thin, emaciated, given over to hatred and grief, Viney stood staring at the ground, pulled off her head rag and twisted it in her fist. "How I know you gonna give me my share? Not just take it all?"

"I guess you have to trust. When every other option is done, trust is all that's left."

She nodded. "I always liked you, Mr. Carter. You was nicer than some of them. Treat us decent. Once when I'se a littl'un I trip and fall carryin' a tray to the kitchen. Cut my hand on a broken cup. Mistress yell at me and make me pick up the mess, even though my hand bleedin' lots. You come along and bend down, help me pick it all up, take me out to the kitchen and bind up my hand. I'se still cryin' so you set me up on the dry sink and give me a piece of hard sugar to suck on. I never forget that."

She rose and walked over to the well, looked down with doubt in her eyes. "All right, Marse Carter. I ain't got no other where to go."

I took a rope from my saddle bag and tied one end around Viney's slim waist, mindful that there was a baby in there. Then I tied the other end around my own waist and stood by while Viney climbed into the well and slowly, hand over hand lowered herself down the side, her face a study in fear. I could still see the top of her head as I yelled directions. The well wasn't very deep and about a quarter full of water with the box lying all the way at the bottom. Viney would have to find it in the muck at her feet, and Viney's old fear of water kept coming back to terrify her.

"I'se hit water, Marse Carter."

"I've got you, Viney. I won't let go. Can you stand and touch bottom?

"I think so, suh. It cold and full of muck."

"See if you can touch bottom. Feel anything?"

I heard some splashing and sputtering.

"I think I found the box. Something metal down in the muck. How I git it up?"

"Locate it with your feet. Then, duck down and see if you can get a hold of it."

"Yes, marse. I found it, but it too deep in the muck. Don't know if I can raise it."

I heard a low moan, then splashing and coughing. I couldn't see her anymore, but each tug on the rope let me know she was still at it. I talked her through it, all the way. Against her fear and better judgment, Viney ducked down one more time and pulled the box up out of the muck. Holding it up so I could see it, she lifted herself out of the well, holding tight to the box, grinning wide. "I done it, Marse Carter. I done it."

I placed the slime encrusted metal box on a stump near the fire, dripping rusty water down over. I picked it up and studied it, turning it this way and that, trying to figure how to open it. It was just an old box, but the last hands to touch it were my father's. I silently thanked him.

Jack, back from his hunt, stood by offering advice. "Just smash it, man. Here, take this rock and smash it."

I could barely feel the hasp or hinges, so encrusted with rust and muck. I turned and twisted the lock, but it wouldn't give, so I placed the box on the stump and told Jack to shoot the lock. He did, but the bullet glanced off, so out of frustration, I took an ax and hit it a few good whacks. The lid collapsed and coins and rusty water rained down over the stump. I grabbed it up with no care for my clothing. I spread it out on the ground and counted it in front of everybody. More than $2000!

The whole troop stood by in amazement, staring dumbfounded at the money. Praising my father's foresight, I wrapped it in a dirty shirt and tucked it into my saddle bag. Viney's share was $400, more money than she could ever hope to amass, and I told her I'd give it to her the next morning when Jack, Emily and I planned to leave. Later when everyone else was taking a nap, I sneaked away with the bundle and stowed it under the back porch of the first cabin, then lay down to sleep myself.

But disturbing thoughts kept me from rest. What would Susannah think of such goings on? I longed to be back in her arms, comforted by her touch. I dreamed of the farm we'd buy and the life we'd have in the Great Cove. How was she doing by herself? Was she worried about me? Surely she hadn't given up hope.

Jack and Emily passed the rest of the day together, walking hand in hand around the plantation where Emily showed him all the sacred spots of her childhood and in the woodlot where only they knew what transpired. I liked Jack – knew he could take care of himself – so if he and Emily found attraction, I could not object, and I suspected it wouldn't matter if I did.

Viney kept a good watch on me all day, just in case I went back on my word and cheated her. For lack of any other company, we talked long about money and how much it took to buy this and that – or had before the war. I couldn't predict prices now, but Viney kept asking me, wanting to know. Deep down, I wished I hadn't promised her so much, for I thought it only fair to offer Jack a share, and Emily's refusal to live in the north meant she would expect a share as well. But fair was fair, and had it not been for Viney, we might not have been able to retrieve the cache, so any thought of cheating her was beyond reason.

That night was a repeat of the first, Jack and Emily off by themselves and Viney and me left to our own devices. If they were coupling, so be it, and when they didn't return from the woodlot I unrolled my blanket and slept on the ground near the fire, using my saddle for a pillow. Viney disappeared into her cabin and I awakened in the morning to an empty dooryard and cloudy skies. I rose and tended the fire, gone out. Looking around for Jack, I found myself singularly alone. I called for Viney. No reply. I went to her door and knocked. No reply. I opened the door to a cabin completely stripped of anything of worth. Two rude beds built into the wall, corn husk mattresses, nothing else.

I tore around to the back of the first cabin, knelt to reach under for the bundle. Nothing. I lay down on my stomach and reached under as far as I could, swishing my arm over the rough ground. Nothing. I stood up and ran around front where I could see Jack and Emily walking arm in arm back across the barren field from the woodlot. I shouted.

"Viney's gone! Took the money!"

Jack broke into a run, leaving Emily behind. "What? Are you sure? Good God!"

We ran back around the cabins and searched in desperation, but the money was gone and so was Viney.

We rejoined Emily, dumbfounded. "I should have slept with it under my saddle. I never thought she'd do such a thing. I thought she'd be happy with whatever I gave her. I can't believe she's done this."

"Well, she's got all she needs to build herself a good life now."

I turned to Jack."We might as well pack up and get out of here. There's no use trying to follow her. She's probably joined up with a gang of ex-slaves or deserters."

Jack stood holding my sister's frail hand, looking ill at ease. "Me and Emily got something to tell you."

175

"Yeah. Yeah. I know. You're sweet on each other. I recognize the signs." I smiled. "Been there lately myself."

"Carter, that's only part of it. Jack and I aren't going north with you. We're going west." Emily fairly beamed with hope.

"West? But I thought… Guess it doesn't matter what I thought now, does it?"

"Sorry, Willoughby. We figure there ain't nothin' to keep us here or anywhere else, so we're just gonna go and see what we find. I guess I'm man enough to make it on my own and take care of a wife, too."

I felt a sinking in the pit of my stomach. Here I stood. Alone. No money. No family. Just my Susannah, waiting for me in that falling down pile of planks in East Sharpsburg, Pennsylvania. I sighed. "Well, better get on the road then."

I embraced my sister for the last time and shook Jack's hand. "Take care of her."

Chapter 23

June 1865
Susannah

Resentment boiled up inside of me, my anger divided evenly between Jonah Riggs and Uncle Thomas. I returned home with little hope and not much else to show for my efforts. Aunt was still abed when I arrived – not a good sign – so I began to gather what little we could take with us into pillow cases. Where would he send us? As far from him as possible, I hoped.

When I told Aunt we had to move, she responded with confusion and fear. "Why would Thomas turn us out?"

"Uncle Thomas didn't turn us out. It was Jonah Riggs did that."

"Oh. Then why is Thomas coming for us? Is Hannah coming, too?"

"He's not coming for us. He's sending a wagon to move us to a new place."

"New place? Where? I don't want to move. I've come to like it here. Tell Alonzo we don't want to move."

"Alonzo is dead, Aunt. Died last winter. You remember. Jonah owns the place now."

She sat down on the settle with a frown – raised her hand to her temple, shaking her head. "That Jonah. I never did like him much."

I took her hand and led her to the table. "Here Aunt, put these things in this pillow case. Uncle says he's sending a wagon, so we

177

have to be ready. I don't know where we're going, but I hope it's far away from both of them. Uncle Thomas and Jonah Riggs."

We worked through the day packing up what little we had and lining up the furniture by the door. Aside from beds, the table and the settle, there wasn't much. When the wagon rumbled up the lane the next day, driven by the ever obedient Anthony, our little pile of goods was waiting for him, Aunt sitting in her rocking chair on the porch in her Meeting bonnet, black gloves and a wool shawl despite the summer heat.

I helped Anthony load the wagon, curious as to where he was taking us. He gave a vague response to my question. "Not far. Just down the road a piece."

"The Hill place?" I asked. I hoped that might be so. Angus Hill was a kind man, a prosperous farmer, and his wife, Hattie, was known far and wide for her good humor and her talent for midwifery.

"Nay. The Singers. Pa says Silas Singer's wife is poorly, so he needs someone to care for his children. That'll be you."

I sighed. Silas Singer was an oaf of a man, a poor farmer and not to be depended on for anything but impregnating his wife. There were half a dozen ragged, barefoot, dirty faced children between the ages of eight and babe-in-arms, even a set of twins as though God was pitching in to make it easier to get to an even dozen. His wife Alice was wearing down with each birthing and hadn't left her bed in the three months since the last one.

I wondered what kind of accommodations Silas could offer Aunt and me, given that his house was already full. We drove up and stopped in front of a chicken coop standing crooked and sagging with a brook running behind.

"This here's it," Anthony announced with a wave of his hand toward the sad little structure. He jumped down and started to unload our things.

"And I thought the Riggs corn crib was a hovel. This takes the cake."

I went inside and immediately turned and came back out. "Don't bother, Anthony. Just stack our things out here. I'll have to clean the place out before we can move in."

Anthony made haste to unload our things and make a quick escape, clearly and justifiably embarrassed by the task his father had meted out. If the place we'd moved out of was barely fit for human habitation, this was unfit to be called a shelter. I sighed and went to the house to ask for a shovel to scrape the chicken droppings off the floor so I could scrub it.

I couldn't bring myself to sleep in that filth, so I made a makeshift tent out of sheets for Aunt and me and we slept on a pallet on the ground that night. Silas Singer didn't even come round to say hello or by your leave, and his bedridden wife stayed bedridden, so I took it upon myself to enter the house in the morning, make porridge and assure some level of cleanliness among the children. Six children under eight can be a handful for anybody, and these had been let run wild for at least three months, so my day was already beyond full.

Aunt couldn't be depended on for much, but she did prove helpful with the baby. I set her rocking chair under a tree and handed her the wrapped bundle that was baby Titus and she sat and happily rocked him the whole day.

It took me three days to turn the chicken coop into a living space for Aunt and me. The pot-bellied stove in a corner promised at least some level of comfort. It was tight, but we squeezed one bed, the table and the settle into the tiny room. I cleaned the only window, sewed a curtain from one of Aunt's old aprons, spread one of her quilts on the bed and called it done. I missed the privacy of having my own room, but this was what we had.

To say the Singer children were unmanageable would be unkind. It's just that there were so many of them. For the first few days, it seemed they were everywhere -- running hither and thither, hanging from tree branches, climbing and jumping off the porch railings. Then there was their mother, worn thin with birthing babies, afraid to get out of her bed for fear of starting a new one, content to direct the household duties from her bed. Silas clumped around doing the farm work and watching his wife, anxious that she get well enough to accommodate him. I thought of Carter, willed him to come home, grateful for the assurance that he would never put me in such straits.

There was certainly enough to keep me busy taking care of the Singers and Aunt who wandered off one day and gave me fits trying to find her and get her back to our tiny home. But Carter was never far gone from my mind. I worried and pondered and ruminated. Where was he now? Why hadn't he at least written me a line? How was I supposed to know if he was alive? Would he get back before the leaves turned? Before our baby came? Ever?

I missed Lizzie Riggs for the Singer place was perhaps a mile and a half from the Riggs place, so it was harder for her to get away, and if she did come for a visit, it would have to take place among six howling banshees. She did come once or twice – bringing a jar of preserves or a compote to please me. We kept in touch as best we could. I even returned to the Riggs place one Sunday afternoon with the whole Singer clan for a picnic in the field by our old house. I sat in the grass while the children stormed about, and looked at the ever leaning stable where my love had laid his head. I missed him so and fought back the doubts that plagued me.

When we returned from our outing, Aunt wandered off again. I put the babies to bed, and told Silas I'd go looking for her. The oldest boy, Abel, volunteered to go with me, and we set out with a lantern, calling her name. We wandered across farm fields and through woodlots, the darkness folding in on us. No Aunt. The ridges were covered by thick forest, and I hoped she hadn't wandered that far. A person could get lost in those woods forever. Still we trekked up and down the hills, calling, noting landmarks so we wouldn't get lost ourselves.

"Abel, take the lantern and go home. I'll keep looking, but I don't want to keep you out all night. Your mother will be worried."

The boy was tired, so he took the lantern and made his way back, leaving me alone in the now overwhelming dark woods. I called again and again, but only the night sounds of the forest responded. I sat down against a huge tree, exhausted, and went to sleep. I awoke to the cool dampness, my bones aching, and continued to call her name. "Betsy! Betsy Lander!"

I looked around me at the dense forest, thinking of the dangers. She might have been snake bit or mangled by a bear or a mountain lion. There was food and water aplenty in these woods, but I wondered if her addled head could still work well enough for her to take care of her needs. I couldn't spend another day away from the Singers. They accepted my need to care for the old woman, but at the same time they expected my attentions to them, so I made my way back to cook breakfast and tend to my duties.

Silas Singer seemed unconcerned about an old woman wandering alone in the woods. He went to his fields after breakfast, taking Abel with him, leaving me with the usual burdens and without a word about sending a search party. So I took it upon myself to go to the neighbors and announce my plight. They passed the word though the neighborhood, and by noon a group of twenty or so boys and young men who could be spared from getting in second crop hay had assembled in the Singers' dooryard. I told them everything I knew, which amounted to nothing, and they divided up into two-man teams and set out.

Later on as the evening descended, I stood watching the line between field and wood when I saw a group emerge carrying what looked like a pile of rags. Aunt had died, nestled against the trunk of a tree, with nary a cut or a bruise. When they laid her down on the table in our tiny abode, she looked peaceful, like the way she'd gone was the way she'd wanted.

I let Uncle Thomas know and he arranged her funeral and burial with the Meeting. She was buried in the family plot in the Friends' Cemetery down at Spring Meadow, home again. Her only sin was being an old maid in a society that only values wives and mothers. She'd done more for me than any other and I recognized that, but still resented the poverty we'd borne over the years. How I longed for Carter as the nagging fear that he might not return nettled me endlessly.

As soon as I could find an escape I ran off on a Sunday afternoon to Lizzie. She welcomed me with sympathy and a prolonged hug, our expanding bellies between us.

"Will Jonah come and make me leave?" I asked.

"Nay. He's gone off to Roaring Spring about a cow."

"God forgive him for doing business on a Sunday."

"He don't care much for religion. Does as he pleases and says God won't hold it ag'in him for making a living. Says they's worse things a man can do than work on the Sabbath."

"I suppose he might be right. But, oh, Lizzie, look at me. I'm so blue. Here is August leading into September and no sign of Carter. I can barely stand to keep on going. What'll I do if he never comes back? My uncle says he never meant to. Come back, I mean. I hate it, but doubt keeps creeping in."

I collapsed into a weeping muddle, reaching out for Lizzie's comforting hand. Her optimism sustained me even though she had to be wondering about Carter, too. The stories that came home with soldiers seemed to never stop. Tales of the dangers of travel now that the war was over came from every direction, and bands of men roamed the roads bent on some kind of revenge or just robbery, especially in the south.

Lizzie stood by the fence soothing me with her words. "I know it's hard to wait, but just keep your eyes on the road and know one day you'll see him there, walking tall and holding out his arms to you."

She could always say the right words to comfort me, that Lizzie. I dried my tears and it wasn't long before we were talking about our babies, excited for them to come. I was in my seventh month and finding it hard to maneuver myself into tight spaces while Lizzie, a svelte four months in, still looked like a girl – mostly.

That first beating Jonah meted out to Lizzie turned out to be the last. Married six months and pregnant with her first child, Lizzie Riggs laid down the law and Jonah became a believer. Many years and ten babies later, she reflected on that beating. "I treated him fair long as he treated me fair. That was the way of it. Once he understood that, things went along all right."

While it took Jonah some time to get it into his hard head, even he came to recognize that he'd bought him a bargain. Lizzie was better than Jonah deserved, but long association with her taught him a thing or two, and looking back, even I could see his search for a good woman had turned out better than he'd ever hoped.

Judith Redline Coopey

Chapter 24

October 1865
The Carolinas
Carter

R iding alone through the devastated country depressed me to the point of desperation. Sometimes I'd just let go and cry for all that was lost, riding along with tears flowing down my face. With no food and no money, I'd no idea how I was going to make it through 700 miles back to the Great Cove. My horse was tired and hungry and I stopped and let her graze as much as I could, but any delay grated on my nerves. I longed for Susannah, dreamed of her at night, whistled her song as I rode along, slumped in the saddle. "Oh, Susannah, don't you cry for me…"

I met all manner of folk on the road, never feeling really safe, for many of them were more desperate than I. A group of Confederate soldiers passed me by, looking worn and hungry, eyes on the ground. Bands of Negroes wandered in both directions, ignorant of location and distance. Everyone was armed and therefore dangerous. I tried to keep to the woods and byways acutely aware of the danger of being picked off and robbed. But I had nothing to steal, and most of them must have discerned that for they let me pass unmolested.

Crossing rivers was dangerous – bridges were out and summer rains had turned the waters into rushing brown torrents. Most of the time I could entice my little mare to swim, but once or twice I had to dismount and swim ahead of her, pulling on the reins and coaxing. When I came to a river I often had to negotiate my way through an encampment of ex-slaves, all armed and menacing. I came upon such a troupe as I approached the Saluda River near Greenville in South Carolina, wanting to cross.

A huge black man, barefoot and barrel-chested, stood in the roadway, blocking access to the water. "You wanna cross you gotta pay the toll," he told me.

"I don't have any money. I can't pay a toll."

"Then you ain't goin' cross." The man held a black bull whip like the ones the slave masters used to discipline their slaves. "You try, you gotta answer to ole Blackie here." He fingered the whip, wrapping and unwrapping it around his hand.

"What do you want from me? I've got nothing. No money, no food, just my horse.

"That'll do."

"What? You want to take my horse? I need her to get along. I'm going home to Pennsylvania."

"Too bad, marse. You whites had your day. Now we have ours. Git down off that horse."

In a fit of defiance I spurred my horse; she reared and turned away from the man as he lurched to grab the reins. Galloping away, I reached for my gun in desperation, but just as I touched it, another man, big as the first, stepped out of the bushes and grabbed the reins stopping my horse hard.

"Where you think you goin', marse? We need our toll money."

The hard stop made me lose my balance and I fell to the ground, my gun clattering on the road. If I'd been faster, I could have ridden downstream a ways and crossed on my own, but they had me now.

"We mighta let you go easy, but you tryin' to get away has o-fended us. Us don't like being o-fended." He wrapped the reins around his arm and led my horse away. A third black man picked up my gun and shot a round into the air. He smiled.

"This a good gun. You got any more bullets?"

"Just what's in the gun."

"Too bad. I'd hate to waste one on you. How 'bout you just git on then?"

"Not without my horse. I've a long way to go."

"You Yankee or Secesh?"

"Both, I guess. Born in the South, live in the north. I wasn't any part of the war."

"Why not? Ain't you got no loyalty?"

"Loyalty to God."

He moved up so close I could smell fatback on his breath. "God? You a preacher man?"

"Yes. Circuit rider."

"Well, ain't that fine? We's in need of a preacher man round here. We got folks need marryin' and babies to baptize. You stay here and be our preacher man."

"I can't stay. My wife is waiting for me in Pennsylvania. Just give me back my horse and I'll be on my way."

Now the other two men, giants both, stepped up. "Gid's right. We need a preacher man. Why you go to Pennsylvania? They's lots of souls to save right here."

"My wife's there waiting for me."

"She can wait. We got at least three couples need marryin'."

"All right. I can do that. And baptize babies, too, if you want." I figured to be accommodating so maybe they'd give me back my horse and let me go.

The first giant smiled. "Yeah. We want. Come on over here and set you up a marryin' place." He pointed to their encampment, spread along the river bank like a trail of the lost and the damned.

Determined not to leave without my horse, I followed them through the encampment to a flat ground under some sycamores along the river.

"What'd you do with my horse?" I asked. "I need my saddle bags."

Someone lifted the saddle bags and brought them to me, a small wizened old man -- looked like he'd given the best of himself to slavery. I reached for the bags, thanked him and spread them on the ground.

One of the giants stood over me with a pistol as I knelt and reached into the bags.

"Careful there. Don't be reachin' for no gun now."

I held up my Bible. "Just this. I need it for marryin'."

Word had spread throughout the camp that I was a marrying preacher and several couples lined up to be joined in matrimony. As I was leading them through the ceremony an old woman brought a broom and laid it down in the dirt. Apparently we were to indulge in some broom jumping. One by one, I went through the marriage ceremony and the broom jumping to the delight of many assembled on the river bank. Except for taking my horse and my gun, they treated me with the utmost respect and thanked me profusely for my services.

When the marrying was over, I looked around for my horse, anxious to retrieve her and get back on the road. I saw her corralled with some other horses, none as fine as she, and walked toward her, but one of the giants blocked my path.

"Where *you* goin'?"

"To get my horse. I must be on the road."

"We still got baptizing to do." His voice was deep and firm. No sense trying to argue.

It was a rollicking baptismal party there in the middle of the river. I did my best to sound sincere, even though this interruption in my journey was more than an annoyance. The Negroes lined up on the river bank, handing me one baby after another until the air was alive with crying babies, incensed at having water poured over their heads. Some adults lined up behind the babies and I spent more than two hours baptizing every Negro in sight. I began to wonder if they planned to demand the ritual for their animals, too.

Now it was about four o'clock and my desperation rose. I sought one of the giants and pleaded to be allowed back on my horse to cross the river.

"You can go now," he boomed. "But your horse and your gun and your saddle bags stay here. Good day, sir. Thank you for your services."

"But, I can't survive out there with nothing. At least give me some food."

"You got trials and tribulations, sir. That's a fact. Now you know how it feels to be in need. You'll get by 'cause you're white. We been hungry and fearful for all our lives. Time you find out how life is for the less fortunate."

I turned and walked toward the river. No one stopped me or even noticed me. There was a party going on – wedding reception, christening celebration, what have you. Strange, I wasn't angry. Except for depriving me of the means of survival, they treated me like a welcome guest. That was more than anyone had ever done for them. I stepped into the water, waded in up to my thighs, fell forward and swam across to the other side. I slogged out of the river, water sloshing off of me, shivering in the cool evening air. Now what?

The trek across South Carolina was long, muddy and hard. I got by stealing food, setting snares for rabbits and going without. I'd lost so much weight, my trousers hung loose on my hips so that I had to steal a length of rope to hold them up. I hid from other travelers for fear of trouble. Everyone on the road was in some desperate state or other, so I avoided contact as much as possible. It took me upwards of three days to pass into North Carolina.

The walking was fairly easy without a pack, but gnawing hunger slowed my pace. I had to stop at least once a day to snare a rabbit, steal a chicken or catch a fish. I wasn't exactly starving, but hunger made me light-headed and weak. Driven by the desire to be reunited with my dear Susannah, I pushed myself as hard and as far as I could, ever mindful that she must be worried beyond reason by my delay.

Once I made it to Virginia my hopes revived and I began to count the days until I'd reach Pennsylvania. Once in every few days, I'd ask someone what day it was. October 10. It was a long slow walk, but I could do it, for every day drew me closer to Susannah's arms.

My boots were beginning to wear out, my socks had fallen into holes, hard calluses gave way to hot spots that gave way to blisters. I never knew how debilitating something as small as a blister could be. I knew men suffered from them on a march, but as an officer I'd always been provided with thick wool socks, so I'd never experienced such. It started small on my left heel, but within one day the soreness had widened and deepened, forcing me to stop and try to relieve it three or four times a day. A blister is such a small thing, I'd never known how serious it could be, what a hindrance to traveling on foot.

I took to walking with a crutch, hobbling along so slow I saw myself as easy prey for the laziest of miscreants. But with nothing to offer them, I was dismissed as a poor target and left alone. Finally after three days of going from bad to worse, I could stand it no longer and I stopped by a farm to plead for help. The farm wife was sympathetic, but so many travelers had interrupted her work to beg for food or medicine that her charity had been about spent.

"Take off your boot. Let's have a look." She said it without pity – just an order. But when she saw the oozing, redness her face fell. "Eeew. That's ugly. I don't know of anything but time sitting down that will heal that. How far you got to go?"

"I don't know. Two – three hundred miles."

"Well you ain't gonna get there for quite a while. My man says people have died from something like that. I ain't got but some camphor and rags to tie on it, but maybe it'll help. She left me sitting on the edge of her porch while she went inside to get the supplies. She poured the camphor on the open blister as I winced in pain; then wrapped long strips of rag around my foot, criss-crossing around my ankle. It felt better, so I put my broken-down boots back on and set out on my trek. The relief lasted for two days before the bandage wore through and the skin was exposed again.

Desperate for a good pair of wool socks, I ventured near a town where I hoped to find some on a clothesline. I scanned yard after yard, skulking along in the back alleys, until I found a pair hanging in plain sight near the fence. I opened the back gate, slipped into the yard, on guard for dog or man.

Just as I reached for the socks, a woman's voice called, "Here! What you doing stealin' my man's socks?"

I stopped. "I'd pay for them, ma'am, but I don't have any money. Please. I've got blisters."

"Everybody's got somethin'. Ain't no pass to steal. Why I've a mind to call the constable on you."

Tucking the socks into my shirt, I turned and ran out the gate and down the alley, right into the arms of a uniformed Union soldier passing by. He stepped aside until the woman, yelled "Stop thief! Grab him! He stole my man's socks!"

The soldier stepped in front of me, blocking my way, and grabbed me around the chest in a huge bear hug. "Wait just a minute, traveler. I want you to meet my boss."

I struggled, but my malnourished condition was no match for him, so I gave up and accompanied him to the Union headquarters where I hoped my story of circuit riding and doing the Lord's work would give me a pass. We entered the front room of a trim little cottage, once the home of some respectable southern citizen, now the cluttered, paper-strewn office of a Yankee sergeant, bent on making these damn Rebs pay for their crimes.

"Name?"

"Car... Uh, Mark Randolph."

"Unit?"

I almost responded with my Confederate troop, but caught myself. "No unit. I'm a civilian."

"Civilian is it? You one of them good for nothing shirkers? Paid somebody to take your place in the ranks?"

"No shirker. I'm a preacher. Man of God. Circuit rider."

The man sneered at that revelation. "Man of God on which side?"

Neither. I chose not to fight because I felt the call to serve the Lord."

"Oh, you did, did you? One thing I know about them Rebs, they wouldn't let no slacker preacher wander around savin' souls 'stead of fightin'. You'd either fight or taste a minnie ball. So what's yer story?"

I told him about serving in the Great Cove, building my little congregations, bringing souls to God. I said I'd gone south at the end of the war to settle my affairs so I could return to my wife in Pennsylvania. Said I was on my way back, told about losing my horse and all my provisions. He listened absently, scribbling notes on a piece of paper.

"Well, now, I'm inclined to disbelieve your story, Mr. Randolph. I think I hear a bit of a southern drawl down deep. Think you might have been up north for a while, and if you was, I figure your business might not have had anything to do with the Lord. Seems to me sayin' you're a preacher would make good cover for a spy now, wouldn't it?"

I stood silent, watching him scribble down more notes. More talk would probably get me nowhere. I waited for him to finish writing.

"So, Mr. Randolph, we got a place for old Confederate spies called Libby Prison. It's in Richmond, Mr. Randolph. The capital of the Confederacy. You should feel right at home there. Guard! Take this man to the wagon bound for Richmond."

Just that quick I was in a fix. For stealing a pair of socks. How stupid of me. I should have waited until dark to steal anything. Should have kept to the byways, out of the way of people. Should have… should have…

Unceremoniously shoved into a wagon loaded down with half a dozen other prisoners, hands tied behind me, I sat looking at the rough floor of the wagon as it lurched and jolted along. Two Union soldiers sat up front in the driver's seat and two sat in the rear with us. All were dusty and tired, with the look of desperation about them. For sure, they were not to be trifled with. After about an hour, I asked one of the guards, "How far to Richmond?"

"Two -- three days. Just sit tight. You ain't going anywheres else and you ain't gonna like it when you get there."

It was readily apparent that these soldiers weren't of a mind to accommodate us prisoners. Tired of war and anxious to get home, they barely tolerated us, and would have lined any or all of us along the road and shot us at the least excuse. The only thing saving us was military discipline. We bumped along through rain storms and sunshine, stopping only for meals of hard biscuits and salt pork. At such times they'd untie us and let us relieve ourselves and eat and drink in fifteen minutes at gunpoint. The other prisoners were a thin, emaciated lot, all Confederate officers, and none ready to accept defeat. There was little talk among us, mostly because our guards preferred quiet and prodded us with rifle butts when our talk annoyed them.

Two of the other prisoners were ill and lay in the bottom of the wagon, one hand chained to an iron ring on the floor. One lay close to me, breathing labored, head lolling in delirium. I tried to talk to him, ask who he was, but his fevered eyes would not focus and his utterings made no sense. One of the others shook his head at me. "Don't bother. He ain't gonna make it to Richmond. Prob'ly better that way."

Suddenly the man on the floor raised himself on one elbow and shouted, "At 'em boys! Give 'em what fer! We got 'em on the run! At 'em!" -- then fell back to the floor, his face contorted. I reached for his free hand to offer comfort, but the Union guard on my side rammed his rifle butt into my ribs, knocking me back into my seat.

"I don't mean any harm. The man needs care. Can't you do something?"

"We got orders to get you damn Rebs to Richmond. That's all. Don't expect nothing more than a ride and food. Now shut up."

We rode in silence hour after hour, for the three days. None of us had the strength to protest or negotiate any more. I was probably the strongest and my strength waned by the day while the prolonged rest gave my blister time to heal. The food we got was barely enough and of comfort, we knew nothing.

When we arrived in Richmond, the venerable capital of the Confederacy, standing in ruins under the hand of the Union Army, the Confederate officers gave a feeble and sickly cheer. Driving through, we saw buildings damaged by artillery fire, windows broken out, walls half collapsed and people going about their business in crowded streets strewn with broken down wagons and caissons. Yankees everywhere. Signs blocked admission to buildings, yards, streets. Soldiers slumped about – mostly young and fresh faced. The real veterans had lit out for home as soon as the peace was signed.

Libby Prison was an old warehouse down by the James River that had been taken over by the Confederates during the war to house Yankee prisoners. As soon as the war was over, the Union commander saw a need for some place to house recalcitrant Rebel officers, so they took over Libby and filled it with Rebs.

Slowly we wended our way along city streets, driving around piles of rubble until we reached a large, three story red brick warehouse on the river bank. The wagon stopped, the soldiers jumped down and came around to unload us. We were led in shackles into the building, all but the sick. They were carried in on stretchers. The building was damp, chilly, and dirty – soldiers milled about with no clear purpose. We were led into an office where we stood for about an hour while a clerk took our names, units, home towns and made notes of any identifiable marks.

"What are we charged with?" I asked, bolder than my compatriots.

"Spying for the Confederacy" came the reply. "Rebellion against the United States," came another.

"Do we get a trial? Do we get to defend ourselves against these charges?"

"You get an appearance before a military tribunal."

"How soon?"

"When your case comes up. Now move on. Follow that soldier. He'll take you where you need to go."

Within five minutes we arrived on the third floor where we were turned loose except for the presence of guards at the head of each staircase. Everyone slept on the floor. No bunks, no doors, no glass in the windows – only iron bars with one bucket at each end of the huge room for slops and another full of water with a dipper for drinking. Men sat, stood and laid around on the floor, their faces gaunt and hopeless. Welcome to Libby Prison.

Judith Redline Coopey

Chapter 25

November 1865
Susannah

Waiting for Carter sustains and exhausts me. I'm fighting doubt, working hard at believing, but as the weather cools and November arrives, I feel my resolve slipping away. Oh, Carter, where are you and when will you come home to me?

All right. I'll give in. He's not coming back. I'm left with his baby and nothing else. If Alice Singer dies, I'm sure Silas will try to fill the empty gap with me. No. I can't let myself think like this. I've got to keep hoping, keep waiting, keep believing Carter will come back. I know if there's a way, he will. So it takes longer than we thought. It's all right as long as he hasn't met disaster. He's strong and smart and he knows how to get out of a tight spot. With a smile I remember the way he turned those slave catchers out. My Carter. He'll find a way.

Without Aunt to worry about, I could give my full attention to the Singer children, and believe me, they needed it. Abel, Timothy and Gabriel were all scholars at the little Apple Bank School a quarter mile down the road. School started in September and I can't say I wasn't relieved to send them off, one lunch bucket among them. Their teacher, Miss Penrose, had the patience of Job, and they came home every day beaming with delight over some kindness she'd showered on them, almost as though she knew how little they got at home.

The four-year-old twins, Faith and Grace, tagged along after me, never more than a step away. Faith was quiet and obedient, but Grace's character belied her name. She was into mischief at every turn, unrolling a ball of yarn around the kitchen to delight a kitten, spilling her breakfast milk down the front of her pinafore, or wandering down by the creek where I found her one day with a frog in each hand. The child truly faced a hard life. I knew. She was just like me.

I had to admit they were nice children, it was just that there were so many of them and here I was getting ready to bring another one into their already overcrowded midst.

My pains began one night near the end of the month, alternating sharp and dull. Again I knew nothing of birthing – wouldn't know if all was well or on the brink of disaster. I tried to sleep, knowing the child might take some time coming. I'd heard of births that took days of laboring, and I'd heard of those that happened in quick time. First babies seemed to set the tone for later ones, so I prayed that this one would be quick and simple. I didn't have the energy for aught else.

By morning, I was still in whatever stage this was, pain alternating sharp and dull at fairly wide intervals. I was pretty sure this was still the early stage. Something told me that I'd know hard labor when I passed into it. I didn't tell anyone I was laboring and went about my work as usual. Then, just after noon I was hit with a sharp, deep pain that bent me over with its intensity. I placed my hands below my swollen belly and lifted it. I could feel the weight and shape of my child and I tried to tell her – yes, I knew it was a girl – everything would be all right. I forced myself to keep on working until Silas came in from the barn where he'd been grinding chop all day.

"I'm laboring. I'll probably deliver tonight."

A grunt and a nod came from the man bent over the wash stand. "I was thinking, perhaps one of the children – Abel? – could go for my friend Lizzie Riggs to help me."

Another grunt. Another nod. I went out on the porch and called for the boy. "Abel, dear, please run for Lizzie Riggs. Tell her I'm laboring. Ask her to hurry."

He looked up with a furrowed brow.

"Laboring, Abel. It means my baby is coming. Hurry on, now."

He scampered away, visibly proud to have been handed such a grave responsibility. I gave Silas instructions about supper and tomorrow's breakfast and returned to my bed in the tiny coop. In my mind, I'd named it the Scant Shelter Inn, and the name stuck. I lay on the bed, willing Lizzie to hurry, even though I was keenly aware that she had no more knowledge of birthing than I did. Abel was back within the hour, but Lizzie wasn't with him.

"She said she had to wait for Jonah to fall asleep so she could sneak out. Said for you to hold on."

I winced at the pesky bug bite that was Jonah Riggs. She would come. He couldn't stop her; Lizzie would come.

I lay there alone thinking of Carter, wishing the door would open and he would be standing there with love in his eyes. The pains intensified, coming close together now and deep with fire. I placed a rag between my teeth so I could cry out without alarming the whole household and lay thus for about two hours, writhing in pain, unsure if this was the way it always went or if I was in trouble.

Lizzie burst in the door, breathless, and took in my condition. "You think it's coming soon?" she asked.

"I don't know. I don't know. It hurts a powerful lot."

She lifted my nightgown and looked for any sign that there was a baby coming. "Can't see nothin'. Wish there was somebody here that knows about this. Do you think Mrs. Singer could get out of her bed and come out? Just to advise us? She's done this afore."

"Well, maybe. Tell her we don't know if it's coming right or wrong."

Lizzie disappeared and was back in five minutes. "She says she's too weak to come out, 'cause if she gets up and around, Silas will want to bed her and she can't take that chance. Hattie Hill's delivered dozens of babies. Mrs. Singer says to send someone to get her."

"All right. Do that."

"I already done it. The Hill place ain't far. I hear she knows her stuff. If she does, I'll get Jonah to go for her when *my* time comes."

Hattie Hill arrived carrying a black bag just like a doctor's and went right to work, pulling up a stool and studying my private parts like she knew what she was looking for. Her voice had a soothing tone and I calmed right down as she talked to me.

"Is it all right? I mean is the baby coming right?" I asked.

"Right as rain. I can see the crown of its head now. It won't be but a few minutes."

Placing my trust in another human being was rare for me. Beyond Carter, I'd never done it before, but now, helpless and ignorant, I knew I had to let Hattie do her work, so I obeyed her and tried despite my pain to do as she directed.

"Push now, Susannah. Push hard. That's it. It's coming. Just a little more, dear. You'll be a mother before midnight."

Exhausted and out of my mind, I cried out for him. Screamed his name. "Carter! Carter! Where are you? Come home now. Please, please come home,"

Hattie reached in, her hands ready, her face intent. One last push, then a rush and a robust cry of protest at being forced so abruptly into this world.

"It's a little girl. Susannah. A beautiful little girl."

"Emily. That's her name. Emily."

As the child joined me in crying, Hattie finished up her work and handed the baby to Lizzie who waited with a basin of warm water and a soft blanket. I lay back on my pillow and stared up at the rafters of Scant Shelter Inn. Welcome home Emily Willoughby. This is where your life began, but I promise you, it will end in a better place.

So now what? I've a child and no husband, endless work for no pay except a tiny, tumble down chicken coop. Is this all I can hope for? He's not coming back. I know it, even though I don't want to know it. Carter Willoughby was but an intruder, a brief interval, a simple distraction. Now I'll go on as before, without prospects, with a child to raise and nothing of her father – not even a memory.

After Hattie finished cleaning up she picked up her bag and let herself out the door, as I turned to Lizzie to voice my fears. "What'll I do, Lizzie? Is this all I'll ever get out of life? Abandoned by the one I love?"

"Susannah Willoughby you shut right up that kind of thinking. Maybe he'll come and maybe he won't, but if he don't, it ain't because he don't love you and this baby. Somethin's keeping him. Somethin' he can't help. Now you can keep on waiting or abandon hope, but you got a baby now and your choices in life just got cut quite a bit. That's the way of it, so stand up like the woman I know you are and get on with your life."

Abashed and embarrassed at my despair, I pulled back and shook my head. I thought of Aunt, living off the charity of others all her life with nothing of her own and no respect. Well, Susannah and Emily Willoughby were not destined for that kind of existence. No. I would do whatever it took to pave the road for us to live in comfort and prosper. That very night I resolved to leave Silas Singer to his propensity for procreation and find work. Some kind of work. Any kind of work. I would save until I could buy a house. From there I'd save again and buy another one. I'd keep saving and buying until I had enough property to sustain us, Emily and me, through life.

Lizzie brought the baby to me and she nestled in my arm and suckled. As I felt the milk stream from my breast I thought of him again. Carter. No, he was neither an intruder nor a distraction.

He'd lifted me up, made me feel worthy, brought love to my life. And now I had his child, a constant reminder of why I had reason to live. I watched her suckle, touched her soft, beautiful hair with just a tint of red in it. Yes, my daughter, you will know your father and you will bring pride to the Willoughby name.

Chapter 26

January 1866
Libby Prison
Carter

They say Virginia has mild winters, but that's only if you have shelter and heat. In the upper reaches of Libby Prison with no fire and no glass in the windows, it was as cold as outside. Deep, penetrating cold and no relief. One tattered blanket barely covered me and I shivered uncontrollably. I knew I was sick. Knew I wasn't getting better. Knew I needed warmth, a full belly and a comfortable bed. Knew I wouldn't get any of it.

Leander Call got up and walked the floor, slapping his arms around his back, wrapping himself in a big hug. He turned and looked at me, his breath coming out in clouds. "You all right, Willoughby?"

I grunted in reply.

"Come on, get up. Walk around some. Get your blood runnin'."

I struggled to rise, reached out a hand to him and he pulled me to my feet. I imitated his action, slapped my arms around my back, walking up and down stepping over men in varied positions, sleeping on the floor.

"Wake up! Reveille! Time for breakfast! A Union guard opened the door at the end of the room, banging a wooden spoon on a steel pot. Every man sat up, grabbed his tin bowl, lined up for

203

his portion of thin porridge and retired to the floor to eat the gruel that was never enough. Since every living prisoner there was a Reb, the Yankees didn't spare us much sympathy. The vast room was quiet except for the clinking of spoons against tin bowls and an occasional cough.

I never saw anyone I knew there. The inmates were mostly Rebel officers, but some, like me, scouts. A scout was just another word for spy, and the guards considered us the lowlifes of the place. Most Union soldiers would have shot or hanged a spy on sight, but now that the war was over, the Army had to decide what to do with us. So far there was only the promise of a trial. I guessed they figured to let us rot in prison, however long that took. Some of the prisoners voiced their frustration, but that only got them shoved back to the end of the line. I kept my head down, hoping my model behavior would count for something.

Now the singing began. What, singing? In prison? Yes, the prisoners sang to while away the hours, even though the guards shouted them down. They'd stop for a while, then the singing would rise again someplace else. My favorite was "Oh, Susannah" for it took me back to the Great Cove and my Susannah, and I joined in any time the song came up. A soft, blended sound rippled through the long room – moving from Susannah to "Old Folks at Home," another Stephen Foster song, a favorite with the southern boys. Once in a while they would rip out a rendition of "Dixie" just to infuriate the guards and be met with threats of "no dinner tonight."

Leander sat down beside me, savoring his porridge. He was a big man, had been burly once, but now he was just a gaunt giant, bony and awkward, but disarmingly gentle, despite the hardships he continued to endure. Having grown up on a small farm, one of a dozen children, he'd nursed his mother through her final illness and was by nature acutely aware of the suffering of others.

"You all right, Willoughby? How's the cough?"

"Right as rain," I replied with a grin. "They ain't got me yet."

I fought the urge to hate my captors, remembering Susannah's assessment of the war and its causes. I missed her sensible, thoughtful view of the world – slow to judge, always seeking justice. Some of her measured way of thinking had rubbed off on me, and I clung to it now in the face of the urge to hate.

"Well, I was thinkin' you and me might make a trip up to West Virginia this mornin'." Leander lowered himself to the floor, leaning against the wall. "I got a good fish story."

It was his way of passing the time, getting our minds off our condition, making us forget the walls that enclosed us, even for a few moments. We would reminisce, telling each other about our childhood, describing every bush and tree we could remember. We embellished our accounts, calling up scenes long-buried, inventing descriptions so vivid we could almost see each other's memories.

So, like me, he was laid up here waiting for he knew not what. Like a gigantic nurse maid, he took care of anyone who was ailing, encouraged those whose resolve was spent, spread optimism over despair.

Leander Call was a Virginia boy, from way up in the hills that were now West Virginia. From common folk, he'd grown up with respect for the Lord and a desire to do what was right no matter if it kept him poor all his life. What had made him join the Confederacy and fight for secession was the influence of a local preacher, a southern sympathizer and enemy of abolitionists everywhere. Leander had grown up in this man's church, listening to his anti-Union rants and his justification of slavery based on quotations from the Bible. So when the talk of the western counties pulling out of Virginia and forming a new state threatened the reverend's take on things, he preached against the move and withdrew his congregation to the Southern side. The new state be damned.

Despite the fact that most of their neighbors approved of the new state, half a dozen young men from the congregation left home and joined the Confederacy, including Leander and three of his brothers. The other three Call boys joined the Union, and, to Leander's everlasting shame, they met on more than one battlefield, grieved by the possibility of killing one of their own.

205

Leander gave his all for the cause, even though doubt crept in from the beginning. He hadn't heard from his family since he enlisted, and, once away from the influence of this ranting preacher, he began to think for himself and came to feel that he was fighting on the wrong side. He deserted and tried to make his way back home, but was captured and accused of spying for the Rebs.

"I got a great story today, he promised on this cold January morning. "It's about once when I was just a bit of a boy, me and my brother Jared – you know, one of the three that went over and fought for the Yankees -- we took our fishin' poles and went down to the Monongahela with a pocketful of worms and hope in our hearts. The waters was clear –so clear you could see down twenty feet, and we took ourselves across to that little island I told you about, Plum Island."

"We set our poles and pulled up a couple of rocks to sit on, figuring to be there a while when right away, somethin' started nibblin' at my line. Nibblin' gentle-like – like it wasn't all the way interested. I watched the line for a bit, then thought to move the bait just to see if the fish was serious. When I moved it, things was quiet for a bit, and then come the nibblin' again, so I figured this here fish had intent, so I gave my line a jerk and, God bless me, that fish reared up out of the water with my hook in its mouth and turned and twisted like to bend himself double. A great big Northern Pike, teeth sharp enough to cut my line, but he didn't. He fought me – fought like a demon – but couldn't spit out that hook."

"I gentled him for about ten minutes, then led him into the shallows where I went to get him off my line. He wasn't cooperative – gouged my fingers good when I tried to free him. He flopped and wiggled so much I thought to cut my line and let him have the hook, but I sure did want to show him off to my pa. So I got Jared to take out a piece of string from his pocket to measure him. That there string wasn't long enough by about six inches."

"I finally screwed up my courage and told Jared to hold him down while I got the hook out. That there fish chewed up my fingers good, but me and Jared finally got the string though his gills and out his mouth so we could carry him home. Momma was sure pleased with the size of him. Big enough for a whole family dinner. My fingers healed pretty good, but I still got one scar."

He held up his pinkie finger to show me a scar that went on the outside from his finger nail down to the second knuckle."

"That's a good story, Leander. Too bad I don't have one to match it. I'm kinda low today, thinking about my wife and wondering if I'll ever see her again."

He looked at me, then turned and picked up a piece of paper. "Here, write her a letter. Tell her all that's in your heart. I'll give it to a guard and get it sent."

"They won't send it. They'll open it and read it and laugh. You remember what they did with Martin Goss's letter? Pinned it up for everyone to see and wrote nasty comments all over it."

"Guards can be awful mean but some of them like an extra nickel now and then. I got me a few extra nickels that can buy me a favor. Not a lot, mind you, but some."

Seized by a fit of coughing, I set about writing to Susannah, telling her all about my adventures and where I was. Regulations limited letters to six lines, but Leander just shook his head when I complained that it was too short. It was the first time I'd even tried to communicate with her in the ten months I'd been gone. I wondered if she'd forgotten me by now. Funny how a plain Yankee woman had managed to take over my heart. All I wanted was to hold her, make sure she was all right and reassure her of my love.

The writing was hard. There was so much to tell – about my trip, about Emily and Jack and Viney, about how I ended up here. I tried to fill it with hope – hope that I would indeed return to her some day. When it was done, I'd used up five whole pages of Leander's paper, so, exhausted, I lay down on the floor to sleep.

I was awakened by someone shouting my name: Mark Randolph!

I rose and stood at attention. "I'm Mark Randolph."

"Follow me. Your case is up."

Excited by the hope of getting released, I trekked down the long room at his heels. He led me downstairs to a cluttered office where a clear faced young major sat at a desk holding a handful of papers that he rifled through without looking up.

"Mr. Randolph, we've little time for triviality, so I'll get right to the point. Your case has been decided by a military tribunal, and you will be released in five days, based on time served."

My delight opened up a coughing fit that lasted a full three minutes and right near pulled me under. "Thank you, sir. Thank you so much."

Back upstairs, I trumpeted the news to the whole third floor, coughing and laughing, yelling and hacking. I fell down on my bed roll, my breathing labored, so weak I couldn't stand up. Leander came over and sat down on the floor beside me.

"You need to rest these five days, so you'll be fit to travel. Wish I could go with you. You need care, 'specially if you have to walk all the way."

"I have to walk all the way," I responded. "Even if a body had cold hard cash for the price, the damn Yankees have rustled up every horse within twenty miles."

He frowned. "Damn them. If they was gonna let you go, why didn't they do it three months ago? Afore you got the lung disease?"

I lay staring up at the ceiling, aware that even this good news couldn't sustain me all the way to Pennsylvania. How I longed for Susannah's arms – her soft gentle touch, her kiss on my fevered brow.

Leander rose, snapping his wide suspenders. "I got it! I'll send her a letter and tell her to come and get you. She might could find a wagon to haul you home in."

"No, Leander. She doesn't have any means – she could never get the money to rent a wagon and take me home."

"Well, maybe somebody would loan it to her. It's worth a try. Ain't she got some rich relatives? Anyway, she needs to know where you are, even if she can't come and get you."

"A letter would never get there in five days. They'll turn me out and she won't be able to find me."

"Hush now with your protestations. Let me take care of this."

So Leander wrote another short letter instructing Susannah to come to Libby Prison, Richmond. In my weakened condition, I couldn't have stopped him if I'd wanted to. The exertion of walking down and up three flights of stairs had done me in, and I lay on the floor for the next five days, barely conscious.

Leander Call

Those five days was the longest I'd ever spent. I nursed him and cared for him the best I could, even sharing my meals with him to build his strength. When the guards came to release him on the fifth day, I stepped up between him and them.

"You can't put him out now. He's too weak to travel. His wife is coming to get him. Just let him lay for a few more days."

"We have our orders. This prisoner is scheduled for release today, so…"

"So nothing. Just leave him be. He ain't no burden to you. Just give his wife time to get here. I'll take care of him."

They went away, grumbling about how this was no government poor house and how a man should stand up and take care of himself. I put my letter into the hands of a young Iowa soldier who'd done me a favor or two in the past and waited.

Judith Redline Coopey

Chapter 27

January 1866
Susannah

It was a gentler winter than the one before, leading me to hope for an early spring. I'd given Silas Singer notice of my intention to leave his employ and walked into Martinsburg carrying Emily. A plan had been taking shape in my head ever since Emily was born. She would not grow up watching her mother muck out barns and dig potatoes. Whether Carter returned or not, I had to find a way to support us. One never knew how conditions might change and it was clear to me that if my life thus far had taught me anything, it was self-reliance. So I was off to make a way for us, Emily and me, in the wide world.

The way was full of slush – a January thaw – and I entered Replogle's store with wet feet and failing courage. Jasper Replogle had been in business for forty-odd years – was known as a skinflint, but a fair man, not a cheat. He was busy with two or three customers – farmers looking for hardware to repair their implements during the slow winter months. I went to the dry goods, standing by while Mr. Replogle picked among the bins looking for the right nuts and bolts.

Emily lay snuggled against me, perfectly content to listen to my heart beat, even though today it went pitty-pat with a faster rhythm than usual. I waited patiently, fingering the fabrics, moving away from the plain, rough cloth the Quakers favored, on to the soft, rich materials the society ladies bought.

"Morning Susannah. What brings you to town on a cold, wet day? Your little one ailing?" It was Amanda Culp, the wife of Richard Culp, the town's prosperous lumber dealer.

"No, ma'am. She's tough like her daddy," I replied, wanting to keep alive folks' memory of Carter as a preacher worthy of respect. "I come to see if Mr. Replogle might have work for me. Clerkin' or sewin'. I'm something of a seamstress, and I know more than a few old women who can't see well enough to thread a needle anymore. So I thought since I got a baby now, I might look for a way to support us. Just until my husband gets back – I could make up a few dresses, aprons, maybe a shawl or two and ask Mister to put them in the store. See if they sell."

Amanda smiled and nodded but went on looking at the goods, touching and holding them up to her face. "Which of these goes better with my complexion? The pink or the peach?"

I took a step back and studied the two choices. We Quakers only wore gray or brown and no ruffles, laces or frills, so I wasn't used to so many choices, especially so many colors. I had to admit both shades were flattering to Amanda's soft coloring, but the pink stood out.

"The pink, Mrs. Culp. Definitely the pink."

I wished I had the money to buy a dress length of either color to make up for a sample of my work, but without Carter's rent money, I was down to no income at all. But being poor didn't bar me from having an opinion, so I allowed myself to give voice to my ideas.

"The pink would look nice with a full gathered skirt and the hem caught up all around," I told her. "And full mutton leg sleeves. I can see you now, wearing it to the Easter services."

"You're right, Susanna. It would outshine ever other dress there," Amanda gushed. "I think I'll take the pink. It's been some time since I had a new dress. Richard frowned upon new and fancy clothes while the war was on, but I think he'd be happy to escort me in this."

"Will you make it up yourself?" I asked, hoping she'd consent to letting me create an original frock for her.

"Well, now, I'm a poor seamstress I'm afraid. But you seem to have a certain eye for fashion. I'd be hesitant to cut such a beautiful piece of goods for fear I'd ruin it, but you -- I'll bet you'd know just how to make it. So you're thinking of turning your skills into a trade?"

"Just until my husband returns, which could be any day now."

She looked from me to the pink cloth. "Do you think you could fashion it just like you said? If I bought the cloth, of course."

Emily began to stretch and mewl about, looking for her mid-morning snack. I looked around for a secluded corner where I could feed her, and Amanda moved on as though my stopping to feed the baby settled the matter.

I watched her fingering a periwinkle blue print but was quick to point out its shortcomings in comparison to the pink. Somehow, from deep inside, I pulled up my confidence.

"I could make the pink dress for you, and if you told everyone I'd made it, maybe they'd want me to sew for them, too."

"Well, yes, but Callie Brumbaugh sews for almost everyone in town. You'd be in competition with her."

Callie was a widow lady, getting on in years, but still considered the best seamstress for miles around. I wondered how her eyes were holding up – and if she might be considering retirement.

I stood, wrapped Emily up tight and nodded to Amanda. "You're right. I think I'll go talk to Callie right now."

Callie's house was right across the street from Replogle's store, a convenience that would hold me in good stead for years to come. I crossed the wide front porch holding Emily, thinking about how any widow without children or with, could make any kind of living on her own. How I wished for Carter to return so I wouldn't have to bear the full burden, but I knew from hard experience that I could.

Callie Brumbaugh opened her door wide when she saw I was carrying a baby. "Why Susanna Lander, how long has it been since I've seen you?"

"More than a couple of years, Miss Callie. Oh, and my name is Willoughby now. I'm married to that itinerant Methodist preacher who was here for a while during the war."

"Oh, yes, that one. People used to talk, you know. Said he was a spy. Was he? You would know." She reached for the baby. "And who is this? Poor fatherless bairn."

"Her name is Emily, and she's not fatherless. My husband had to go south to settle his affairs, but he's coming back as soon as he can."

Callie took the baby from my arms, nodding as though in total agreement with my assessment of things. "I'm sure he will. Now what can I do for you this morning?"

Stepping aside to let me in, Callie took possession of Emily, giving me to wonder if I'd be able to wrest my child free to go. I'd known Callie Brumbaugh all my life. She was a childhood friend of my mother's so she knew all about my plight and was steadfast in her kindness toward me. Always taken with babies, Miss Callie welcomed us in and poured us each a cup of hot tea while I screwed up the courage to explain my errand.

"I've come to talk to you about work."

"Work? What kind of work?"

"Seamstress work. I wonder if you have any extra that I could do. I sew a fine seam, but I know there is much more to learn."

"Hmmm. Sometimes I wonder if God has his ear trumpet turned in my direction. Yes, I could use some help. My eyes ain't what they used to be, so I need somebody to do the finishing work."

My heart got up to pitty-pat speed in less than a second. A huge relief flooded my soul. "I could do that, Miss Callie. And you could teach me all the finer points so I could take over your business when you're ready."

Preoccupied with the baby, Callie held her and talked to her and cooed at her until Emily cooed back. "That sounds like an answer to my prayers, but what about this one? What's she going to do while you're sewing?"

214

"I was hoping that between the two of us, we could sew and care for her. I know you don't have any grandchildren, so maybe Emily could fill that gap."

"Mayhap. One thing I'll tell you for sure. Be glad you've a daughter. All I had was three sons, and believe me, they're only good to have while they're boys. Once they marry, they're not much good to their Ma."

"So I've heard. A son's a son 'til he finds him a wife..."

Callie looked at me, her eyes bright. "If you need a place to stay, I've got an upstairs room you and the baby could share."

It was a wonder to me how all you had to do was ask. Some folk were just waiting for someone to ask, and if you laid out a plan, folks would be willing to help. I'd spent my life waiting for someone to help me – take up my cause – not really expecting anything. Now here they were, more than willing to help, just for the asking. I didn't know if my work would sell, but at least I was given a chance. People really were good at heart. I'd always known that. Now I could keep my promise to Emily. Carter might return or not, but I would build us a life out of sheer determination and the help of kind folk.

I'd no idea I'd find work and shelter all in one day. 'Ask and it shall be given unto you.' Thank you, Lord. Elated, I rescued my baby and started back to gather my things at the Singer farm. As I crossed the street in front of his store, Jasper Replogle stepped out onto the steps.

"Susannah! Mrs. Willoughby! Come here. I've got a letter for you .Come yesterday from some place in Virginia."

Stunned, I climbed the stairs and reached for the letter, half afraid to touch it for fear of breaking this morning's good luck. Holding Emily against me with one hand free, I struggled to tear it open. My hands shook as I tried to hold the letter still enough to read. It was from a man named Leander Call, writing on behalf of Carter, lying ill in a place called Libby Prison.

He said Carter was free to go, but was too weak to travel, and couldn't I come and get him? He assured me that my presence would work the miracle of healing and that once Carter saw me, he'd regain the will to live.

I shook with fear that I'd not be able to get there before Carter passed out of this life. Where would I get a wagon? Or the money to rent one? Or a train ticket to Richmond? I turned and headed out of town, working out a plan in my head. Carter had not deserted me. Is that what I'd been thinking? He needed me. I was still his wife and I had to get to him.

I trekked through the slush back to the Singer farm where I gathered what few possessions I had, all the while contemplating how to get to Richmond. Then I remembered the two greenback ten dollar bills Carter had left with me – the ones I'd hidden under the stair tread in the old house where Aunt and I lived. Immediately I set aside my things, picked up baby Emily and made my way up the rut-frozen road to the Riggs farm.

No one had lived in the Riggs's shack since Aunt and I moved out, so I hoped against hope that the money would still be there. The snow in the field was up to my knees, wet and sloppy, so walking was doubly hard carrying the baby. She didn't seem to mind, lying against my breast wrapped in an old wool shawl that Aunt used to wear.

High stepping across the field, I realized that the house, left open, had gone downhill since I left. The front door barely opened, hung up on the damp and swollen floor boards. I threw my weight against it, forcing it open about a foot. Inside, the room was dark and I had to feel my way until I found the stairway and felt for the bottom tread.

I pried the tread up and reached into the opening. Nothing. There was no lamp to light, not even a piece of kindling to burn for a torch. I bent down, reached deep, feeling around among the dirt and splinters but the hole was empty.

Jonah! Jonah Riggs must have found my money and taken it. I rushed out the door and down the lane toward the Riggs house in a panic. I didn't know if the two ten dollar bills were enough to take me to Carter, but it was all I had and nothing on God's green earth would keep me from getting to that Libby Prison. Wet up to my knees and numb, I waded across the field through the deep sloppy snow to the Riggs place.

"Susannah! My word, God hears prayers, for sure." Lizzie, great with child, met me at the door.

"Lizzie! Where's Jonah? I have to see him right now."

"Gone to fetch the mid-wife. I'm laboring. Why? What do you need him for?" She reached for the table to support herself as a pain grabbed onto her and held for a full minute.

With a pounding heart, I explained my errand. Lizzie lurched back to her bed, listening, sympathetic. "Jonah never said a word about no money. I doubt he took it, but when he gets back, we can ask him."

Frantic to find the money and be on my way, whatever that way turned out to be, I poured out my story, begging for any help I could get while Lizzie lay abed holding onto her protruding stomach. In my anguish, I overlooked her stress, but once I'd voiced my fears, I turned my attention to her. She lay on her side, knees drawn up, wracked by pain every five minutes or so.

"How long have you been laboring?" I asked.

"Since last night. I know birthing is supposed to hurt, but I'm scared, Susannah. Scared it ain't comin' right. Scared it won't come alive or even come at all."

I felt suddenly afraid myself. With my limited experience, if there was a problem, I might not notice it or know what to do. "How long has Jonah been gone?"

"Couple hours. He should have been back by now."

"All right. When he gets here with Hattie Hill, everything will work out for the best. You just relax. This will all be over soon."

I hoped my quavery voice didn't betray my fear. Lizzie looked awful. I did what I could to make her comfortable, forgetting my own troubles for the moment. Emily needed to be changed and fed, and I did that, all the while wondering what was keeping Jonah. When he arrived an hour later, wet, bedraggled and alone, I confronted him.

"Where's Hattie?" I asked. "And where's the two ten dollar bills you took from the under the bottom step in my old house?"

"Gone off to another birthing. I tried to get Emma Barefoot, but the ice was so slippery in her lane that my horse couldn't get any traction. Almost fell." He stood dripping snow off his slicker, then turned to me. "What are you doing here?"

"Never mind about me. Lizzie needs help, and you need to find somebody who knows about this birthing thing. Go back out and find someone – anyone who can help. What do you think will happen here without a midwife? An angel from heaven will come down and deliver this child?"

Jonah stared down at his boots, arms crossed against the tirade he knew was coming. Now I demanded an answer to my other question.

"What about my money? Don't pretend you didn't take it."

"I ain't got your money. Don't know nothing about it. And don't you go accusin' me of no robbery."

Frustrated by Jonah's slim relationship with honesty, I turned back to look at Lizzie, lying there ghostly white. She'd lost consciousness. I turned her over on her back and lifted her nightgown as though I knew what I was looking for. Jonah turned away.

"Wait a minute, Jonah. You can't leave now. You and I are going to have to do this together."

Jonah Riggs, never the brightest nor the bravest, stared at me, dumbfounded. "You mean I...? No. Oh, no. I ain't gonna deliver no baby."

"You *have* to help me. That's all there is to it. You have to. Now go wash your hands."

I lifted Lizzie's nightgown and looked again. What I saw sent a stab of fear through me. I could see that the baby was coming – backwards – stuck upside down in as tight a spot as you ever saw. I'd no idea how to deal with this.

I'd heard of breach babies, but what could I do? Instinctively, I began to knead Lizzie's stomach, slowly, gently, trying to turn the baby around. At first I thought it might work. The baby seemed strong enough, and once Lizzie revived, she did what she could to help. But after about an hour of kneading and pushing, everything stopped. It felt like the baby was near about turned around, but it wasn't moving on its own and Lizzie was too exhausted to push. Now I worried that I might lose one or both of them. I turned to Jonah.

"Go out again. If Hattie's still not home, get anyone – someone. I don't know what to do. I'm afraid the baby might be dead already. Go all the way into Martinsburg and get the doctor if you have to."

Jonah's face went slack. He stepped back from Lizzie's bedside, hands helpless at his sides. "If she dies, it'll be on you. She was doing good afore you got here and started pushing her around. Now look what you done."

"Just go for help, you slack-jawed fool. You can be mad at me later. Now, go!"

Once he was gone, I lifted the nightgown again and saw the crown of a tiny head, right where I thought it should be. "Now, Lizzie. Now push. Just one more good big push and the head will be out. You're doing good. Just keep it up one more time."

She gave it all she had and the child moved on down toward the world. First the head, then the shoulders, then the whole slippery, writhing, mewling human child. "That's it, Lizzie. You're done! You've got you a son."

I looked at her over her raised knees and saw grayness, stillness, exhaustion. I wrapped the baby in a clean cloth and laid him aside. Lizzie didn't respond to my touch or my voice. I put my hands on both sides of her face, rocked her head back and forth. Nothing. So I slapped her – hard.

"You listen to me, Lizzie Riggs, this here new baby needs you. He can't be left to Jonah to raise. You wake up and tend to him. I know it's been hard, but you're the only one can save him. It's been hard on him, too, and he needs his ma."

Lizzie moaned and let her head loll off to the side. I slapped her again. "Wake up, Lizzie. You wake up right now."

Slowly her eyes opened, foggy and vague. After a few seconds they seemed to focus and she blinked. By now the baby was letting the world know he was there, crying out a lusty baby roar. I

219

picked him up and laid him across his mother's belly while I wiped him off and wrapped him up tight. "Sounds like he's healthy. Not happy so much, but very healthy."

Just then the door swung open and Jonah entered, followed by Hattie Hill. After a brief look around, Hattie pronounced it a job well done and proceeded to tend to Lizzie's needs. Jonah stood by, looking peaked, like he was out for a walk in the woods and found himself between a mama bear and her cubs. The man was helpless – he didn't know what to do.

He approached me, hands in his pockets, head down like he was ashamed and said, "Thank you for saving her, Susannah. She'd never have made it without you – and my son. You saved my son."

I nodded, not sure what else there was to say. Then Jonah dug deep in his pocket and produced two ten dollar greenbacks. As contrite as I'd ever seen, he stood looking at the baby, shaking his head, then handed the money to me.

"I'm sorry for the meanness over the years. I was lying afore about this here money. I found it a long time ago, but I didn't figure to give it back. I never seen a baby born. Don't know what I'd a done if you weren't here. Is there anything I can do to repay you?"

"Yes, Jonah, there is. You can hitch up your wagon and drive me and my baby to Altoona so we can catch a train to Richmond."

Now both Emily and the new baby decided it was time to eat, and they put up quite a chorus until we two mommas satisfied their hunger. That done, I wrapped Emily in her shawl and herded Jonah out the door to the barn.

Jonah was back in five minutes hovering over his newborn son. He picked the child up, held him close. "Wait a minute, Susannah. We gotta figure out a name for this boy. He needs a special name."

I stopped by the door, nodded and waited. Lizzie had a budget full of names picked out, so this could take a while even though I was frantic to get going.

Lizzie pushed herself up on one elbow to look at the baby resting in his papa's arms. "I know his name," she said. "His name is Mark Randolph Riggs. Mark's a Bible name, ain't it?"

Jonah looked stupefied, not sure how to react. "Mark Randolph Riggs." He let the name roll off his tongue, then smiled. "Sounds like a squire or a general or maybe even a president." He lay the baby down in the crook of his mama's arm and turned to me. "Me and Lizzie and little Mark here can't thank you enough, Miz Willoughby."

I reached into my apron pocket, touched the two ten dollar greenbacks, picked up Emily and followed him out the door.

Judith Redline Coopey

Chapter 28

January 1866
Susannah

Riding in Jonah's wagon over the bumpy, slush-laden roads I worried over how to do this. I hoped I had enough money to take a train from Altoona to this Libby Prison which Leander Call said was in Richmond, Virginia. But how much would that cost, and how much more to bring Carter back? And would he be able to make such a long trip? What if I could borrow a horse and wagon? No. The train would be faster. And what about Emily? Even though she was healthy and robust, I was hesitant to take a three-month-old on such a trip. Anything could happen.

I longed for someone to ask – anyone who knew a thing about travel beyond Altoona. Uncle Thomas? He rarely traveled except to Yearly Meeting in Baltimore. Not likely that he'd be of a mind to help. Lecture maybe, but help? I asked Jonah to pull up at Replogle's store, stepped down and went inside to warm my frozen feet.

"Mr. Replogle, do you have any knowledge of trains?" I asked.

"Trains? What about them?"

"Like how much does it cost to travel on one?"

"That depends on how far you're going."

"I don't know how far it is to Richmond, but that's where I've got to go."

"Richmond? In Virginia? That's maybe two hundred miles. Cost you upwards of seven – eight – dollars, I'd guess. What would you want to go to Virginia for?"

"That letter you gave me this morning? It was about my husband. Seems he's sick down there in Virginia and I need to go get him and bring him home."

Mr. Replogle cocked an eyebrow. "Pardon me for asking, but do you have any money at all, Miss Lander?"

"Willoughby. My last name is Willoughby, and yes, I have some. Not much, but some. Maybe enough to get there. Don't know if it's enough to get back."

"Well, first you got to get to the railroad station in Altoona. They can tell you the cost and you can decide. But what about your baby?"

I was determined to take Emily with me in spite of the complications she presented. I wanted her pretty blue eyes to take in the face of her father, if only once. I wanted Carter to see the fruits of our love. Now the child began to fret and I picked her up to soothe her, held her close, fighting back my fears. "I don't know if I should take her or leave her here with Callie."

Jonah waited outside while my mind, filled with apprehension, bounced back and forth between one plan and another. Callie Brumbaugh could care for Emily, for sure, but I was filled with the need to make sure she got a chance, however small, to know her daddy. I picked her up, clutching my two ten dollar bills, and rejoined Jonah in the wagon.

I didn't own a coat, so Emily and I shared Aunt's ragged old wool shawl. Jonah drove the horses right down the middle of the road, trying to dodge the frozen ruts. He tried to keep up a conversation, though I was too distraught to hold up my end. He said he was sorry he couldn't do more to help, but I assured him he was doing enough.

I'd only been to Altoona twice before – once to visit a cousin who lived there in what I considered splendor – and once to spend a week with an ailing Quaker lady who died the second day I was there. The train depot was huge and noisy, but rich and opulent in every way. The Logan House, a big hotel right at the depot, stood impressive before me. I didn't dare think of what it must cost to stay there, so I got down from the wagon, thanked Jonah, clutched my baby close and stepped up to the ticket window.

"How much is a ticket to Richmond, Virginia?" I asked.

The clerk studied his time table and fare schedule. "Eight dollars and fifty-seven cents, ma'am."

"And how much would it cost to come back?"

"The same, ma'am."

A quick calculation told me I didn't have enough money to bring Carter back with me, but, something urged me to go on and worry about the return trip later. I dug out one of my ten dollar bills and held it, hesitating.

"How long will it take to get there?" I asked.

"Train leaves here at 2:00. Sure, you could be there early tomorrow morning."

I shoved the greenback across the marble counter into his hands. He did some figuring and wrote out a ticket to Richmond and shoved it back along with some change. I picked up the ticket, put it away in my reticule and settled myself on a hard wooden bench, breathing fast. Emily lay asleep against my bosom.

Oh, Carter. Please hold on 'til I arrive. I brought our baby, so you could see how beautiful she is. Please! You have to hold on until we get there. Without a thought about food or any other creature comfort, I sat upright the whole way, holding the baby, marveling at the breakneck speed at which the train hurtled me through the afternoon shadows toward my love.

The bench was hard, the ride bumpy, the progress slow for the train stopped at practically every hamlet, if only to take on wood for the boiler. Around 6:00 in the morning I felt the steaming monster slow to a crawl as the conductor made his way from car to car announcing our arrival in Richmond.

It was as dark as only a cold January night can be, but still there was much activity around the station. Black men and white wheeled iron carts from here to there, unloading freight and throwing wood into the steaming behemoth. Looking around in awe, and unsure where to go, I searched in vain for any sign pointing to Libby Prison. I passed into the station, brightly lit and full of people even at such an early hour, all seeming to know where they were going. I found a ticket window with no line in front and waited while the clerk thumbed through his stack of tickets and finally raised his eyes to me.

"Excuse me, sir. Can you direct me to Libby Prison?"

"Go outside and get ye a horse car going south. James River car. Ride to Carey Street, just above the river, and get off at 20th. You'll see it from there. Red brick building, bars on the windows. Soldiers all around."

I followed his directions out into the dark street. This was the biggest city I'd ever seen, dreamed of, even, busy and bustling at 6 o'clock in the morning. The cars weren't running yet. Not until seven. I stood outside the station looking around in awe. I, Susannah Lander – no, Susannah Willoughby – standing here in the capital of the Confederacy, watching people come and go as though coming and going were as routine as breathing. I felt alone, uncertain, and yet I knew he was near. How near, I couldn't tell, but Carter was here in this city, waiting for me. I could feel it.

Emily fussed for her breakfast and hunger gnawed at my stomach, so I went back inside and woke up a snoozing woman selling baked potatoes in a corner of the station.

"How much are your potatoes?" I asked.

"A nickel, ma'am."

"I'll take one."

She leaned over and reached deep into her basket and handed me a potato, still warm from its place beneath the others. I took the potato and handed her my nickel then settled myself on a bench to eat. Emily chose that moment to put up a louder demand for her breakfast. The potato woman smiled.

"Seems like yer not the only hungry one."

I rendered up a half-hearted smile, wondering where I could find a quiet place to nurse her.

"Yer welcome to use my wagon, round back. It ain't much, but it's private."

I thanked her and gratefully took up her offer. I was so excited at the prospect of seeing Carter I could hardly hold still. Would he greet me with love in his eyes? Would he pick me up and swing me around and kiss my cheeks for joy? No. The letter said he was ill. How ill? He might not even recognize me. Still, I would nurse him back to health, tend to his every need, hold him close until he was himself again.

It was cold in the train station and I pulled my shawl around my shoulders, shivering from the cold or from anticipation, I didn't know which. I was so close to seeing him, touching him, holding him. I watched the big station clock as the hands crept around toward 7:00. Done tending to Emily, I walked around to the street side again, looking up and down for the horse cars.

At seven fifteen, a car stopped right outside the station door "Are you going south, toward the river? To Carey Street?"

The driver shook his head. "Next car. Be round in ten minutes."

I stepped back and stood on the sidewalk, stamping my feet against the cold. Dear Emily, asleep again with her stomach full, snuggled close, oblivious to the cold. Worried about how I'd get us back home, I wished I had something – anything – to sell. I opened my reticule and touched my last ten dollar bill. One step at a time.

When the next car rounded the corner by the station, I climbed aboard, shaking, took a seat, tucked the shawl tighter around the baby and watched the city pass by. I sat right behind the driver so I could hear as he called out the names of the streets. People got on and off, all intent on their own business. We crossed so many streets, I wondered if I'd missed my stop. "Is Carey Street coming soon?" I asked.

"Two more. Going to the market?" the driver asked.

"No. To Libby Prison."

"Visitin'?"

"No. My husband is being released."

"Oh, good fer you!" He sounded genuinely pleased. "He's a man of the South, then. The Yankees took Libby over, so there's only Confederates there now, officers mostly – and spies."

The thought dismayed me. I'd never really thought of Carter in that way, even though it was a hard truth. It was a struggle to imagine him wearing gray and swearing loyalty to the land of cotton.

The car rumbled to a stop at the corner of 20th St and Carey. "Right over there, ma'am." The car man pointed to a huge red brick building, plain, unadorned, stark and guarded by Union Soldiers, all of whom looked less than joyful to be here on extended duty beyond the surrender.

I stepped down from the horse car, my heart beating a tattoo and adjusted the shawl around Emily so that her little face was just visible. Walking unsteadily, I entered the only door I could see and found myself in a wide hall at the foot of a broad wooden stairway. A young Union soldier stood by a frosted glass door, rifle at his side.

"Ma'am?"

"Yes. My husband is a prisoner here. I've come to take him home."

The young soldier nodded. "I'm sorry, but my commanding officer doesn't report until nine o'clock. You can sit down and wait here." He indicated a row of hard wooden chairs lined up against the wall across from the frosted door.

At least the hallway was warm, and thanks to the potato, I wasn't hungry. But I was impatient. Tired of waiting, even though I'd no idea where we'd go once Carter was released. I sat down and waited the hour and a half until a handsome and dapper officer arrived, greeted the young soldier and let himself in the frosted door to the office On any other day I'd have been proud of these Union soldiers, handling the details of putting the nation back together, but this day I wanted nothing but Carter. So I waited, barely able to contain my wildly beating heart.

When the young soldier disappeared behind the frosted glass, I waited, sure my turn was imminent. When he returned, he stepped up and asked my name and my husband's name, wrote them down, then disappeared behind the door again. Five minutes later, he stepped out of the office and mounted the stairs without looking in my direction. I listened to his tread, all the way to the top. It took another five minutes for him to come back down, and I could tell by the sound of the tread that he was not alone.

I straightened up in my chair, then, unable to stay seated, I rose in anticipation of greeting Carter with a very unQuakerly embrace. Instead, a giant of a man in tattered uniform pants and a sweat-stained undershirt accompanied the young soldier to where I sat and stopped before me.

"Susannah. My name is Leander Call. I'm a friend of Carter's." He stood almost at attention, hands at his sides. "I feel like I already know you. Willoughby described you so well."

"Where is he?" I asked, desperation alive in my voice. "My husband, Carter Willoughby. Where is he?"

The giant lowered his eyes. "He's still abed, ma'am. I'm afeerd I can't take you up there and he's too sick to come down."

I felt myself falling into blackness. I couldn't hold myself up. The big man caught me in mid-swoon and led me back to my chair as Emily, disturbed by my near fall, put up a wail.

"What's this?" the man asked. "A baby? Why Mrs. Willoughby, ma'am, I'd no idea there was a baby."

"Carter didn't know. She's three months old. Her name is Emily."

"After Willoughby's sister? Oh, god, he'll be overjoyed."

"Can't I see him? Please. Don't you have a sick room here?"

"The whole place is a sick room, ma'am. Everybody here's in some state of illness. I hate to say it, but you'd better get that baby out of here afore she catches something."

I looked down at Emily, smiling and cooing against me. "I've no place to take her. No one to care for her. Please, sir, see if there's anyone."

He stepped away and spoke quietly to the young soldier. Surely there was a kitchen, a laundry, any place where women congregated and could care for the baby while I...

The youth disappeared down the wide hall behind the stairs and returned shortly with an aproned grandmotherly woman, arms bare to the elbow as though she'd just been pulled away from the laundry tubs. She smiled a weak smile and reached for Emily. I handed her over, full of apprehension about illness, but unable to keep myself from taking the chance.

Turning to Mr. Call, I pleaded. "Please, please take me to him."

Call looked questioningly at the young soldier. "Can't we?"

The youth, clearly befuddled by such irregularity, looked over his shoulder at the frosted door.

"I can't, Call. You know that."

With that, Leander Call turned and mounted the steps in giant strides, two or three at a time. The young soldier stood planted at the foot of the stairs looking uncomfortable, but making no move to stop him.

Within minutes, Call reappeared carrying what could have been a bundle of rags, but which was, to my everlasting grief, my husband. Call carried him over to the line of chairs and laid him gently down. I couldn't take in the frail, emaciated collection of dust and ashes before me. Carter? Was this my husband? How did they know this unrecognizable body was Carter Willoughby? I touched his feverish face, held back my tears and whispered his name.

His blue eyes opened, closed, opened again. His head lolled back, his mouth agape. "Susannah?" It came out, barely a whisper, so weak it could have been anybody's voice. Or nobody's.

I leaned in and spoke, louder so he could tell it was me through the fog. "Carter. It's Susanna. I've come to take you home. You'll feel better, dear, as soon as we get some nourishment into you. Hold, dear heart. Hold fast. All will be well."

I raised my eyes to Leander Call, standing guard like a defending angel, ready to do, to give, to stand fast for his friend. Soldiers came and went, barely noticing the make-shift pallet of chairs. No one spoke and Leander and the young soldier formed a wall between Carter and the rest of the space. Leander's eyes said it all. Carter was too far gone. He shook his head.

"I knew he didn't have a chance. I thought if you could just get here, but..." He covered his face with big, calloused hands. "That's why I wrote the letter. Thought maybe – just maybe."

I pulled up another chair and sat down by Carter, taking his hot dry hand in mine. "Oh, Carter, try. Try to hold on. You'll be all right as soon as I get you home." The image of Scant Shelter Inn passed before my eyes – or Callie Brumbaugh's upstairs bedroom – either a sad, pitiful place to die. But no bother now. I could see the life waning, the will to live slipping away. "Carter! Listen to me now. I'm taking you home. Hold on just a little while longer. We're going home."

I turned to Leander and motioned toward the door where they'd taken Emily. "Get her, please. I want him to see her."

Leander nodded to the young soldier who sprang into action, opening the door and calling for someone to bring the baby out.

The same woman hurried into the room, carrying Emily, and handed her to me.

"Carter! Oh, dear Carter, look. Open your eyes and see your daughter."

I watched as his eyelids fluttered, then closed. I sat back down on the chair, holding Emily close, talking to her all the while. "See, baby? See your papa? He's going to get better and come home with us. He's a very strong man, and he'll be good as new as soon as we get home and take care of him."

Carter's breathing became ragged, his chest barely rising and falling with each breath.

"Carter, can you hear me? This is our daughter. Our baby. Her name is Emily, Carter. Isn't she beautiful? Her eyes are blue, just like yours. Oh, Carter, she needs her papa. Please, just hold on. I'll get you home by tomorrow."

Emily began making baby sounds as though she were talking to him. His eyes flickered open once more, and he turned his head toward the sound of his daughter's voice. I saw him focus, look steadily at the child and lift his hand as though to touch her. He was too weak, the effort too great. His hand dropped, and his head turned to one side. One more deep and ragged breath, then nothing.

I stared up at Leander Call, still standing vigilant. Gone. Oh, God no. Gone. I handed the baby to him, buried my face in Carter's emaciated chest and sobbed. Gone. So much that might have been. So much I'd longed for, gone.

"Do you have the funds to get back home?" It was so like Leander Call to think of the details – what was needed, what was important.

I stopped to wipe my tears before I replied. "I think so – it wouldn't have been enough to take Carter along, but it's enough for just me."

He reached into the pocket of his ragged uniform pants. "Here." He handed me a crumpled dollar bill. "It ain't much, but it's all I got. I don't want you to go home hungry."

I stood looking at my husband's body, clad in what was left of the clothes he'd worn when he rode away ten months ago. "Such a waste. What will they do with him now?" I asked.

Leander shook his head. They got a plot out back. Just a common grave. No markers or flowers. I'd do something for him if I could, but being a prisoner..."

I took out my reticule and emptied it into the palm of my hand. I counted out $8.57 and put it back away. Then I turned to the young soldier who'd stood guard with Leander as Carter died. "This is all I have, but maybe you can get someone to carve a stone for him. He was such a good man. He deserves at least that."

The young man took the money and nodded. "Yes, ma'am. I'll see to it."

I turned back to Leander. "What of you? Do you have hope of getting back to your own people?"

"I ain't sure they'd want me back, them being Yankees now, but I 'spect to be gone from here in a week or two. Time I was settlin' down, getting' started with my life."

"Where will you settle then?"

"West maybe. Ain't thought much about it."

I don't know to this day why I did it, but I reached out to him, prodded by the image of Carter smiling at our baby. "Why don't you come to Pennsylvania then? You could get farm work there and maybe someday buy your own place."

He smiled and looked down at his shoes, worn and broken. "I'll think on that, ma'am. Gotta get out of here first, but I got no place better to go."

Suddenly in a great hurry to get back home with my child, I patted his arm. "Good-bye Mr. Call. Thank you for your kindness to Carter. I know he would want me to repay you for the care you gave him."

Leander Call reached out and wrapped me in a bear hug, his bushy beard scratching my face, the smell of him lingering on my clothes. There really was no reason not to go and yet I stood looking into his kind brown eyes, grateful for his presence in this time of need.

"I'll tell Emily all about you so she remembers you for taking care of her father."

"Emily -- for his sister -- huh?" He smiled. "Emily. That's a fine name."

Judith Redline Coopey

Chapter 29

July 1872
Martinsburg, Pennsylvania
Leander Call

Ever since I met her at Libby Prison, back in '66 I've thought of little else but Susannah Willoughby. We been writin' each other letters ever since. I think I was in love with her before I even met her for Willoughby talked of nothing but his Susannah day and night. I'd always wanted a woman like her – kind, caring, smart, loving. More than I deserved, I knew, but my ideal, just the same. Now here I am to visit, meet young Emily, see if maybe I could find me a farm for sale.

My fortunes have taken a good turn since the war. I did go west, like I said I might, and I got me into the cattle business, kind of like by the back door. I met up with Charlie Cutler, another West Virginia boy with nowhere to go and nothing to stop him. We worked a couple of cattle drives and pooled our money to buy us several head of cattle. Then we joined up with another company and drove our cows with theirs. Made a little more money. Kept doing that and saving our money until we had a good sum set aside. Then me and Charlie divided it up and went our separate ways.

Charlie's still out there, partnered up with an old Reb and three Mexican cowboys. I guess they're doin' all right, but I kinda had to follow my heart back here to Pennsylvania. I knew it that cold

235

day in January in Richmond. Mrs. Susannah Willoughby had me roped and tied the moment I met her.

I rode into Martinsburg, down the main street and right there before me was Replogle's store. I knew from her letters that she often sold her dresses there – one after another, as fast as she could make them. I turned and looked across the street at the house with the big front porch, also as described in her letters, and saw a little girl swinging high as she could go on a wooden swing. I stopped.

"Might you be Miss Emily Willoughby?" I asked.

"Yes, sir. And who might you be?"

"I am Mr. Leander Call, a friend of your mother's."

"And of my father's, too." She dragged her foot to slow the swing. "I know you. My mama told me how you took care of my papa in his last days."

The swing stopped and the child hopped off and crossed the yard to the fence, where she stooped to pick a yellow faced Pansy that she held out to me.

"Thank you, Mr. Leander Call for being a kind and caring friend. My mother and I will always be grateful."

I took the flower and tucked it into my button hole.

"Come, sir, my mother is in the house sewing a dress for Mrs. Riggs. Mrs. Riggs has four children, you know. My momma just has me. I wish I had a brother or a sister. Maybe someday I will. I hope so."

I smiled. "Yes, Emily, I hope so, too."

I followed the blonde-haired, blue-eyed child through the gate and into the house.

About the Author

Judith Redline Coopey writes historical fiction about Pennsylvania. Her interest in history can be traced to her father, Kenneth Redline, an avid reader and student of history as well as an author in his own right. Born in Altoona, PA Ms. Coopey holds degrees from the Pennsylvania State University and Arizona State University. She has spent her life reading, researching and loving history. As an author, she finds her inspiration in the rich history of her native state and in stories of the lives of those who have gone before. She lives in Mesa and Happy Jack Arizona with her husband and a beautiful German shepherd named Sadie, but when it comes to deciding what to write about, she always comes back to Pennsylvania.

About the Horseshoe Curve

Built by the Pennsylvania Railroad and opened for rail traffic in 1854, the Horseshoe Curve is a huge horseshoe-shaped bend that reduces the grade and allows trains to negotiate the climb from Altoona to the crest of the Allegheny escarpment at Cresson. One of the engineering marvels of the 19th century, the curve is 2375 feet long with a 9 degree 15 minute degree of curvature. The grade rises at 91 feet per mile from 1594 feet to 1716 feet making it possible for locomotives to haul a heavily loaded train up the otherwise steep incline.

It was designed by J. Edgar Thomson, then chief engineer of the PRR and built over a period of two years by about 450 Irish laborers using hand tools -- picks, shovels, hand carts, mules, wheelbarrows -- and black powder.

Originally accommodating two tracks, the curve was expanded to four tracks before 1900 to serve the needs of a growing economy. Steam locomotives built and serviced in Altoona negotiated the Horseshoe Curve for 100 years before they were replaced by diesel engines in the 1950s. Its long history includes stories of human achievement, tragedy, intrigue and determination – all hallmarks of America's Industrial Age.

Because of its importance in transporting troops, supplies, weapons and war materiel, the curve was guarded by Union troops during the Civil War to prevent its destruction by Rebel forces. More recently a group of German saboteurs was arrested during World War II and charged with planning to destroy this American transportation landmark.

In continuous operation since it was built, the Horseshoe Curve is open to the public via a small museum and observation post. It is a National Landmark located in a scenic mountains of western Pennsylvania. For more information, contact the Railroaders Memorial Museum at http://www.railroadcity.com or visit the National Landmark Museum at the Horseshoe Curve.